continued . . .

The Sun Witch

Prince of Magic

LINDA WINSTEAD JONES

BERKLEY SENSATION BOOKS, NEW YORK

THE BERKLEY PUBLISHING GROUP
Published by the Penguin Group
Penguin Group (USA) Inc.
375 Hudson Street, New York, New York 10014, USA
Penguin Group (Canada), 90 Eglinton Avenue East, Suite 700, Toronto, Ontario M4P 2Y3, Canada
(a division of Pearson Penguin Canada Inc.)
Penguin Books Ltd., 80 Strand, London WC2R 0RL, England
Penguin Group Ireland, 25 St. Stephen's Green, Dublin 2, Ireland (a division of Penguin Books Ltd.)
Penguin Group (Australia), 250 Camberwell Road, Camberwell, Victoria 3124, Australia
(a division of Pearson Australia Group Pty. Ltd.)
Penguin Books India Pvt. Ltd., 11 Community Centre, Panchsheel Park, New Delhi—110 017, India
Penguin Group (NZ), 67 Apollo Drive, Mairangi Bay, Auckland 1311, New Zealand
(a division of Pearson New Zealand Ltd.)
Penguin Books (South Africa) (Pty.) Ltd., 24 Sturdee Avenue, Rosebank, Johannesburg 2196,
South Africa

Penguin Books Ltd., Registered Offices: 80 Strand, London WC2R 0RL, England

This is a work of fiction. Names, characters, places, and incidents either are the product of the author's imagination or are used fictitiously, and any resemblance to actual persons, living or dead, business establishments, events, or locales is entirely coincidental. The publisher does not have any control over and does not assume any responsibility for author or third-party websites or their content.

PRINCE OF MAGIC

A Berkley Sensation Book/published by arrangement with the author

PRINTING HISTORY
Berkley Sensation mass-market edition/March 2007

Copyright © 2007 by Linda Winstead Jones.
Cover art by Danny O'Leary.
Cover design by Lesley Worrell.
Hand lettering by Iskra Johnson.
Interior text design by Stacy Irwin.

ISBN: 978-0-425-21448-0

BERKLEY SENSATION®
Berkley Sensation Books are published by The Berkley Publishing Group,
a division of Penguin Group (USA) Inc.,
375 Hudson Street, New York, New York 10014.
BERKLEY SENSATION is a registered trademark of Penguin Group (USA) Inc.
The "B" design is a trademark belonging to Penguin Group (USA) Inc.

PRINTED IN THE UNITED STATES OF AMERICA

10 9 8 7 6 5 4 3 2 1

All these books focus very much
on the importance of family.
It's a theme I come back to again and again
in all my stories, no matter what type they might be.
This book is dedicated to
my brother Tom and my sister Sandy.
Love you much.

I

THE EMPEROR WAS DYING.

Emperor Arik had been on his deathbed for months, but it was a well-kept secret. A few ministers were aware of his condition, as were two of his priests. Other than that handful of trusted men, only one woman knew how grave the situation had become.

Ariana Kane Varden had been the palace healer for a little more than two years, since just after her twenty-fourth birthday. Against the wishes of her parents, who both had bad memories of the Imperial Palace in Arthes and wished for their daughter to stay far away from the cursed place, she had rebelled and answered the emperor's call.

"Drink this, my lord," she said, offering the thin, aging man a cup of steaming hot liquid.

Today the emperor felt well enough to sit by the window and look out on his city. It was not a cool day, yet his legs were covered by a thick blanket to ward off the chill he felt. He took the cup with hands too frail for a man of his age. He was years yet from sixty, and yet at the moment he looked as if he might be a hundred.

"Do you think he's out there?" the emperor asked before taking a sip of the bitter liquid that was keeping him alive.

Ariana knew very well of whom he spoke. Arik's only child, Prince Ciro, had been missing since the first cold night of winter, months ago. Summer approached rapidly, and still there was no sign of the prince and heir. It was for that reason that no one outside the palace could know the emperor was so very ill. If he died without an heir, the country would once again be thrown into the chaos of war, as ministers and warriors and distant relations tried to make a case for taking the throne.

"I'm sure he is, my lord," Ariana said kindly.

Arik turned his head to look up at her. He was very ill, but there were moments when the spark in his lively eyes belied his condition. Now was one of those times. "You lie no better than your mother."

Ariana did not care for being compared to her mother, and the emperor knew that well. But he was the emperor, and was therefore entitled to speak his mind. "We cannot know where Prince Ciro is, my lord," she said honestly.

She was not the only magical servant in this palace. In the months since Ciro had disappeared, Arik had called to his side many who embraced magic. Thus far, none of them had been able to shed light on the mystery of what had happened to his son.

Ariana's gift was not divination, so she could not offer assistance where Prince Ciro's fate was concerned. She was a healer, taught at her mother's knee from the age of four to remove pain, prolong life, and restore health. Some of this was accomplished through the use of herbs and magical spells, but there was more to her gift than chanting and mixing potions. There were times when the healing power came alive within her, and all that was needed came from a magical place deep inside.

She'd tried to heal the emperor in that way, but so far had been unsuccessful. He said that some things were simply meant to be, but she refused to accept that answer. She would try again . . . and again. Her efforts were barely keeping him alive. She was beginning to suspect there was more to his infirmity than age or a simple, explainable illness. If an unknown dark magic was making him ill, it was no wonder that her healing abilities were insufficient.

Arik finished his medicine and handed Ariana the empty cup. "You would make a fine daughter."

Her heart leapt, but she did her best to hide the reaction. It was not the first time Emperor Arik had mentioned his desire that she marry his son, the heir to the throne. At least the emperor had never commanded that the match take place. If Ciro was found and Arik so ordered, what would she do? She could not, would not, marry the prince.

"As I've told you, my lord, I will never marry."

He smiled wanly. "Yes, you've said that many times, but I don't believe you. When the right man comes along, you will change your mind. You could learn to love Ciro, with time. He might be that right man, Ariana."

She had met with Ciro a number of times before he disappeared, usually thrown together by his father, the emperor, whose intent was plain to see. Ariana did not know the prince well, but her instincts were finely honed and she was quite sure she would never be able to love such a spoiled, arrogant boy. Most males could be considered men at twenty-two, but not Ciro Elias Brennus Beckyt. He would forever be a boy. Arik had spoiled his only child, as had everyone else in the palace. Ariana supposed the prince had been doomed from the start.

"Perhaps Prince Ciro will return to the palace with a fine bride who will become a wonderful daughter to you," she offered cheerfully.

"I suppose that's possible," the emperor said, and yet he did not sound as if he believed his own words. Something was wrong. They all felt it. "I should've married after Cylia died. I should've had lots of children, the way your parents did."

Ariana shuddered at the thought. There were nine Varden children. Six girls and three boys. As the eldest, Ariana had helped to raise them all. She had tended the younger ones, changed more than her share of diapers, bathed them, fed them, and taught them. And when the Fyne sisters had one of their frequent reunions and Aunt Juliet's six children and Aunt Isadora's three had been added to the mix, the chaos had been unmanageable. And there Ariana was, the eldest of all the cousins and the one who was held responsible for every spill, prank, and fuss. It was no wonder she so often argued that she did not want children of her own. She'd already had a hand in raising seventeen!

"You are young still, my lord. When you're well, you can find yourself a young bride who will give you all the children you desire."

The emperor didn't answer. He knew, as she did, that this illness was killing him. Besides, if he'd had the inclination to remarry, he would've done so long ago, when his young wife had died. He must've loved his Empress Cylia very much, to grieve for so long.

They did not discuss the blatant lie that the emperor was young enough to breed another heir before death claimed him, as Ariana laid her hands on his shoulders. She attempted once more, again in vain, to draw out the illness which was slowly and surely killing him.

SIAN PACED IMPATIENTLY, BOOT HEELS CLACKING loudly against the stone floor. His eyes remained focused on the closed doors of the emperor's suite. If not for the presence of half a dozen armed guards, he would storm the suite in spite of the sentinels' insistence that the emperor was not to be disturbed. He could make his way inside no matter how diligently they tried to stop him, but it might get his visit off to a bad start.

"This is quite important," he said under his breath.

"So you have said, sir," one sentinel responded calmly. "When the emperor is finished with his business, we will announce you. Perhaps he will see you. Perhaps not."

The words were meant to rile, he imagined, but Sian did not respond. He had no doubt that the emperor would see him.

"What was your name again?" another green-clad sentinel asked.

"Sian Sayre Chamblyn," he said, his teeth all but clenched.

"And your business with the emperor?"

"I will discuss my business with him. No one else. What's taking so long?"

One of the sentinels smiled.

Sian had not been to Arthes and this palace for many

years. He'd been caught between being a boy and becoming a young man when he'd experienced the wonders of the Imperial Palace for the first and last time. Little had changed since his visit more than twenty years ago. He'd been told that during Emperor Sebestyen's reign the royal family had resided on the top floor. Level One. At that time there had been a wondrous lift to transport those of importance ten floors up, but the man who had the keeping of the machine that powered the lift had disappeared during the last day of battle in the War of the Beckyts, and Arik had never set men to work on reviving it.

Since shortly after Arik had become emperor, the royal family had taken up residence on Level Nine, which would have been the second floor in a normal house. Of course, much in this palace had changed since Arik had become emperor.

Sian remembered running up the winding stairway, all the way to Level One. No one had resided there at that time. There were too many bad memories on the top Level of the palace; too much bad energy. He'd heard rumors of secret passageways and hidden doors, but as a boy he had not been able to find them. Perhaps they didn't exist, but were merely tales, much like the tales of Emperor Sebestyen and his many unfortunate empresses.

Sian suspected most of the tales were exaggerated, but there had to be some truth in them. Odd that a good man like Arik could share blood—a father—with a man as evil as the long-departed Emperor Sebestyen.

Finally, the door to the emperor's room opened, and a pretty girl stepped into the hallway. She quietly closed the door behind her, as if she'd left the emperor sleeping and did not wish to disturb him. Sian noted that she was tall, for a woman, and possessed unruly, curly blond hair and a curvaceous figure any woman would envy and any man would admire. As she turned, she revealed a flawlessly beautiful face and lively green eyes.

"I've been left waiting for the emperor to finish his business with this piece of fluff?" Sian asked harshly. "I told you, my purpose here is momentous." He had expected that at the very least he'd been waiting for the exit of a highly placed minister or perhaps a priest.

The woman turned to look him in the eye. She started visibly, as many people did when they first saw his face. It was the eyes that gave her pause, he knew. "What did you call me?" she asked.

"Fluff," he answered without hesitation. "The fate of the country hangs by a thread, and I am left waiting in the hallway cooling my heels while you service your lord and master. The least you could do is to be quick about your responsibilities."

She was not outraged. Her slowly spreading smile was one of amusement, not anger or seduction. Perhaps she was not a concubine, after all. What was her purpose, then?

One of the sentinels entered the emperor's suite to announce Sian's presence. Sian waited impatiently to be summoned. The woman who had just left the emperor continued to study him with curious eyes. "The fate of the country, you say. Do you care to elaborate?"

"To you? No." Sian stared at the door as if willing it to open. How would the emperor receive him if he barged in before being summoned? He was sorely tempted to find out.

"Emperor Arik does not receive many visitors these days," the woman said cordially. She took a step closer to him, unafraid and openly curious. "He's very busy. What makes you think he will see you?"

"He will see me."

She looked him up and down, taking in his travel-dusty black clothing and the disheveled black braid that hung over one shoulder. He likely made a sharp contrast to her, as she was very clean and properly dressed in a pale gray frock which was pressed and free of road dust. Perhaps he should've bathed and dressed more properly before presenting himself to the emperor, but he hadn't felt he had the time. No, there was no time for niceties. This message was *important*. Dreadfully so.

The blonde reached out and touched Sian's cheek. He almost recoiled; he was not accustomed to the touch of strangers. But the caress was light and easy, not at all threatening or seductive. It might be the touch of a mother, or a sister. A caretaker of some sort, surely.

A healer. Yes, he knew the touch of a healer when he felt it. There was power in that tender touch, and though he did not share her power, he could certainly sense it.

"Dirt," she explained as her hand dropped. "One cannot be presented to the emperor in such a sad condition."

Before he could respond, the door opened. The sentinel who emerged closed it again, and walked solemnly toward Sian. It wasn't until he reached the weary traveler that he said, almost reluctantly, "The emperor will see you now."

With more than a touch of impatience, Sian lifted his right hand and twisted the fingers. The double doors to the emperor's chambers opened swiftly and fully, banging back against the stone wall with great force. The sentinels in the hallway stepped cautiously away from him, awed and frightened by his display of magic.

The woman didn't react at all. She didn't even flinch.

Sian strode toward the emperor's chamber, making his

way through the opened doors to find the man he sought sitting by the window. Good God, Arik looked so old and feeble. No wonder he had need of a healer.

One of the sentinels tried to follow Sian into the room, but he had been stunned by the display of magic and lagged behind. Sian turned, and with another twist of his fingers, the doors closed as forcefully as they had opened, and the latch fell into place, leaving him alone with the emperor behind locked doors.

His last glimpse of the crowded hallway was of the blonde's impassive face.

Alarmed, the sentinels began to pound against the door. Sian knew that if they succeeded in gaining entrance to the room, he was a dead man, and that couldn't happen. Not yet.

"It's all right," Emperor Arik called in a voice that was loud enough to carry, and yet sadly weak. "Sian is a friend. Stand down." The pounding stopped, and Arik smiled. "Always the showman. I see nothing has changed."

"I wish that were true," Sian said. In fact, everything had changed, or would in the days to come.

"Your mother?" Emperor Arik asked, his voice touched with melancholy. "How is she? I used to hear from her regularly, but over the past few years the letters came less and less frequently. It's been a long time since I had a communication from her."

"She's been gone almost five years."

The emperor seemed to flinch, though so mildly it was difficult to tell what had happened. "I'm sorry to hear that. I liked your mother very much." Sadness showed on his too-thin face. "I should've heard of her death, but you live so far from Arthes and we had lost touch. She did write now and then, but I was not the best at returning

those letters. I must confess, the years fly by too quickly."
He sighed tiredly, as if he felt every one of those years.
"I always thought I had more time, I suppose. Your grand-
father?" Arik changed the subject abruptly.

"He passed away three weeks ago, but not before penning a final prophesy," Sian answered. "I promised him
that I would deliver it to you."

The emperor turned his gaze to the world beyond his
window. For twenty-four of the twenty-five years Arik
had ruled, Columbyana had been a better place than it
had been under Sebestyen or his father or his grandfather.
During the past year the country had experienced a decidedly dark turn. Sian carried the explanation for that turn
in the inside pocket of his dusty traveling coat.

The emperor was obviously in no hurry to hear the
prophesy. Did he know the news would be bad? Likely
so. Prophesies were rarely of the joyful sort. The news
that Sian had made the long trip in less than three weeks
should also tell the emperor that the news he carried was
of great importance. To journey from the southernmost
tip of the Eastern Province to Arthes could easily take
twice that amount of time if one traveled at a moderately
leisurely pace.

"Before we get down to the business which brought
you here, tell me something of yourself, Sian." Emperor
Arik folded his trembling hands on his lap. "Are you
married? Do you have children? You're how old now,
twenty-eight?"

"Thirty-four."

"Yes, of course. Thirty-four. Imagine that." He
glanced out the window, as if studying the fine, sunny
day with some interest. "Surely by now you've taken a
wife and produced many fine children. Do they have

magic, like their father, their grandmother, and their great-grandfather?"

Sian had not expected to find himself in a position where he had to relive his failures. There were so many of them . . . "I married many years ago." Before the emperor could make joyous inquiries, Sian added, "My wife died giving birth. The child also died."

"And you never remarried?"

"No," Sian snapped. "Did you?"

The force of Arik's gaze was powerful, ill or not. "No, I did not, as I'm sure you well know. Did you love her so much, then?"

Sian withdrew the prophesy from his coat and unfolded the paper his grandfather had scribbled upon in his final days. "My lord, the matter which brings me to Arthes is of such importance, I feel we must press forward. Personal conversations must be set aside for another time."

"Of course." Arik gestured, rolling two fingers of his right hand in a manner which very clearly said, *Go on, and be quick about it.*

" 'A darkness creeps beneath Columbyana and the lands beyond,' " Sian read. " 'This darkness grows stronger each and every day, infecting those who have an affinity for evil. As it grows stronger, it will also begin to affect those who are of weak mind, and eventually it will grow so strong no one among us will be able to defeat it. If this darkness is allowed to grow to that point, the world is doomed to eternal shadows, where evil will reign.' "

Arik lifted a silencing hand. "What does that mean, a *darkness*? Is this a person? A group of people? Is it a metaphor or an actual dimness?"

"I do not know," Sian admitted. "Prophesy is not one of my gifts."

Again, Arik made the gesture that commanded Sian to continue.

" 'Only the firstborn children of three fine women have the power to stop the darkness and restore the world to light." Sian folded the paper. There was more written in his grandfather's hand. More detail about the ugliness of the battle and the monsters which would need be defeated in this war. More promise of death and darkness, along with a few scribbles in the margin which made no sense at all. "Beware Serrazone," with no hint as to who or what Serrazone might be. "He who walks through fire may show the way." There were other references to the children of the fine women as soldiers. Warriors. Scrawled along one margin were the words, *Those who are called must choose between love and death, between heart and intellect, between victory of the sword and victory of the soul.* Some of the scribblings seemed to be nonsense. Others were no more than doodles. Still, Sian was certain they were as important as the carefully worded prophesy which filled the center of the page. He just didn't know how. Not yet.

Given Arik's fragile condition, it was likely best that he not be bombarded with an excess of unpleasant details at this time. " 'The firstborn children of three fine women' isn't very specific, I'm afraid, but he made it very clear to me that they would be crucial. Grandfather was very ill in his final days. I'm sure if he'd had more time . . ."

Arik smiled crookedly, a strange response given the dire prophesy. "Your grandfather was specific enough, Sian."

"There are many fine women in Columbyana and beyond, my lord. How will we know where to look for their sons?"

Arik shook a too-thin finger at Sian. "You see the

prophesy, but I hear it. I imagine your grandfather heard it, too, in his own way, so he can be excused for making a mistake."

Sian's spine went rigid. A mistake from his grandfather? Unheard of.

"F-Y-N-E," Arik spelled slowly. "Fyne. I suspect the prophesy refers to the firstborn children of three *Fyne* women. I didn't hear the word 'sons,' though you used that word."

"As these children are meant to be soldiers in the coming war, I assumed it to be so."

"If sons were required, I believe your grandfather would've made that plain. No, his one mistake was in the misspelling of Fyne."

While Sian hated to admit that his grandfather might've made a mistake, given the old man's physical condition in his final days, it was certainly possible. "Do you know where these Fyne women and their children can be found?"

For the first time, Arik's smile seemed real, and familiar. He looked not quite so ill, not quite so old. This was the man Sian remembered. "Yes. Yes, I do."

ARIANA RAN DOWN THE HALLWAY, HER BREATH CATCH-ing in her chest, her skirt held off the floor so it would not impede her progress. Something was wrong. She would not be called to the emperor so soon after her last visit if he had not taken a turn for the worse.

She wanted desperately to save him. Everything inside her told her that was impossible, and still . . . that was what she wanted. Not only had she come to care for the man, much as she cared for her own father, but she felt a responsibility to the country she called home. Under Arik, Columbyana had known many years of peace, with nothing more than infrequent local skirmishes and Tryfyn criminals who crossed the border to call his soldiers to battle. When he was gone, what would follow? Prince Ciro would not be a good ruler, as his father had been, and if Ciro was not found, anything was possible. War was not only possible, it was likely.

She had to keep Arik alive. He should have many years left! What could've happened so soon after her visit to require her presence? He'd been doing well, considering his condition. The wizard was surely to blame. The purple-eyed, beak-nosed man in black who'd made such a show of opening and closing the doors. He must've done something to the emperor. If only she'd seen the danger coming. If only she had known . . .

As she approached, waiting sentinels opened the door to Emperor Arik's chamber. Ariana did not slow down, but burst into the room, breathless and scared, and more than a little determined.

The man in black stood near the window beside the emperor, who looked no worse than he had when she'd left him. In fact, there was new color to the emperor's cheeks, and he smiled up at the man with the odd purple eyes. She could not forget the man's eyes, even now. The color itself was unusual enough, but it was the way the colors shifted constantly that had made her heart skip a beat when she'd first seen him. His eyes looked like dark skies on a stormy day, with clouds drifting and ominous rain threatening.

Ariana came to a quick halt in the center of the room. Both men looked at her, and then the emperor gestured to his sentinels, ordering silently that the doors be closed behind Ariana.

The wizard—for what else could he be, given those eyes and his trick with the doors?—lifted imperious eyebrows. "Her?" He sounded surprised and more than a little disappointed.

"Yes, *her*," the emperor responded calmly. "Sian Sayre Chamblyn, may I introduce Miss Ariana Kane Varden, firstborn child of the witch Sophie Fyne Varden, and a Fyne witch no matter which name she chooses to call her own."

Chamblyn looked down at the seated emperor. "But . . . she's a healer, and not a particularly good one at that."

Ariana stepped toward the men. "I beg your pardon . . ."

"Apologies," Chamblyn said in an offhand way that conveyed no real regret. "I should have said not a particularly *powerful* one. I'm sure you're adequately trained with potions and such."

He spoke of her in such a dismissive way, an uncustomary ire rose up and threatened to choke Ariana. How dare this dirty, arrogant, hawk-nosed, purple-eyed wizard insult her. How dare he dismiss her as if she were insignificant? "I'll have you know . . ."

Without even looking at her, Chamblyn lifted his hand and twitched his fingers, and with that simple move he stole Ariana's voice. She continued to try to speak, but no sound came from her mouth. She stalked toward the offensive wizard, and he lifted his hand again.

"Don't make me freeze you. I understand it's very uncomfortable."

Ariana wanted to say, "You wouldn't dare . . ." but she couldn't.

She came to a halt, and Chamblyn returned his attention to the emperor—who had been watching the exchange with no small amusement.

"We are talking about war, my lord. Not a war like the one in which you and my father fought together, but a struggle between light and dark. There will be monsters in this coming war. The blood of innocents will be shed before it's done, not the blood of soldiers and rebels who chose the life of combat, as you and my father did so long ago."

Ariana stopped trying to regain her voice and listened as the wizard raised his hand again and pointed at her. She wondered . . . what would he do to her this time? But he merely pointed at her, without so much as looking her way. "She will be eaten alive if you send her into this battle. Perhaps figuratively, perhaps literally. In either case, she will die a very ugly death, and I wish no part in sending her there. Only the strongest of wizards and witches have a chance of stopping this darkness before it claims the world we live in."

"She has potential," the emperor said. "If you teach her—"

"I am no tutor," Chamblyn snapped, interrupting the ruler of Columbyana with his sharp voice.

"You could be," Arik argued.

Chamblyn sighed, and raked a hand through long, black hair that had come loose from his braid to brush his face. "Let me take her place," he said more calmly. "I have the skills she does not, and I'm willing to fight in her stead."

Arik looked Ariana's way, and she was taken aback by the depth of sadness on his face. He'd had no reason to be happy of late, but she had never seen him look so completely disconsolate, as if the wizard had robbed the emperor of his last hope. "You read the prophesy, Sian. It doesn't work that way, and you know that well."

Chamblyn studied Ariana from head to toe with that annoyingly dismissive gaze. His purple eyes—heavens, she had never known such eyes were possible—seemed to glow from within. They danced and the color shifted from dark to light and back again. Set above a nose that was too sharp and too long, and above cheeks that were too lean, the eyes were captivating . . . and the only truly beautiful feature on a masculine and somehow bleak face.

"My grandfather made a mistake in the spelling of one word. Perhaps those who are required are not firstborn children, but firstborn sons. Did Sophie Fyne have a son?"

"Duran Varden," Emperor Arik answered. "He's a sentinel, one of my best. When Ariana came to serve me, her parents would not allow her to travel alone or stay here without family nearby, so he accompanied her."

The wizard seemed to relax. "What are his magical gifts?"

Arik shrugged. "Like his father, he has none. He's a fine soldier, however. Quite the swordsman."

Chamblyn began to pace. "Magical powers will be necessary for this fight." He stopped pacing and waved his hand carelessly in Ariana's direction. "Perhaps we should ask the healer what she thinks."

"I . . ." Ariana touched her throat as the word left her mouth. The wizard had returned her voice to her as quickly as he had taken it. "If this man wishes to sacrifice himself to monsters in my stead, I won't stand in his way." She looked bravely into his odd eyes.

Unexpectedly, he smiled at her. She did not find him at all attractive, but he had a nice smile nonetheless. It transformed his face in a way she had not expected.

Ariana dismissed the wizard and his smile, much as he had dismissed her, and turned to the emperor. "My lord, perhaps you would be so kind as to tell me what's happened to make this man speak of monsters and war and the death of innocents."

"Of course."

Ariana moved closer so that the emperor would not have to raise his voice when he grew weary. She suspected this would take some time, and he did tire easily these days. He took her hand, and in a lowered voice began. " 'A darkness creeps beneath Columbyana and the lands beyond . . . ' "

2

THREE *FYNE* WOMEN. IT DID MAKE SOME SENSE, HE SUP-
posed, especially as the Fyne women Arik was acquainted
with were powerful witches. That did not mean, however,
that their firstborn children were equally powerful, or that
those children would be adequate in battle against the
darkness that was rising. If only the firstborn son had
some sort of power inherited from his mother, perhaps
Sian could convince himself that this woman before him
wasn't meant to sacrifice herself to save others.

"So, what kind of wizard are you?" The Fyne witch
Ariana—Varden, she preferred to be called—paced in the
large Level Five room Arik had assigned them for their
lessons. This had once been a suite for guests or family
members, if he remembered correctly, but lately it had
been used as some sort of meeting room. A long table,
dark wood with a decorative inlay on top, had been
placed in the center of the room. The large fireplace was

dormant on this warm day, and a wide window allowed sunlight to illuminate the room. The rest of the room was ordinary. There were chairs—a mixture of comfortable and austere—and tables—some useful and others decorative. There were mismatched framed pictures on the walls, carried here from different parts of the palace where they were no longer wanted. Some were of long-ago imperial residents, others were landscapes that had lost favor from their original wall-spaces. Much of the spacious room was empty. In the coming days of training, he and Ariana were to have anything they asked for.

A miracle would be nice.

"I'm an enchanter," Sian replied.

"Tricks and illusion," Ariana responded airily. "You might scoff at the power of healing, but at least my talents provide a substantial difference in the lives of those I assist."

"I do not scoff at the power of healing." There had been times when he would have put aside all the powers of enchantment for such a gift, not that he would admit as much to Ariana. "That power is, however, insufficient when it comes to battle, unless you're present to tend to the wounded."

She tried to appear nonchalant, but the too-firm set of her mouth gave her away. "Perhaps it is a metaphorical battle against evil that your grandfather spoke of. We all must choose good or evil at some point in our lives."

"There's nothing metaphorical about the prophesy," Sian said sharply. "The battle has already begun, and if you open your eyes, you'll see it for yourself. Emperor Arik's illness, Prince Ciro's disappearance, a village two days' ride from Arthes decimated by plague, a perfectly ordinary man killing his wife and then eating her heart, a mother murdering her own children . . ."

"Enough," Ariana said gently. "I know that things have not been right in the past few months, but that doesn't mean evil has infected the people of Columbyana."

"Doesn't it?"

Ariana pulled a chair—one of the plain, hard ones—to the long table that dominated the room. She sat, and then leaned forward, propping her elbows on the table and resting her head in her hands. She had healer's hands, soft and white and delicate. How had he ever mistaken her, even for a moment, for a concubine? She remained in that position just long enough to take two long breaths, and then she lifted her head and looked at him. She was stronger than she looked. Most women, when informed that it was their duty to fight monsters, might shed a tear or two, or bemoan the inconvenience or the danger. Not Ariana. She did not like the idea, but she was willing to take it on.

"What is my part in this to be?" she asked steadily.

"I do not yet know," Sian responded, not yet ready to tell her all that he knew. "Much of the prophesy is yet to be interpreted." Should he even tell her that she must be a warrior? That in spite of her talents for healing, she would be called to take up the sword? Perhaps not at this time. He could not tell her near everything he knew just yet. "Our first task will be to discover the nature of the evil, so that we can fight it effectively."

"How best to accomplish that?" There was no panic in her voice, no wailing. She got straight to the business at hand, and for that he was grateful.

"I'm not sure." Neither his gift nor hers would be of any help in identifying the source of the darkness. "Tell me about the other two firstborn children of the Fyne women."

"Keelia is a year younger than I," Ariana said. "She's been Queen of the Anwyn for ten years, and she's a very powerful seer, as well as a shape-shifter. She can tell us the source of the evil, I'm sure." Her voice grew slightly lighter as she revealed this belief. "We're weeks away from the Anwyn mountains—the Mountains of the North—and the journey there isn't an easy one, but I know she'll be of great help once we tell her what's going on."

Sian began to relax. At least this cousin would be of some use. "And the other?"

"Lyr Hern. He's twenty-three years old and has just taken his father's place as Prince of Swords. Have you heard of the Circle of Bacwyr?"

"Yes, of course."

"Lyr has his father's gift for swordplay, as well as inherited magic from Aunt Isadora. Even as a child, watching him practice with his knives and such was like watching a dance."

"His magic?"

"Time," Ariana answered. "Lyr can freeze time, for a moment or two. He can move through it, but everything else remains stagnant."

"A useful gift for a swordsman."

"Oh, he never employs his magic while fighting. Lyr's father, Uncle Lucan, forbade it long ago. He said it wasn't sporting."

"When fighting evil, one doesn't have to be sporting."

Ariana sighed. "Lyr is, of course, a long journey in the other direction from Keelia, halfway across the country of Tryfyn. Must I collect them myself, or should I send couriers to them both with the news?"

Sian shook his head. "Once the prophesy is revealed to the masses, people will panic. When that happens, the darkness we're trying to fight will have yet another foothold. It's possible the enemy doesn't yet know that you and your cousins are destined to fight them, and that you might even win. If the news spreads to the wrong ears, I'm afraid it will only accelerate the coming battle." And they were not ready. "I'm encouraged to hear of the talents of your cousins."

Ariana wrinkled her nose in an almost girlish way. "I will admit, compared to Keelia and Lyr, my own talents are rather puny."

"I will teach you what I can," Sian said solemnly.

She faced her fate bravely. "Why don't you retire to your quarters for a while? After your long journey I'm sure a nap and a bath would be welcomed."

His own personal comfort meant little, given the circumstances, but he suspected that Ariana needed some time alone herself. She did not want him to see her dread of what was to come. Perhaps she wished to shed a few tears in private. He could allow her that indulgence, as long as her tears didn't last too long. They had much work to do.

And she still did not know the worst of the prophesy.

BY THE TIME ARIANA RETURNED TO THE WORKROOM, it was well past dark. A fire had been lit in the stone fireplace, and the dancing flames warmed the room nicely. Sian Chamblyn paced in front of that fire.

He looked somewhat better, after bathing and changing into fresh, clean clothes. Again he wore all black, but at least the trousers and wide-sleeved shirt he wore this evening were clean. He'd loosed the braid, and his long black hair fell free. Straight, silky strands moved sensuously as he paced.

There was so much tension in his long, lean body, she doubted he'd followed her advice about taking a nap.

The enchanter was not a pretty man, not at all. And yet, there was something fascinating about him. Sian Sayre Chamblyn was all man, and in spite of the too-long nose and the odd purple eyes, he was sensually appealing. If Ariana cared about intriguing men, which she didn't, she might take a moment longer to admire that fact.

She entered the room quietly, and he barked at her. "It's about time."

"I apologize for the delay. I wanted to see the emperor once more before we got started."

Sian's head snapped around and he glared at her.

"Never fear, wizard, I didn't ask too many questions about you." Well, she had, but the emperor had been oddly stubborn, insisting that Sian himself would tell her what she needed to know. "I needed to make sure my patient was situated for the evening. It's been a trying day for him, and he no longer has the energy to face trying days."

"Is there another healer in the palace?" Sian tried to sound cold, but Ariana could tell that he cared about the emperor's condition. He just didn't want anyone to know that he cared.

"No," she answered. "None of sufficient skill, at least. I've sent for my sister Sibyl. She's only eighteen, but she's quite talented. It will take her some time to get here, but at least if I have to depart the palace in order to fulfill my part in the prophesy, I won't be leaving the emperor unattended."

"Two healers in the family. How odd."

"There are nine of us. Many of us share the same ability." Some of the Varden children had more than one natural magical talent, and two of the boys had none at all.

Sian recoiled slightly, and then he shuddered. "Nine children? How awful for you."

Ariana smiled. "Thank you. Most people go on and on about how lovely it must be to have such a large family when they find that I have five sisters and three brothers."

"And you don't agree?"

"I love my siblings, but solitude was almost nonexistent when I was growing up. I've always favored my privacy."

"So have I."

"And how many siblings do you have?"

"None," he snapped. "I'm an only child. Now that this useless repartee is done, can we get to work?"

"Of course."

Work, at least for tonight, began with an examination given by the wizard. His disdain for her all-but-useless abilities was evident, as he ascertained everything which she could not do. He made notes on a sheet of paper, perhaps planning for her lessons in the days to come. When the sheet was full, he turned it over and began again, scribbling on the backside and muttering to himself.

"Shouldn't our first order of business be to identify that which we will be fighting?" she asked as Sian set the very full sheet of paper aside.

"That would be helpful. How do you propose we accomplish that?"

Ariana placed one hand on the table. Her fingers touched the colorful and elaborate inlay. "I have been studying this while you were interrogating me."

Sian's eyebrows arched slightly at the word "interrogating," but he didn't respond.

"It's difficult to tell until you know what this is, but what we have here on the table is a map."

Sian grunted, and the sound seemed to be affirmative. Perhaps he could now see what she had discovered as she'd stared at the table. "I understand that at one time Emperor Sebestyen concocted battle plans for his generals using this very table."

Sian cocked his head to one side and studied the inlay. Precious and semiprecious stones were set here and there in colorful polished marble. Tryfyn was green stone; the land of the Anwyn was in gray, as was all the unexplored land beyond the known borders. Columbyana was represented in a soft pink, with cities and lakes and rivers marked in other stones of varying colors. It was quite beautiful.

"Who told you that tale? A smitten sentinel?"

Ariana smiled. "A smitten grandfather. Maddox Sulyen was once Sebestyen's Minister of Defense."

"Until he joined Arik in the revolution," Sian said. "Sulyen is your grandfather?"

"Yes. His fighting days are behind him, of course. He's well and married and lives near my parents. Before I came here, he told me many secrets about this palace. He told me to look for this table if I had the chance. He found it quite beautiful. A work of art, he said."

"It is a fine work of art," Sian agreed sharply. "How does it help us in our work?"

"This is the palace." She pointed to a red gem near the center of the map.

"I see," he responded, his voice low as usual.

"All evening, I have been thinking about what you said. The plague, the emperor's illness, the . . . other incidents." Even though war was coming, according to the wizard, she could not bring herself to speak about a mother killing her children or a husband eating his wife's heart. "I did of course hear about those incidents when they occurred. The emperor is informed regularly of the happenings in his country, and in the past several months I have been spending more and more time in his company."

"As he grows more infirm," Sian added unnecessarily.

"Yes." Ariana pointed to the palace, and then drew her finger out along a thin road that headed almost straight north. "Here is the village where the plague killed everyone and then vanished." Her finger returned to the gem that indicated the location of the palace where she and Sian now worked. Again, it trailed along a road—south, this time. "It was here that the man murdered his wife so violently." She did not feel the need to say more as once again her fingertip returned to the palace. "The woman who . . . the mother . . ." Again, she traced a road east and stopped. "Here."

She had Sian's full attention. "They are an equal distance from the palace, though in diverse directions."

"Yes. And all three incidents occurred at about the same time, not long after Prince Ciro disappeared and Emperor Arik fell ill. I'm going to imagine that whatever it is I'm meant to fight, it started somewhere and grew. A darkness creeping, your grandfather called it."

"Yes."

Ariana once again placed her fingertip on the red gem that marked the location of the palace. "I think it started here."

FYNNIAN SAT BACK IN HIS FAVORITE CHAIR AND watched the boy, as he did most evenings. Ciro favored his mother, his long hair fine and pale, his eyes a hypnotic pale blue. There was nothing feminine about the boy, though. He might be young still, but he was a man.

A man with no soul, but still—a man. A man who would one day rule Columbyana and all the land beyond the country's borders. Fynnian would be with him when the time came. The boy would be a puppet emperor, just as he was a puppet now.

As they had in months past, the two men passed the evening in the study of a vast and well-built house which sat upon an isolated part of the northern mountains of Columbyana. A fire burned in the large stone fireplace. Summer was coming, but here in the mountains the nights remained cool.

During his lifetime, Fynnian had managed to surround himself with many beautiful things. The furnishings were the finest, and exquisite paintings graced the walls. There were not many windows in this part of the house, and the colors in this study were primarily dim. If not for the interference of his daughter, Rayne, the room might be quite gloomy. Instead, it was brightened by a few colorful vases filled with flowers she had grown in her garden and carefully arranged with her own hands, as well as decorative pillows in shades of red and gold.

Perhaps it was not the Imperial Palace where Ciro had been born and raised, but it was Fynnian's palace . . . smaller but certainly adequate for any man, prince or not.

From the short sofa where he sat, near the fire where he might take in some warmth, Ciro lifted his head and looked Fynnian in the eye. "I'm hungry." His voice was lifeless. Dead. Hollow, just as the man was hollow.

"You will be fed soon enough." The necessary feedings were coming more frequently now, a sign that the boy's power was growing as it should.

"You know what I want." Ciro cocked his head to one side, and his eyes narrowed. Firelight flickered on long flaxen hair, and on a pale cheek, and for a moment it seemed the lifeless eyes glowed red. Another man might be afraid, but Fynnian was not. The transformation was not yet complete, but Ciro was already his. Fynnian had made himself father, mother, friend, and mentor to the lost prince.

"You cannot have her," Fynnian responded. "Not yet. Not until we're finished with all we have to do. You cannot have her in the way that you wish, but . . . would you like to have a look?"

"Yes, please," Ciro whispered.

Evidence that Ciro's transformation was not yet complete was clear in that spontaneously spoken "please." A true beast did not use such a polite word. A soulless fiend took what he wanted without the word "please" passing his lips.

Fynnian lifted the silver bell which sat on his side table, and rang it briefly. In moments, Rayne appeared.

"Yes, Father?"

"My guest and I would like some tea."

Rayne glanced nervously at Ciro, who grinned at her like a man who did not have *tea* on his mind. "Of course, Father." She fled from the room as quickly as she could, her skirts swishing, her breath held.

"More," Ciro muttered when she was gone.

"Rayne will soon return with the tea. She'll stay longer next time."

Fynnian was not blind to his daughter's beauty. The girl looked very much like her mother. Dark hair, dark eyes, innocently beautiful face, body ripe and still untouched. She would make a fine empress when the time came.

Rayne was as much a prisoner here as Ciro. Neither of them realized they were being held captive. It was an art, one at which Fynnian was quite adept—and well practiced.

Rayne returned quickly with the tea. As was expected, she served Ciro first, since he was their guest. She did not know he was the Prince of Columbyana, or that he'd been officially missing for months. How could she know? Rayne had been sequestered here in this fine house for her entire life. If she had been given to wandering, she would not have gotten far. They were a long way from any village, and the closest neighbor they'd had in her nineteen years had met with an untimely accident—as did anyone else who came too close. Rayne knew nothing which her father did not tell her.

She did not like the tall, fair-haired man who had been with them for so long. Fynnian could tell by the way she served the guest so quickly and then moved away that he made her uneasy. He could not blame her. Ciro looked at the woman he lusted after as if he wanted to eat her alive. His hands wandered too close to her body, though he did not touch. He had been told he could not . . . not yet.

When the time was right and Rayne had served her purpose, Ciro could do whatever he wanted to her.

After Rayne had served Fynnian his tea, she nodded gently. "If you don't think you'll need me again this evening, I'll retire for the night."

"So soon?"

"I don't enjoy the late-night hours the way you do, Father."

No, Rayne was a morning person, like her mother.

"We'll be fine, dear," Fynnian said, patting his daughter's hand gently. "You go on to bed."

Rayne said good night, cast a suspicious glance at Ciro and nodded shyly, and all but fled from the room.

"She doesn't like me," Ciro said when Rayne was gone.

"She will learn to like you in time."

"And if she doesn't?"

"Then when she's served her purpose, you can kill her, the way I killed her mother when she grew tiresome."

Ciro shrugged slightly, accepting that as a possibility. "It was nice to look upon Rayne for a few moments, but watching her only made my hunger more keen," he said.

These days Ciro was always hungry, but that was to be expected as the transformation took place. Fynnian rose from his chair and headed for a small door at the rear of the study. He could not feed the boy as often as he'd like, not without some considerable trouble. Eventually the prince would be able to feed himself, but until then these weekly feasts would suffice.

Fynnian opened the door, and found the girl waiting. She was thin, young, and frightened. His personal soldiers had delivered her just that morning. She cowered in the small room that was little more than a closet, her dark hair mussed, her face smeared with tears and dirt.

"Come, child," he said, offering her his hand and a genuine smile.

"Why have you brought me here?" she asked. "What do you want with me?"

"I did not bring you here," Fynnian said calmly. "You poor child. What happened?"

The girl stared at him suspiciously. Armed men had kidnapped her; a maid as timid as she had seen to her through the day. Perhaps she thought he was going to save her. Foolish girl.

"I was traveling to my sister's house, and—"

"Traveling all alone, I imagine," he said.

"Yes, as I have done many times." Her voice was quick. "Her house isn't far from mine, less than half a day's walk. But this day some . . . some horrible men snatched me up and I was on the back of a horse for—"

Still smiling, Fynnian backhanded the girl. The sound of his hand against her cheek was followed by a surprised gasp that came deep from her lungs. "You talk too much." He grabbed her arm and dragged her into the study. Her eyes flitted this way and that, as if she had never seen such elegance in her lifetime. She likely had not, given the state of her dress and her worn walking shoes. Her gaze eventually landed on Ciro and stayed there.

The prince was a handsome fellow, tall and broad-shouldered and pretty of face. The girl was fascinated for a moment. There were no more tears, no demand for explanations. She was enchanted . . .

"This is Prince Ciro," Fynnian said. "Have you heard of him?"

"Of course I have," the girl said. Her brow furrowed. "Is that why I was brought here in secret, because he is a prince?"

"Yes, dear." Fynnian could almost hear the gears turning in the simple girl's mind. She was thinking of romance, and Fynnian reached into her mind and nudged gently, feeding the enchantment. The girl imagined, quite vividly, that the handsome prince had seen her about town and had ordered her delivered to him so that he might slake his lust. She would gladly spread her legs for a man like this one, and it wouldn't be the first time she had done so.

She approached the prince almost coyly. "It's a pleasure to meet you, my lord." The girl was not beautiful, not like Rayne, but neither was she entirely homely. She knew how to flirt in a crude way. She tossed her mussed dark hair, and smiled—forgetting the tear tracks and smudges of dirt on her face—and thrust out her chest to show off her wares.

"Would you sit on my knee?" Ciro asked, patting the knee in question.

"Of course, my lord." The girl perched prettily on Ciro's knee, and placed a hand on his shoulder. "What is it you desire of me, Prince Ciro?"

Ciro had likely never been subtle, and in his new state all semblance of patience and princely comportment had been dismissed. He thrust his hand between the girl's legs and rubbed hard. Without so much as a word of protest, or a moment of pretending to be a demure lady, she closed her eyes and rocked against that hand. She spread her legs and shifted so that the prince touched her where she wanted to be touched.

Fynnian watched, a silent observer. Neither of the participants in this groping encounter paid him any mind, so he was free to watch. Not only to watch, but to study Ciro's moves, the expressions on the boy's face, the way his breathing changed as the girl moaned and thrust her bosoms close to his face.

"I want your body and your soul," Ciro whispered.

The girl smiled, and reached down to caress the prince's erection through the tight crimson trousers he wore. Her fingers trailed there lightly for a moment, and then she stroked hard and bold, much as he stroked her.

"Body and soul, you shall have them both, my lord."

"Freely given?"

She gasped in pleasure as his stroke grew harder. "Very freely."

"Thank you," Ciro whispered.

The prince placed his mouth against the girl's throat, and while he continued to stroke between her thin thighs, he broke the tender flesh at her neck, feeding greedily on her blood and on the soul she had so foolishly given him. Ciro slurped and grunted as he fed, moaning like a man in the throes of passion.

Thanks to her enchantment, by the time the poor girl realized that something was wrong, it was too late. She was weakened by loss of blood, and Ciro was much stronger than he had been when he'd first invited her to sit on his knee. She struggled to get away, but the prince held her fast and attempted to fill his own eternal emptiness with someone else's soul.

Fynnian knew that it would work for a while, but eventually Ciro would be hungry again. Soon he would be strong enough to take a soul without permission, and when that happened . . . when that happened, there would be no turning back for Ciro, and together he and Fynnian would be unstoppable.

After the girl was dead and her soul had been emptied into Ciro's body, the prince continued to fondle her with one hand while he gnawed upon her ruined throat with leisure. Fynnian was both fascinated and repelled by the sight. When the transformation was complete, would Ciro be more beast than man? Or would he be entirely beast?

Finally, Ciro allowed the husk of the girl to drop to the floor. She landed there limp and forgotten.

"Thank you," Ciro said, sated and appearing quite sleepy. With the back of his hand, he wiped away the few drops of blood that stained his lips. In the early days his feedings had been quite messy, but he had become much more adept at the ritual. "I feel better."

"Of course you do."

When the Isen Demon stole a living man's soul, the resulting hunger was tremendous, or so Fynnian had heard. The ancient writings which had led him to this place in time had been written more than a thousand years ago. It had been that long since the demon had risen. The soulless man would feed upon other souls endlessly, searching for relief, but the souls he ingested were never his to keep. The Isen Demon took them all eventually. The Isen Demon took the souls its vessel fed upon, and it became stronger with each feeding.

So did the vessel.

The Isen Demon had been defeated in the past, so long ago when it dared to attempt to gain power. Of course, Fynnian hadn't been there to guide and care for the demon, more than a thousand years ago. The vessel it had possessed had been killed before the demon could build sufficient power. That wouldn't happen this time. Fynnian would see to that.

Some men might be afraid to share such close quarters with an animal such as Ciro had become, but Fynnian had everything under control. Ciro loved Rayne, and Fynnian controlled his daughter. That alone would be enough to keep the future emperor in line for a while longer.

Ciro didn't have to know that the love he felt for the beautiful Rayne was the product of an enchantment, any more than he needed to know that it had been Fynnian who'd offered the boy's soul to the Isen Demon.

3

AFTER AN ALMOST SLEEPLESS NIGHT, SIAN FELT ODDLY energized. He ran up the winding steps, the snap of his boot heels clacking and echoing off the stone walls. His mission made sense in a way it had not before. His grandfather had sent him here not simply to deliver the prophesy to Emperor Arik, but to discover the very foundation of the new enemy. This palace was the source of the evil that threatened the world. *This* was where the seed of darkness had taken hold.

A faint, breathless voice reached him. "I cannot run any longer," Ariana called. "If you are determined to run all the way to Level One, please proceed. I'll meet you there."

Sian turned to wait for his pupil. True, she was a woman and as such was not accustomed to physical exertion. Her legs were shorter than his, and her cumbersome gown was not fashioned for moving with ease. He frowned as he watched her climb slowly. When the time came, Ariana would not fight only with her magic. She would face monsters in a very real physical battle, and she could not do so wearing fine palace fashions.

She needed more than magical tutoring. Her physical stamina was not sufficient for what awaited her.

"You were the one who suggested Level One as the location to begin searching for a seed of darkness."

"True, but I did not say that I wished to race you to the top of the palace." Her face was flushed, her hair in disarray. That wild disarray seemed to be a usual condition for her, thanks to all the curls that wound this way and that. She'd made an attempt to restrain the curls, pulling them back and pinning them down, but they would not stay in place. She was composed in the face of her new calling, and she dressed in an austere manner. But her hair hinted at another aspect to her personality.

Sian shook off the odd thoughts. It was just hair. Why did he allow his imagination to run wild where this woman was concerned? Perhaps he was trying to avoid the more obvious challenges. He could strengthen her magic; he could teach her a few new tricks. But how on earth would he prepare her for the physical tests to come?

They continued the climb side by side, and at a slower pace. "My mother always said this was an evil place," Ariana said, her eyes focused on the steps ahead. "Emperor Sebestyen was horribly wicked, she said, and his last empress Liane . . . We don't talk about her much. She was my father's sister."

A shiver of pure surprise danced through Sian. "Truly? I did not know."

"Few people do. She and her baby fled after the palace fell in the final battle of the War of the Beckyts, after Sebestyen died. They were killed by thieves."

"I know the story," Sian responded. "It's quite tragic."

"So tragic my parents refuse to so much as discuss Liane or the baby. They did tell me that this palace was Liane's ruination. She was captured at a young age, and made a concubine against her wishes. Her circumstances changed her. This palace and the people in it destroyed her soul and her heart."

"Your parents think of this palace as evil, they swear it destroyed your aunt, and yet they allowed you to come here?"

Ariana smiled. It was a nice smile, bright and real in spite of the dangers she was about to face. "They didn't so much *allow* me as not tie me down when I told them what I wanted to do. They did send my brother Duran with me, and they said if I ever decided I wanted to come home, he would be my escort. I think in their mind I'm still six years old and helpless."

"I suspect they simply wanted something different for you."

Ariana sighed. "My mother was certain that the only way I would be happy was if I lived as she did. She wanted me to marry and have children. Lots of them, if she had her way. She said I could use my talents as a healer right there in Shandley. When I told her I wanted to do more with my life, she didn't understand. My father simply didn't want me out of his sight. He's rather overly protective."

As many fathers were, where daughters were concerned. Sian wondered, momentarily, if he would have been such a father. Best not to allow his mind to wander there. "I thought every woman desired above all what your mother wanted for you."

"That goes to show how very little you know about women," Ariana teased.

"True enough," Sian admitted.

After a few more steps, Ariana turned her head to look at him. "Are you married?"

"What difference does it make?"

"It doesn't. I'm just curious."

They reached Level One, and thankfully that put an end to the questioning.

These days, the once fine hallways of Level One were deserted. Not only deserted, but very obviously abandoned. Anything that might be of use had been carted off long ago. Spiderwebs and the scurrying of small critters made the long dearth of human residence quite plain.

Ariana did not seem to be bothered by the conditions of Level One. As she walked toward an uncovered window and the light it allowed to fall onto the stone floor, she trailed her fingertips along the walls and gazed about curiously. She was not squeamish, and that was good.

He still couldn't imagine this woman fighting battles of any kind. His mother and his long-deceased wife were the only women he had ever known well. Others came and went, but he didn't *know* them. He didn't understand them at all. Nor did he want to. In spite of their varying circumstances, females were all delicate and fragile and given to moments of weakness. Even his mother, who had been quite strong when it had been required of her.

Did Ariana have that sort of strength inside her? For her sake, he hoped so.

The hallways were eerie, but were nothing to compare to the vast emptiness of the grand ballroom. Side by side, Sian and Ariana walked through the opened double doors. If the tales were true, it was here that Emperor Sebestyen had tortured and killed the men and women who displeased him. If evil could linger in the walls, in the air, then it was very possible the darkness they had yet to fight had taken root here.

Ariana walked to the center of the room and looked up. Sian copied her move, wondering what she was searching for. A large section of the ceiling had obviously been patched. The stones there were smaller in size, and the grout had not aged in just the same way.

The wild-haired healer pointed up and smiled. "My mother did that. She stood face to face with the emperor, when he was trying to force her to marry him, and blew a hole in the ceiling."

"Did she, now?" If her mother was that powerful, it was no wonder Emperor Arik had immediately thought of the woman when he'd heard the word "fine." "And then what?"

Ariana shrugged. "I don't know. Poppy would never let her tell us the rest. I can guess, though. Mama's talent is fertility."

"Then I suppose the fact that she has only nine children is a blessing."

"I suppose," Ariana said absently as she glanced around the cavernous room. "We're here. Now what?"

Sian crossed the room to join Ariana. "Have you ever studied the gift of healing, or do you simply accept what comes naturally to you?"

"I've studied the design and use of potions and poultices. I understand that I have a gift for healing that goes beyond medicines that anyone can produce, but that gift simply *is*. I call on it when I can, but such a gift can't be taught or learned. What else is there to study?"

"Much," he said softly. Sian preferred to keep his distance from women like this one, but if he was to do what needed to be done, he would have to touch her. He stood behind Ariana, reached around her slender body, and took her wrists in his hands. He forced her to turn those hands palms up. "Healing, like all magic, is rooted in manipulation of energy. Energy is everywhere. It's all around us. Bright, dark, weak, powerful. We all abound with energy. Most illness is an imbalance of that energy, and a true healer can bring those energies into alignment with the touch of a hand." He raked his thumb down the palm of Ariana's right hand, and as he did so, he shifted some of his own power into her. She felt it. He knew that to be true because her body twitched. "The gift that you say simply exists inside you can be practiced, enhanced, and ultimately vastly improved. Look around you, healer." Her hands were soft and small and gentle, but not without their own sort of power. "What do you see?"

Ariana looked up first, and she gasped. "Oh, my. After all this time . . ."

"What do you see?" he asked again.

"My mother, I think. All around the repaired place in the ceiling is . . . warmth." Was it his imagination, or did Ariana suddenly grow warmer? The body close to his, the gentle healer's hands . . . yes, she did grow much warmer. "I see a yellow glow, like a softly glowing sun. Love."

Which made it unlikely the darkness they sought had started in this room. Still, this was a good and powerful lesson, one Ariana needed. "And in the rest of the room? Tell me what you see. Concentrate."

Ariana stood in his arms, relaxed and rejuvenated, more comfortable than she'd been when he'd first touched her. They were oddly and comfortably connected, their energies melding. "I see red. Passion. Yes, I think passion. There's also a dirty gray . . . hate. There's a knotted energy, muted colors tied up in a tight little ball. That's confusion, I believe, or maybe anger. I can't be sure. Oh, there's so much energy here."

Sian could amplify her abilities with his touch, but he did not share them. He did not see what his pupil could see. "Is there blackness?"

Ariana studied the room carefully. "I see some spots of black, but they're small and overpowered by the other energies. They hide from the yellow, and from the red, and from the white. Did I tell you there's white?"

He released his hold on Ariana, and as he backed away, she spun to face him.

"How did you do that?" Her green eyes were lively, her lips rosy and slightly parted. She was lovely, and he could not afford to notice that loveliness.

"In time you will be able to see energy without my help."

"You can teach me that?"

"I hope so." If she could read energy, it would give her a decided edge. "In any case, this room is not the source of the darkness that threatens us. From what you described, there's more positive energy than negative, and if the darkness had begun here, then the spots of black you saw would either be gone or dominant. From your description, they were neither."

"If not here, then where?"

Sian crossed his arms and glared at his pupil. "You tell me, healer. You have seen many different types of energy, here in this room. We're looking for darkness. We're looking for a dominance of black. We're looking for an absence of love, hope, and passion. Where in this palace does the darkness reside?"

Ariana closed her eyes and took a deep breath. She turned her hands over so the palms were up. She was a quick study.

Sian wished he could believe that his interpretation of the prophesy was wrong. His grandfather had rambled, scribbling in the margins, quickly penning what he saw. What he knew. Some parts of the prophesy were unclear, but Sian understood what was penned there too well. Ariana Varden should live the life her mother wanted for her. A husband, babies, laughter. Safety.

She would have none of those in what remained of her short life.

Finally her eyes flew open and she gasped. "Of course." With those two inadequate words, she turned and ran from the room.

Sian followed, stalking after her, refusing to run as she did, since he had no idea where she was headed, or why. "Where are you going?"

Ariana cast him a bright smile over her shoulder, and at that moment she looked much too young and innocent to take up this fight. "Level Thirteen!"

"THERE IS NO LEVEL THIRTEEN."

With a newfound energy, Ariana moved down the stairwell as quickly as she could. Sian was able to keep up with her easily.

"Yes, there is," she responded.

"Level One is the top floor, Level Ten is the ground floor, Level Eleven houses lowly positioned soldiers and servants, and Level Twelve is a prison. There *is no* Level Thirteen."

Ariana stopped on the landing at Level Five, and turned to face her tutor as he came to a halt close beside her. Her face was overly warm, and she was breathless. Her heart was beating so hard she could feel it pounding in her chest. "My Aunt Isadora was imprisoned in Level Thirteen for a time, twenty-five years ago. It might not have been in use during Emperor Arik's reign, but that doesn't mean it no longer exists."

Sian's stern expression was that of a man who was rarely wrong, and who didn't like to admit it when he was. "Perhaps your aunt spun a tale for your amusement."

"Unlikely." A part of Ariana wanted to continue running downward, but in truth she needed to catch her breath. Besides, she wasn't sure she was ready to face the reality of Level Thirteen. Aunt Isadora had not spoken much of her time in the pit beneath the palace, and if a few of the elder cousins had not heard a portion of a conversation that had not been meant for their ears, she might never have known of its existence.

Nothing in life happened entirely by chance. If her days as a healer had taught her nothing else, she knew there were no accidents. Every small moment, every choice, led to something. Perhaps she had been guided to a position where she might overhear that long-ago conversation solely so she could understand what was happening now.

Perhaps it was her turn to do a bit of teaching. Ariana sat on the top step, looking down at the winding stair she'd be taking in a few moments, and patted the stone beside her. Sian was hesitant, but he did eventually sit beside her. His expression was as stony as the walls of the palace, and she had to wonder if he had ever been young and carefree, like her brother Duran or her Anwyn cousins. He did not look like a man who had ever been a boy without cares.

"When Sebestyen was in power, he thought nothing of tossing his enemies into the prison on Level Twelve."

"This I know," Sian said dryly.

"But for some, prison was not sufficient." Ariana leaned back, resting on her hands. "Have you heard of the drug Panwyr?"

That question elicited a response. Sian's long black-clad body twitched. "Yes, of course. Nasty stuff. Dreadfully addictive."

"So I hear. Emperor Sebestyen would drug his enemies, as well as the wives who had lost their appeal, and then he'd toss them into this hole beneath Level Twelve. Every day or two the guards would toss down Panwyr and food, but not enough for everyone. The prisoners fought and killed one another for the drug or their food. They lived in the dark, like animals, and eventually became little more than animals."

"And yet your aunt survived this place?" Sian sounded as if he did not believe her, and in truth she couldn't blame him. Level Thirteen sounded very much like a tale whispered to children to make them do as they were told. *Eat all of your peas, or the ghost of Emperor Sebestyen will snatch you up while you sleep and drop you into Level Thirteen . . .*

"There was a wizard, Thayne," Ariana explained. "He's Aunt Isadora's father, actually, and last I heard he still lives, though he was old then so now he must be ancient. He's a wizard for the Circle of Bacwyr. Long ago there was an unpleasant prophesy, and Sebestyen had Thayne, who delivered that prophesy, tossed into this pit in the ground. Thayne protected some of the innocents who were thrown into Level Thirteen, including Aunt Isadora, and eventually they escaped. After the end of the war, Emperor Arik closed Level Thirteen. My mother says he's a good man who would not make use of such a terrible place. It's dormant, I suppose, but if dark energy lives in this palace, surely it lives *there*."

"If the tale is true, it makes sense."

"Of course it's true. Aunt Isadora wouldn't lie. As it is, I don't think she told us everything." She'd never forget the look that had crossed the usually stoic Isadora's face when Duran had boldly asked her about Level Thirteen.

Sian sighed. "I suspect you might be right, then. We'll examine this Level Thirteen, or what remains of it, but not right now. First we need to do something about your wardrobe."

Ariana felt a woman's immediate ire at having her attire criticized. "What's wrong with this gown? The fabric is quite sturdy, and this shade of green doesn't show dirt, and—"

"Stand up," Sian ordered as he rose to his feet and moved back to stand in the center of the landing.

Ariana stood and faced the wizard. Now that she was certain Level Thirteen was the root of the rising evil, she was anxious to conduct a proper examination. Perhaps there would be clues there as to how to stop the evil. Perhaps there would be a sign to indicate exactly what she'd be fighting.

"Kick me," Sian ordered.

Ariana looked up so she could study his face. He didn't look as if he was joking. "I beg your—"

"Kick me," he said again. "Surely a woman who has eight siblings and an immense number of cousins has kicked someone in the past."

"I don't want to hurt you."

"You won't."

"I'm stronger than I look," she argued.

His purple eyes narrowed. "Must I inflame you before you'll do as I ask? Fine." His nostrils flared slightly, and the small wrinkle between his nicely shaped eyebrows deepened. "The fate of the world is in your hands, and that bothers me greatly. I fear for our future, now that I know *you* must play a part in the war which is to come. I have never known a less competent warrior, and that is what you must be, little girl, a warrior. A soldier. I do not believe that you have the strength to do what must be done. You don't have the magical strength or the physical strength. I can only hope your cousins are better equipped . . ."

"Fine," Ariana said, her indignation rising as Sian had no doubt intended. She drew back one leg slightly, as if preparing to kick the man who'd ordered her to do so. He was prepared for her toe to meet his shin with as much force as she could muster.

He was not prepared for her fist to come up swiftly and catch him in the jaw.

Sian's head snapped back, and he stumbled. He muttered a vile word as he regained his balance.

Ariana shook her hand. Connecting solidly with his hard jaw had been painful. "I have three brothers," she explained.

"They taught you well." Sian cradled his jaw in one hand for a moment, and then he dropped his hand and managed a brief, crooked smile. "You've proven the point that you are not entirely unprepared, but my point is that you will be better able to fight, and to examine places like Level Thirteen, if you wear trousers and a loose-sleeved shirt which allows more freedom of movement than the fashionable frock which you now wear."

"Trousers? Women don't wear—"

"Conventions must be set aside for what's to come, Ariana. Women don't do a lot of things. They don't wield a sword, they don't wear trousers, they don't fight battles. You must do all that, and more."

"You did not tell me that I had to go into combat." He'd said she'd be called upon to fight, but fighting could take many forms. Combat, on the other hand, was another matter.

"You must be prepared for anything."

"If it comes to that, I don't see why I can't fight in a skirt," Ariana grumbled. She could only imagine what people would think of her if she took to running about the palace in men's clothing! Not that they didn't already think she was odd. Still, she did have her dignity, and she wasn't anxious to toss it away.

"This is why." Sian moved quickly. He grabbed her skirt and yanked, and she stumbled. "Escape, Ariana. Get away."

She slapped ineffectively at his hand for a moment, but he had a large amount of fabric caught in his very large, hard fist. Again she tried to punch him in the jaw, but he was prepared this time, and he avoided the blow. In fact, he yanked her around again, and she landed on the floor. Hard. He crouched, and every time she tried to stand, he yanked her back down again, with very little visible effort. Since his arms were so much longer than hers, she was unable to free herself, and he made it all look so easy.

"You're wrinkling my skirt," she complained.

"I don't care."

"Fine. You've proven your point. A traditional skirt offers too much fabric for an enemy to grab and manipulate. If it comes to that, and I don't think it will. If I'm to play a part in this war, then it must be through casting spells and healing and such. That's what I do."

"You must be prepared to fight in a more traditional manner, I'm afraid."

It was impossible to free herself, and she soon became frustrated with the efforts. "Perhaps I should fight naked. Then there would be nothing for the opposing soldiers to grab."

Sian's only response was a lift of his eyebrows, and a twinkle of awareness in his purple eyes. The color darkened and shifted, as if she were looking into a fast-moving indigo rain cloud. "My, what a picture that paints in my fertile imagination."

That was not what she'd intended! She'd only wished to point out that his ideas about her fighting were ridiculous. "I'm not a soldier."

"That is one of the things you must learn, so you'll be prepared for anything."

Her brothers were adept at fighting. They had been trained almost from birth to use swords and knives, bows and arrows, and their fists. She had not. If she had to fight in this manner, her part in the battle to come wouldn't last very long.

For the first time the truth hit Ariana, hard. If the prophesy Sian had delivered to Emperor Arik was a true one, then she was likely going to die. Nobly, perhaps, but still . . . she was going to die. She prided herself on being a strong woman, but she was not a soldier. She was not a fighter.

She quit trying to free herself and sat on the landing. Sian continued to clutch at the fabric of her skirt, so that it rode up to her knee. The position was less than lady-like, but she didn't much care at the moment. Being told that one had a part to play in a war against darkness was shocking enough. The moment when the words finally felt *real* was enough to take her breath away.

"Will I survive this?" she asked softly.

"I do not have the gift of sight."

She yanked her skirt from Sian's hand, and he let her have it. "What kind of teacher are you?" she snapped. "You're supposed to tell me that if I'm a good student I will survive. You're supposed to promise me that if I try very hard I will win this fight and the world will not move into darkness. You're supposed to give me faith that I can *do* this."

"Any faith you have must come from your heart, not my words."

His calm manner annoyed her. "I don't want to die."

Sian sighed and leaned back against the stone wall, adopting a casual pose that belied the severity of the situation. "No one wants to die, but to be afraid of death is like being afraid of nightfall. It comes, for all of us. Fear does not hold back the night, nor does it hold death at bay. That fear can only make you weak, and you cannot afford weakness, Ariana Kane Fyne Varden." He looked at her, his purple eyes boring into her, seeing through her. "Would you live a life filled with fire and purpose, or would you hide yourself away in a place that's safe but uneventful? Would you leave this earth in a battle against all that is wicked, or would you cower behind the safety of solid but isolated doors? Will you die proudly with a warrior's scream of excitement, or will you live long and afraid with a whimper forever on your lips?"

Ariana took a deep breath and blew it out slowly before answering. "I'm rather fond of whimpering."

"I am to be your teacher. You must promise not to lie to me."

"Fine," Ariana said sharply. "I've never been at all fond of whimpering."

"I thought as much."

She was in no hurry to rise and continue down the stairway. Beyond this landing there waited trousers and swordplay and a wizard's lessons and Level Thirteen. She remained in a seated position and looked at Sian, studying the sharp planes of his face and the strength of his neck and the ruggedness of his hands. He was a powerful wizard—a powerful man. She could do worse, where teachers were concerned. He had the power to manipulate some physical objects, like the doors to the emperor's suite. Could he teach her to do the same? She had a feeling she'd need every advantage she could muster.

Sian had once offered to take her place in battle, fearing for the world if the fight was left to her. He was likely a good swordsman, and though many enchanter's tricks were little more than illusion, he had some substantial talents. He had taken her voice, that one time, and had threatened to freeze her. Now, that would be a useful trick to have when battle came upon her. She suspected that was the sort of magic that was either inborn or took a lifetime to perfect.

"When the time comes, will you fight with me?"

"No," he answered without a moment's hesitation. "This is your battle, not mine. You will have need to raise an army, but I am no soldier. When you are properly trained, I will return to my home."

And she would continue on without him. She barely knew the man, and still that thought made her heart leap.

"I did not ask for this responsibility," Ariana said sharply as she rose to her feet. "I did not ask to be burdened with the fate of the world!"

Sian stood much more smoothly and gracefully than she did.

"Heroes rarely do."

WHEN ARIANA HAD BEEN DISMISSED FOR THE DAY—Level Thirteen as yet unexplored—Sian went to his assigned room and barricaded the door behind him. He lit a single candle, and sat before the weathered desk near the head of his bed.

Sighing, he withdrew the prophesy from a deep pocket of his coat. He didn't dare leave it lying around for just anyone to find. There were promises here he was not yet ready to share. Not with Arik, not with anyone.

He gently unfolded the document which was already showing signs of wear, it had been folded and unfolded so often. His long fingers raked down the left edge of the paper, stopping to rest over the passage that haunted him. His grandfather had been wrong about the fine women. Perhaps he was wrong about this as well.

Probably not.

Of the three fine warriors who are called to this battle, one will find and wield the crystal dagger. One will betray love in the name of victory. And one, the eldest, will die at the hands of a monster who will hurtle a weary soul into the Land of the Dead.

Ariana Varden was the eldest, and by sending her into battle, he was sending her to her death.

❧ The Prophesy of the Firstborn ❧

A darkness creeps beneath Columbyana and the lands beyond. This darkness grows stronger each and every day, infecting those who have an affinity for evil. As it grows stronger, it will also begin to affect those who are of weak mind, and eventually it will grow so strong no one among us will be able to defeat it. If this darkness is allowed to grow to this point, the world is doomed to eternal shadows, where evil will reign.

*

Only the firstborn children of three fine women *[later translated as Fyne]* have the power to stop the darkness and restore the world to light. These firstborn will be the warriors who lead the fight. Our fate rests in their hands, and in the hands of the armies they will call to them.

*

Of the three fine *[Fyne]* warriors who are called to this battle, one will find and wield the crystal dagger. One will betray love in the name of victory. And one, the eldest, will die at the hands of a monster who will hurtle a weary soul into the Land of the Dead.

*

Many monsters will rise from among us in this unholy war, soulless monsters such as the world has never seen. Heroes will be born and heroes will die. Death and darkness will threaten all those who choose to fight for the light.

Scribbled in the lefthand margin, in an almost illegible hand:

Beware Serrazone,

and beside it,

He who walks through fire may show the way.

Scribbled in the righthand margin:

*Those who are called must choose
between love and death,
between heart and intellect,
between victory of the sword and victory of the soul.*

The remainder of the prophesy is illegible scribbling and indecipherable sketches. A scraggly tree; a bird with wings too large; a flower; a heart; a dagger. *[The crystal dagger, perhaps?]* Do they have meaning or are they simply a dying old man's insignificant doodles?

4

SINCE THEY WERE LITTLE MORE THAN A YEAR APART IN age, it was only natural that Ariana and her brother Duran had always been close. Still, they were different as night and day. She had been born to magic, like their mother; he had no supernatural talents, like their father.

But it was more than magic—or lack thereof—that made them so dissimilar. Duran was carefree, taking each day as it came without worry. Ariana was a planner, and a worrier. She could not take each day without careful planning of her schedule and her wardrobe. Until Sian had shown up to throw all her plans into disarray, she'd already planned what each day in the following week would bring. Duran simply followed his feet, and went wherever they led him.

There was another way in which they were very much not alike, but Ariana suspected this difference had more to do with gender than anything else. In other words, it wasn't always Duran's *feet* which guided him.

Duran loved women, and they loved him. He had been sent here to keep his sister safe—against her wishes but at the insistence of their parents. His two years here had been spent as more than a brother and a bodyguard. He was a fine sentinel. One of the best. His skills with a sword had improved greatly in his time in the palace. He was also very popular with the maids and laundresses, as well as one particular minister's daughter who was not the perfect angel her father thought her to be.

Sian had insisted that the fewer who knew of the prophesy, the safer she'd be. Word could not reach those she'd be fighting against until she was ready. They could not be forewarned. Anyone who knew of the danger would be in great peril, as those dark forces that threatened Columbyana would not hesitate to do away with anyone who might rouse troops before they were ready to fight.

Ariana wasn't sure she'd ever be ready, but the other argument, the one that put her carefree, life-loving brother in mortal danger, kept her silent. When the time came, he'd learn of the prophesy. Until then, he was better off not knowing anything at all.

She was surprised that he paid her a visit in her quarters, late in the evening. He often worked the evening shift, and if not, then he was always busy with one woman or another, or failing that, a game of cards.

No, she wouldn't put an end to his carefree lifestyle until it was absolutely necessary.

He paced before her fireplace, obviously anxious. Duran did not wear his hair as long as many of the other sentinels, but preferred a shorter style. His dark curls didn't even reach his shoulders. She'd always thought it terribly unfair that his hair was so much prettier and more manageable than her own.

Ariana sat in a comfortable chair near the fire and continued to sew while her brother paced and asked cordial questions. Had her day been a pleasant one? Had she been able to walk outdoors to enjoy the nice weather? What had she eaten for supper?

Duran *never* asked such questions.

Ariana stilled her hands and looked up, to find Duran glaring at her. It was also not fair that he was more beautiful than she was. Right now he looked fierce, but he was still beautiful. Was it possible that somehow he knew all her secrets?

"What do you really want?" she asked.

"I have heard rumors," he said, his voice not as genial as it had been moments earlier.

Ariana's heart hitched. "What sort of rumors?" Had someone overheard them speaking of the Prophesy of the Firstborn? Only she, the emperor, and Sian knew. At Sian's insistence, it was a secret. For now.

"Today you spent a significant amount of time in the company of a stranger. A wizard, if what I heard was correct."

"Oh." Ariana returned to her sewing, relieved. The rumors that had her brother fuming were of the ordinary sort. "His name is Sian Chamblyn, so he's not a stranger."

Duran's eyes narrowed. "And what exactly were you doing in his company?"

The overprotective nature of the question was amusing and annoying at the same time. Ariana didn't look up as she answered, "He's tutoring me."

"In what subject are you being tutored?" Duran asked, his teeth clenched.

Ariana put her hands down once again and looked up. At this moment, Duran looked so very much like their father. She had seen this expression of ire and impatience—and yes, love—from Kane Varden more than once.

But Duran was *not* her father. "Sex, of course. Today's lessons were quite ordinary, but I understand tomorrow we're going to study the more deviant aspects of sexual relations. We have been told that in some segments of Level Three there remain a number of potentially pleasurable devices and instruction manuals that describe in great detail . . ."

Duran turned away from her and stalked toward the door. He mumbled under his breath, and she only made out one word. "Kill."

Ariana dropped her mending to the floor and leapt up, giving chase. She caught Duran by the shirt sleeve as he opened the door. Laughing, she said, "He's teaching me magic, and nothing else."

Duran turned his head and glared down at her. "Why?"

"Because he knows much of magic that I don't, that's why." She reached past her brother, and pushed the door shut. "I promise you, I'm as pure and untouched as I was when Sian Chamblyn arrived here this morning."

Duran leaned against the door and crossed his arms defiantly. His expression and the set of his tense neck spoke of withheld suspicions.

"I was only teasing you because I'm twenty-six years old and you have no business quizzing me as if I were still twelve and you were Poppy."

"I am here to protect you," he said in a low, serious voice.

"I do not need your protection," she insisted. Not yet, in any case.

"Poppy will kill me if anything happens to you."

"Unlikely. And if he were to try, Mama would stop him. Probably."

Duran didn't look as if he were inclined to engage in sibling banter at the moment.

"I'm fine, truly," she said seriously. "You know how desperately I want to hone my skills. The enchanter who tutored me today will help me to reach my goals in that area of my life."

"If he tries anything untoward—"

"I will alert you immediately so that you may administer proper punishment."

Duran's eyes were narrowed, his mouth tight and thinner than usual. "You make light of my concern."

Ariana laid her hand on Duran's arm. "Of course not," she said gently. "I just want to make sure you understand there is no need for concern."

She felt and saw him relax, gradually but unmistakably, and then he said, "If you do need me, you know where I can be found."

"Of course."

Duty to family done for now, Duran left Ariana alone with her sewing. She sighed in relief when he was gone, and when she sat down in her chair once again and lifted from the floor the garment she'd been mending, she held it up to fully survey her work.

Trousers. Roughly made, dark and plain, but soon to be well fitted. If Duran had realized just what type of clothing she was altering, his meddlesome questions would've continued for quite some time.

GOOD HEAVENS. SIAN KEPT HIS EYES ANYWHERE BUT ON Ariana as they made their way down to Level Twelve. She preceded him, and he found it best to look over her head, or at the stone walls that surrounded them.

He had never imagined that a woman wearing trousers would look just so. A woman's rear end simply did not fill a pair of trousers like a man's did. There was a roundness to her hips and backside, a tempting curve that could undo the staunchest of men.

There had been many tales over the years of women who disguised themselves as men in order to travel where they should not, or fight, or deceive. He'd always found them amusing stories, and wondered if they were perhaps based in truth.

If the tales were true, the women in question had not been built anything like Ariana Varden. No one would ever mistake that backside for male.

She was actually excited about their foray into Level Thirteen. Her hair was loose and wild, her cheeks overly pink, her lips . . . well, there was no reason to study her lips. They had nothing to do with this excursion. She'd donned an ornately decorated vest over a plain white shirt, perhaps in an effort to disguise her breasts. The plan had failed . . . but again, her breasts had nothing to do with this search for the source of the evil which threatened the entire country, and even the world.

Sian bit back a vile word. The firstborn Fyne could not have been a man, a soldier, a brute who would welcome a battle with evil. Oh, no, instead it had to be this slip of a girl who had no business fighting monsters.

Level Twelve was dimly lit and somber, home to murderers and thieves and a handful of apparently lax guards. Heavy wooden doors with small grates built into them lined the stone hallway. Sian ignored the prison cells, shutting out the whispers and shouts from beyond the heavy doors and following Ariana down a long hall. There was a chill in this place, a chill he didn't like at all.

She seemed to know where she was going.

"Here." She stopped at the edge of a worn, stained carpet that was oddly placed on the prison hallway floor.

"Pardon me." A young guard stepped forward. He and a cohort had been conversing with animation at the opposite end of the hallway, until they'd seen the visitors to Level Twelve. "This is no place for . . ." He looked Ariana up and down, taking in the vest, the trousers, the serviceable boots. "Who are you?"

"Ariana Varden, healer to the emperor," she said confidently. "What lies beneath this rug?"

The guard looked taken aback. "Nothing."

Ariana sighed, and lifted one hand as she turned to face Sian. "There is definitely something here. It's . . . dark." Fear touched her eyes, but Sian did not see panic.

"Is it safe?" he asked simply.

"I think so."

"Stand back," Sian ordered. With a wag of his hand, the guard obeyed the command. When no one stood upon the nasty rug, Sian once again waved his fingers. The rug rolled up as if guided by invisible hands. The guards were now visibly afraid.

Ariana was amused. "You are such a show-off," she whispered.

He did not respond, which was just as well. This was no time for teasing. Beneath the rug was a trap door built into the floor, a portal aged by time and neglect.

"Level Thirteen?" Sian asked.

"Yes, I believe so," Ariana answered softly.

With a whispered word and a twist of his fingers, the heavy trap door swung open, slamming against the floor with a loud whack, and offering a glimpse into total darkness. One of the guards began to inch away from the scene, no doubt planning to run.

Sian lifted his hand and pointed at the cowardly guard. He used no magic, but still the man halted, as if frozen. "Stay."

"Yes, my lord," the young man responded.

"We're going down. I expect you two to stand guard. If we don't return in a reasonable amount of time . . ." He glanced at Ariana and lifted his eyebrows in silent question.

"One hour," she said.

He doubted Ariana would last a quarter of an hour in that pit. Still, this was her call. She was the chosen one, and he was here just to assist her in charging toward her destiny. "If we don't return in one hour, go to Emperor Arik and request that he send sentinels in to assist us."

"Yes, my lord," the two guards answered simultaneously.

They were soldiers, and yet they were cowed by his display of magic and the revelation of the pit. Ariana would be at least as good a warrior as either of these two. Perhaps the fact that she was a woman was not the worst of circumstances. She did have a strength about her that he could not deny.

It seemed the unseen prisoners that surrounded them were disturbed by the revelation of the pit. The prison noise increased, and one man screamed. Did they realize that Level Thirteen had been uncovered? Did they feel it?

One soldier collected a length of rope and, when instructed to do so, tied it to a hook on the backside of the trap door. A hook which might have been installed for that very purpose. Sian tested the knot, not entirely trusting the guards, and then he began his descent.

"Don't you want a torch, or a candle?" one of the guards asked.

"That won't be necessary," Sian responded.

He made his way quickly down, using his feet and his hands to give himself a sturdy command of the rope. A fall from this distance would not kill him, but neither would it be pleasant. When he was close to the ground, he released the rope and dropped onto the packed dirt floor.

As Ariana began her trip down the rope, Sian placed himself directly beneath her. If she lost her grip, he'd be able to break her fall. He wouldn't always be around to catch her, but for today she was his responsibility. For today, he could catch her if need be.

The view from this angle was quite interesting, especially as he cast a spell and the wizard's light, purple and illuminating, was born and grew. Her descent was slow and deliberate, but not without the display of some small strength. The trousers seemed to tighten considerably as she worked her way down and toward him.

"What do you see?" she asked when she was perhaps halfway down the rope.

He could not very well tell her where his eyes were

drawn. "Nothing," he answered. "Nothing at all. We'll explore the area when you complete your dreadfully leisurely descent."

Ariana glanced around and down, just so she could glare at him. She did glare for a moment, and then she began to laugh. "You are not half so fearsome as you pretend to be, I believe."

Heaven above, he did not want her to laugh. He did not want her to look fetching in her inappropriate clothing. He did not want to care about her.

Ariana was not his to care about, after all. She was a doomed witch, an ill-fated warrior. If all went well, one day there would be heroic tales written about her. She would be the subject of songs and poems of goodness and bravery. It was his calling to prepare her for what was to come. He could not allow even the vaguest of emotions to cloud his intent.

ARIANA WAS GRATEFUL FOR THE WIZARD'S LIGHT AS SHE examined the pit that had been—that *was*—Level Thirteen. The ground was littered here and there with what appeared to be bones. Some were obviously from rodents. Others were larger, and very likely human. The walls were natural stone, as if they had descended into an irregularly shaped cavern. That stone was much colder than was natural; it was rough and stained with what might be . . . no, what *was* . . . blood. She shuddered as she looked into the dark corners beyond the purplish light that reminded her, so very much, of Sian's eyes.

She was cold well beyond the actual chill of temperature, so far beneath the surface. It was as if ice formed on her very skin, as if it seeped beneath her skin. Steeling her spine, she made herself step toward the edge of the light Sian created. One step, and then another.

"Stay close," he ordered, his voice gruff.

She looked back and up to see his face. Sian Chamblyn was a man of great magic. A stoic man. A teacher of great things.

And he was frightened of this place.

"I cannot see what I need to see when I am protected by the light you create," she explained. "The energy you taught me to see hides from the power of your wizard's light. I must move beyond it." She glanced up, to see the faces of the two frightened, curious guards looking down. "I hate to say it, but that door above must be closed as well." She needed darkness in order to do what had to be done. She also needed the touch of Sian's hand. As he had done in the great room on Level One, he would assist her by lending her a touch of his power.

Sian did not snap the hatch closed with a twist of his fingers, but ordered the guards to see to the chore. When that was done, the purple light began to dim. It faded, slowly but not slowly enough. Right before the light was entirely gone, Ariana reached out and snatched Sian's hand.

Maybe she did need the darkness, but she did not want to be alone. Not down here in this awful place.

Sian seemed surprised that she'd taken his hand, even though he must know that she needed his help to see the energies in this dark, dank place. He did not shake her off and insist that she attempt to discover the lingering energies on her own. Thank goodness. The darkness here was so complete, she could not see the man she touched. Maybe in time her eyes would adjust to the darkness, but that had not happened yet.

As Sian had taught her to do just yesterday, Ariana searched for the energies that abounded in this place—with his assistance, of course. His power combined with hers was extraordinary. It was as if he fed her natural abilities in some way she didn't entirely understand. What would she do when he left, as he had promised he would?

Even though all was black, she could still see—and sense—the evil dark energy that lived here. Upstairs, in the ballroom of Level One, there had been light and dark, love and passion, hate and happiness.

Here, all was dark. There was despair, and hate that reached such depths she had not known such was possible. Ribbons of a sexual anger also lived here, but there was no passion or love mingled with it, just raw, angry need.

Ariana closed her eyes and held on to Sian's hand a bit tighter. He did not ask what she saw . . . not yet. Even with her eyes closed, she could see the evil that existed here. She felt it; she experienced it. Men—and yes, a few women—had ended their lives here. Some of them had lived a long time in filth and misery and blinding need. A need for the drug, for the light that never came, for food. A deep, unquenchable need of a body. Of a man, of a woman.

She jumped when it seemed that something . . . someone . . . touched her leg. No, that was not possible. No one had been down here for a very long time. What she felt was the energy that remained from some poor soul. A ghost, perhaps, or the shadow of a pain so great it survived death.

Tears. Screams. Violence. As Ariana stood there, she felt it all, and the sensations did not abate, they grew stronger. Her heart began to race. Sweat formed between her breasts and on her throat. Her fingers trembled.

Souls had been lost here. No, not lost, stolen. *Taken*. By what? Or whom?

A terrible darkness crept around and inside her, cold fingers touched her, and still she felt protected. It was Sian's hand in hers that protected her, she knew. That large, warm, strong hand that would produce light if she needed light. Protection, if it became necessary. Solace, if the darkness tried to claim her. She had something precious that none of those who had lost their souls here had possessed. She had the hand of a friend, and it kept her from seeing all that she needed to see.

Could she see anything of the horrors here without his hand in hers?

Moving quickly, so he wouldn't know what she was going to do, Ariana snatched her hand from Sian and stepped away, so that she was truly alone. She heard him curse, and out of the corner of her eye she saw a soft glimmer of purple.

"Not yet," she whispered. "I'm close to something, but I can't quite grasp it. What I need is just out of reach, and if I hold your hand or take comfort in your light, it won't come to me. Let me try to do this alone, Sian. Let me try. I'll call if I need you."

Again he cursed, but no light was produced.

It was more frightening than she had imagined was possible, to be alone in this place. The darkness was suffocating, and the black corners seemed to stretch into forever. Ariana stepped away from her companion, her teacher, her protector. This was something she had to do alone. There could be no comfort, if she were to discover the secrets of Level Thirteen.

Without Sian's touch, without his added power, she could no longer see the energies here. But oh, she could feel the pain and terror. She could feel them as if they were her own, and with every breath she took, they grew.

Nothing warm lived here. No yellow light, no sunshine, had ever touched these walls. She took a few more steps, separating herself from Sian and grasping for the knowledge that remained just out of reach. She opened herself to the souls that had been lost here; she felt the pain of their addiction and their longing.

Everything she knew of herself, everything that made Ariana Varden the woman she had become . . . the love of her family, the care of a teacher, the position of respect she held in this palace . . . it was all gone. It was stolen by darkness and cold fingers and the pain of the dead that survived. In the dark, she heard a piercing, echoing scream, and for a moment she wondered where it came from.

And then she realized with an icy coldness that crept inside her that the scream was hers.

Sian called her name, his voice sharp and oddly distant. She tried to answer, to guide him to her with the sound of her voice, but no voice would come.

And then everything went black, inside and out. Someone else was here, and Ariana Varden was gone.

5

How had Ariana moved so far away in the short time they'd been separated? Sian threw wizard's light in all directions, searching for the woman. No, searching for the scream. It had been a horrible scream, filled with terror and pain. He hated screams almost as much as he hated tears, not that he'd had occasion to hear many of them.

Finally, *finally*, he saw an arm move into the light he created.

Above, the doorway to this hell opened, and a concerned guard asked, "Is everything all right down there?"

All right. The man was a moron. Nothing was all right, nor would it ever be again. As Sian was about to order the moron to descend and assist, he caught sight of Ariana's face. Thank the gods and goddesses, she was unhurt. In fact, she smiled strangely. Her eyes darted upward, and she whispered, "Tell them to go away."

The woman before him sounded well enough. She

sounded very calm, in fact. The problem was, that wasn't
Ariana Varden's voice. Not precisely.

The answers they had come here to seek might be
right before him. "Everything is fine," he snapped to the
guard. "Close the doorway."

The man above obeyed, and Sian stepped toward
Ariana . . . or whoever this woman might be. The smile
and the voice were female enough, so he felt safe in as-
suming whatever was inside Ariana was female.

He saw no need to play games. "I am Sian Sayre
Chamblyn, enchanter and tutor to the woman you possess. And you are?"

She walked toward him slowly, not at all afraid. "Once
I was empress. My loving husband tossed me down here
just because I tried to have him killed. Now I am almost
nothing, but not yet nothing. I am pain and sorrow and
desperation. I am lost."

"The empresses who were believed to be dead were
released at the end of the War of the Beckyts," Sian argued. "Who are you, truly?"

Her mouth, Ariana's mouth, thinned and hardened. "All
but *one* was released. All but *one* was rescued. I remained.
A piece of me still remains."

"Your name?" There was power in a name, and he
might yet need power over this thing before him.

"I was called Diella, for a time."

"What do you want with the woman you possess,
Diella?"

The eyes closed, the lips parted sensually. "I want to
live again. I want to feel something good. Something . . .
fine and right. I want to experience something besides
pain and horror and craving."

"Your time is past." For Ariana's well-being, he should

order this ghost, if that's what it was, from her body. But there was more at stake than one woman's well-being, and he could not forget that fact. "I will allow you to remain in that body for a few minutes longer, if you will tell me what I need to know."

"You will *allow*?" she laughed, and there was too much confidence in the laughter. This former empress called herself a piece of something lost, but she still had power. Power, in this dark place.

Sian lifted his hand and whispered a word. Ariana's body froze. Perhaps he could not command the spirit away, but he did have control of the physical.

Even though she was frozen, he saw the anger on Ariana's face. On the Empress Diella's face.

"Yes," Sian said calmly. "I will *allow*." After a few moments, which he knew to be uncomfortable if the woman who had use of Ariana's body experienced physical sensation, Sian released her. She no longer smiled quite so widely.

"What do you want to know?" she asked, her voice throatier than Ariana's, older and angrier.

"Something evil has escaped from this place. What is it?"

Again Diella smiled, stepping forward. By the wizard's light, her face seemed not as pretty as Ariana's, and still . . . she was Ariana. Ariana and not. Good and evil. Lost and yet to be lost.

"If you do as I request, I will tell you."

He had no intention of giving this creature anything, but he asked, "What do you require?"

She approached him bravely, unafraid and obviously happy to be in possession of Ariana's body. "I want a kiss."

Sian had expected almost anything, but the request surprised him. "A kiss? Why?"

Ariana—the creature Diella who had possession of Ariana's body—all but leaned against him. Her breasts brushed his chest. Her breath, warm and human, touched him. "When I lived, when I was here, I had the use of many men who serviced me as I required. The drug Panwyr causes a mighty surge of need which no man can truly satisfy, but they did try. With their inadequate cocks and their tongues and their fumbling hands, they gave me what I demanded of them. Sometimes I returned the favor when they had such a need. Sometimes I did not." Her voice turned cold. "Sometimes I killed them with my bare hands. More than once I killed for a dose of the drug I came to love better than any man. I would kill for it now, if I had the chance. Does that surprise you, that a woman has the ability to do such a thing?"

"No."

"Good. You should never underestimate the power of a woman. This one is strong, but . . ."

"But what?" Sian snapped.

Diella closed her eyes and took a long, deep breath that made her breasts swell. "I smell death on her. I smell the promise of the land I have not yet been allowed to pass into. Do you think it will be beautiful there?"

Not for you, I imagine. "I don't know."

"Neither do I," she whispered. "Sometimes I long for that passage, but at other times I am afraid. I know not what awaits me there. Ah, I've been sidetracked. My kiss. You wonder why, when I have possession of this body and information that you require, I ask for something so insignificant as a kiss."

"Yes."

She rose up on her toes and whispered, "I want to feel again. I'm not talking about the meeting of two bodies. I'm not talking about sweat and invasion and release. Animals mate. Men have been known to take what they want with no consideration for the woman who lies beneath them. But a kiss is special. It's sensation and affection and promise and . . . and life, all in the meeting of two mouths."

"I have no affection for you," Sian said coldly.

"No, but you do have some affection for this body." She leaned in and whispered. "I saw you watch her. You want her. She wants you, too. I know, because even though I am at the surface at this moment, she is not gone. She's very much here, and I can access the deepest reaches of her mind. Not all, not everywhere, but I can touch much of this woman and I know you make her tremble deep inside. I know she wonders what it would be like if you were lovers, if you came to her bed at night and made her scream. Not the way I made her scream, you understand, but—"

"Do not lie to me, demon woman. Ariana is a demure maiden who would not think of—"

The woman began to laugh before he could finish. "Demure maiden? I thought you knew her, but apparently you do not. She is no maiden, I assure you, and deep down she occasionally thinks of taking a lover to satisfy her womanly needs. In the back of her cluttered mind, she believes that you would do quite nicely."

He did not intend to stand here and discuss Ariana with this thing that had taken control of her body. "Tell me what I want to know."

"Kiss first," she said, and then she grabbed his shirt front and dragged him down, placing her mouth on his and taking the kiss she demanded.

Sian did his best to remain distant and unaffected.

This was simply the price he had to pay for the information he needed. But it was not so easy to remain detached. The creature before him smelled like Ariana. She tasted like Ariana. The body that molded to his was Ariana's. The hand that very boldly grabbed him where a demure maiden would not was Ariana's. Against his wishes, he grew to fill that hand. Still kissing, she laughed, and she squeezed lightly.

He pulled away, and she didn't seem to mind. The kiss was over. "You're going to send her off to die without even a proper bedding. Not very generous of you, enchanter."

He did not want to hurt Ariana, but this creature before him was not his student. She was not the firstborn Fyne child. She was one of the monsters Ariana had been chosen to fight. Sian grabbed her by the throat and held on tight. "Your price has been paid, so speak. What happened here?"

As if immune to the power of his hands, the creature smiled. "The Isen Demon happened here. It was born from a seed left dormant long ago. It grew strong here. The demon you seek is a stealer of souls and feeds from the dead, a creature from which other creatures hide once it grows as strong as this one."

"How can it be stopped?"

With his hand on her throat constricting her, the empress answered, "It cannot be stopped, enchanter. With every soul that's taken, the Isen Demon becomes stronger. It grows stronger and darker and hungrier with every passing day. You can't stop it. She certainly can't stop it. Perhaps you can make it hurt for a while if you take away the Panwyr, but the demon will find a way to possess what it needs. Souls and the drug that gives it life." Her smile grew wide. "I'm glad I'm already dead. What's to come isn't going to be pleasant." She closed her eyes and took another deep breath, a breath which was ragged, thanks to his grip. "I smell the Land of the Dead on her, but not on you. You'll get to see it all, enchanter. You'll live a long time, as wizards often do, and you'll get to watch everything that matters to you crumble and die."

SIAN'S HAND WAS ON HER THROAT, AND SHE COULDN'T breathe. She couldn't breathe! Ariana reached out to slap at the man who held her. What had happened? One minute she'd sensed a darkness surrounding her, and then . . . this.

He didn't seem inclined to let her go. Ariana grabbed his sleeve. Beneath that sleeve was muscle hard as stone, firm and warm and strong. Much stronger than she. He was right; she was not made for fighting.

She lifted her face and looked into his eyes. The wizard's light was a pale, gentle purple, but his eyes were dark and rich. They were enchanter eyes, and even in the dim light she could see the shift of color. Those eyes looked like a vast, deep ocean she could very easily fall into, and they were filled with life and power and pain. She had not seen the pain before, but when their eyes locked, she saw more of her new teacher than she had seen before.

He was not so cold as he pretended to be.

He flinched, and with suddenness he released his hold on her. "Ariana," he said. "You're back."

"I didn't go anywhere," she responded, lifting a soothing hand to her throat.

"Yes, you did," he snapped. "Why on earth didn't you tell me that you're an empath?"

"It's part of the healing. I assumed you'd know—"

"Not all healers are empaths," he interrupted. "Someone

with your sensibilities should steer clear of dark places like this one, and you should've known that. You're much too open to influences of all kinds."

Influences like the darkness she had felt. "So I was—"

"Possessed," Sian said sharply. "Yes."

It was frightening to realize not only that another spirit had been in control of her body but that she didn't remember a single moment of the encounter. Ariana was so very grateful that Sian had been here, and that he'd realized she was not herself.

"Did you learn anything?" she asked.

"I'll tell you all about it later." Sian shouted for the guards who waited above, and demanded that the rope be lowered. He then insisted that she climb up first, and she did not argue. She wanted out of this place. She wanted never to see—or feel—Level Thirteen again.

Climbing the rope wasn't as easy as descending it had been, but Ariana managed. Anything to escape Level Thirteen. It was difficult to believe that Aunt Isadora had spent *days* in this place. When she reached the top, the guards assisted her. When she glanced down, Sian—who moved much more quickly than she—was already halfway up the rope. He moved with assurance and anger, as anxious to escape as she had been.

She knew Sian was here only to prepare her for what was to come. He could be a soldier if he so wished, but he had told her with certainty that he would not fight with her when the time came. It was her calling to fight this war, not his.

Sian needed no assistance to bound from the hole in the floor. There was a touch of magic in the way he left Level Thirteen, almost as if he flew—a short distance and just for a moment.

He took her arm and together they walked toward the stairwell. Why did an enchanter have need of such strength? The man had muscles like the finest sentinel. Muscles he hid beneath a loose-fitting shirt. Muscles he had used to grip her throat—which was still sore from his tight hold. Of course, she did understand that at the time he had not been gripping *her*.

"Well?" she asked as they entered the stairwell and left the guards—and Level Twelve—behind. "What did you learn?"

He moved too quickly, all but dragging her up the stairs. "We're in trouble."

ARIANA HAD INSISTED ON MINISTERING TO THE EMperor before Sian informed the man of his discoveries. Emperor Arik, seated by the window and visibly frail, was taken aback by Ariana's unusual state of dress. Sick as he was, and old enough to be her father, Arik eventually smiled weakly and simply watched her. Ariana herself seemed oblivious to the way the emperor's eyes studied her, not as a patient, but as a man.

The demon below had shared Ariana's mind for a few moments. It was possible that she'd lied—those who embraced darkness were not wedded to the truth, after all— but it was also possible that she'd been telling the truth. Could it be that Ariana was no innocent maid? Was there more between her and the emperor than the healing Arik so desperately needed? Not now, certainly, when he was so ill, but in the past, perhaps?

Her hands did not seem hesitant to touch her patient, even though Arik was emperor, a man of the greatest authority. She smiled at him now and then, and the smile seemed kind enough—and also familiar, as if she considered him a friend.

Not that he cared, of course. Ariana was his student in the arena of magic. His job was to prepare her to march to her death. Her sexual liaisons past and future were of no concern to him. So, why did the very idea of her lying with this old man incense him?

Finally, after many long minutes, Ariana assured herself that the emperor was well enough for this conversation, and she stepped away from Arik.

The old man looked to Sian, his eyes full of questions.

"It started here," Sian said simply. "Beneath the palace, in Level Thirteen. A demon, an Isen Demon, grew potent there and escaped, taking with it the souls of those who died in that horrible place."

"How?" Arik asked.

"I don't know. I've studied a bit of demonology over the years, but I am not an expert by any means. I'll research the matter."

"Do we have time enough for research?"

Sian could only be honest with the emperor. "Probably not. Not enough, anyway. If I can locate a wizard who is acquainted with the Isen Demon, it will save valuable time. Otherwise I'll be searching through documents for months, and I suspect we don't have months."

Ariana spoke up. "There are many fine wizards in the Circle of Bacwyr. Perhaps we should collect Lyr before we go to Keelia, and while we're there, we can interview the Circle wizards and find one who's familiar with demonology and the Isen Demon."

"Perhaps," Sian said. "I have not yet decided."

"There are many journals on Level Seven, where

witches and wizards of the palace have always practiced. Perhaps you will find what you need there."

"I'll study these journals." Sian liked the idea of exposing Ariana to battle less and less. Maiden or not, she was a woman. A healer. An empath. How could an empath do battle? How could an empath kill, as Ariana would surely need to do? He might as well walk her to the edge of a cliff and toss her over the side. She'd have as much a chance of survival, and suffer much less pain. "As for the other suggestion, it is too soon. We will not be making our journey to Queen Keelia or to Lyr in the very near future."

"But—" Ariana began, ready to argue with him.

"You are not ready." With that, he turned his back on her and walked away, opening the doors with a flick of his wrist and making haste for his quarters. He had lessons to plan, and he could not offer all of them himself. Ariana would need the tutoring of a swordsman, an herbalist, a foot soldier, and a shaman if she were to survive long enough to do her part in this dreadful war that was coming.

CIRO STOOD AT THE WINDOW AND WATCHED RAYNE work in the garden. A part of him wanted to join her, but he no longer cared for the sun. It burned his skin and all but blinded him. No, these days he was much fonder of the night.

But he was also fond of watching Rayne. She was beautiful, but what appealed to him went deeper than that. She was so fine, so good, a light shone from her soul. He could see it now, as if the light of her soul radiated from her body and became as tangible as the breasts, the hair, the long, fair limbs. The light of her soul kept Rayne from him for now, but soon he would be strong enough to take it from her.

He wanted more from her than her soul, as any need-ful man would, but her body would only be an appetizer, something to whet his hunger for her soul.

When he was strong enough, he would take both at his leisure.

He heard footsteps in the hallway outside his room. Strange how his senses had heightened in the past few months. He knew the footsteps were coming to his room. Fynnian's step he recognized. The other . . . the other was a woman. A frightened woman who took quick, light steps toward a destiny of which she was blissfully unaware.

Watching Rayne below was nice, but he needed more. He was so hungry.

Fynnian did not knock, but walked into the room with confidence. He'd have to speak to Fynnian about that ac-tion. It was rude. It was not befitting the power Ciro now possessed.

The girl was half-hidden, standing behind Fynnian with her eyes downcast. Her hair was an ordinary brown, as was the dim light of her soul that made Ciro hurt to be fed. Until now, he had only been able to take a soul—gray or dark—with permission, but he felt stronger today, and this woman's soul was so tainted it was possible . . . very possible . . . that he could simply take what he wanted without asking.

"Prince Ciro, this young lady is Elen. I purchased her for you."

"My own slave," Ciro said as he walked away from the window, taking care not to step into the sunlight that streamed through the window. "Let me have a look at her."

Fynnian grabbed the girl by the back of her ill-fitted frock and pulled her forward. Ciro could not see her face, as she kept her head down. Her hair was lank and in need of washing. Her clothes were worn, dirty and torn at the hem.

"I said, let me have a *look* at her!" Ciro said sharply.

The girl lifted her head slowly, and Ciro was pleasantly surprised. Her face, while dirty, was very pretty. The features were even and the skin was pale and smooth. Her eyes were bright, and a fetching shade of blue. If she'd been a slave for very long, her work had not been of the outdoor sort.

Fynnian smiled and stepped into a corner of the room, where he took a chair and settled down to watch. The man was smug. Confident. Yes, this was the wizard's house, but he had been taking too many liberties of late.

Ciro motioned for the woman to move into an opposite corner, and turned his attention to Fynnian. "You are dismissed," he said with confidence.

Fynnian's smile faded quickly. "You have never objected to my presence in the past."

"I object *now*," Ciro said. He didn't want Fynnian to know if he was now able to take souls without being granted permission. He also didn't want the old man watching if he attempted such and failed. "Leave us."

Moving too slowly and with great caution, Fynnian rose to his feet. He looked at the girl, then at Ciro, as he made his way toward the door. "If there's trouble, I must be here to—"

"There will be no trouble," Ciro assured his mentor. "Leave us. Now."

Unhappy about the situation, but unable to do anything more, Fynnian left the room, closing the door behind him. Ciro bolted that door, in case the old man had any ideas about returning uninvited.

Ciro turned and leaned against the door. The girl trembled, but just a little. "Close the curtains," he commanded.

Elen scurried to do as he said, yanking the heavy drapes closed so that no sunlight shone through. It took only a moment for Ciro's eyes to adjust completely to the new darkness. Outside the sun shone, but in this room there was not a hint of daylight.

"Remove your clothing," Ciro whispered.

Elen quickly did so, not even bothering to pretend to be demure, not even caring to cover her most private parts as she revealed a body fine enough to match the pretty face. How many men had she spread her legs for? How much tainted seed had she taken into her body? He did not know how or why, but something deep inside warned him to beware of tainting his body with that which was possibly diseased.

When the day came that he could feed himself with untainted souls, he would be unstoppable, and he could do no damage to this body. As the process was not yet complete, he still had to take care.

"Undress me." He stood in the middle of the room, arms lifted, so that Elen could do as he ordered. She thought he would bed her, and he allowed her to continue to believe that as she unfastened buttons and ties and very carefully laid his clothes aside. She couldn't see as well as he in the dark room, so her hands occasionally fumbled as she completed her task. He could not help but notice, as her trembling hands groped in the dark, that she was very small. Not only small, but insignificant. Of no more importance than a spider or a flea.

This encounter could be over quickly, but he did not want to rush. It might be days before Fynnian delivered another meal, and Ciro did not want this to be done too soon. He wanted to savor what was coming. As the last of his clothing was put aside, he anticipated the taking of the soul that would satisfy him, and the blood that would sustain him.

Pretty as this slave was, she was not Rayne. Rayne, who was beautiful and pure of body and soul. Rayne, who would be his empress when the time came. He closed his eyes and thought of the woman he wanted most of all, as the slave Elen knelt before him and took him into her mouth.

A part of Ciro was demon, and he realized that fact too well. But another part remained human, at least for now. He was still a man, and he pictured Rayne as she had been in the garden as the slave used her mouth and her tongue and her hands on him. She no longer trembled or fumbled.

No, Elen's previous duties had *not* been of the outdoor type. She was talented, this one was. If he cared more for the needs of the body than the needs of the demon who resided inside him, he would keep her alive for a while longer. But his demon hunger was more powerful than his hunger as a man, and he knew that would not happen.

Ciro fisted one hand in the slave's hair, and in his mind it was Rayne's dark hair he gripped, Rayne's wide mouth pleasing him, Rayne's gentle hand working with the mouth. One day it would be his beloved who knelt before him, naked and trembling. It would be Rayne, with her beautiful face and her slender pale hands, and her flawless soul, who became his slave. Rayne would be his wife, his empress, and mother of his son.

The thought was unexpected, and Ciro realized that it was the Isen Demon who spoke to him as the slave continued at her task. The demon whispered promises, as it sometimes did. There would be a son, the offspring of the demon, and Ciro, and Rayne. All three would be necessary to create the remarkable child who would be both a monster and a man, who would grow to rule this ruined earth and feed upon those who dared to attempt to bring the light back to what had been destroyed.

His completion was strong and quick. It had been a long time since he'd had a woman kneel before him this way, and the needs of his body were not yet dead. He suspected they might be soon, but not before he made Rayne his bride in every way. Not before he created his son.

Our son.

Elen stood, breathing deeply and wiping her mouth. "All I ask is that if I please you when you desire it, you do not hit me."

She thought he would be agreeable now, and what man wouldn't be after such a display of skill?

Ciro's answer was to backhand her, so that she flew across the room and landed on her backside, naked and shaking.

"You do not dictate to me," he said. "Stand."

She scrambled to her feet, shaking and cowering.

"Lie on the bed."

Elen, his slave, took care not to come too near him as she passed by, but she again did as he commanded. She sat on the side of the bed for a moment, and then she reclined on top of the coverlet, legs spread and trembling. One hand caressed the cheek he'd slapped, and a single tear slipped from one fetching blue eye.

As he approached, it occurred to him that she was a bit too skinny to be truly beautiful. Her previous owner hadn't fed her properly. Her breasts had not suffered too badly. They were full and taut, the breasts of a young woman who had not yet given birth.

As he stood over the slave Elen, Ciro wondered if the demon inside him would completely wash away all that was left of his human desires. When Rayne became his bride, when he planted his son inside her, would the experience be a chore, or the pleasure he dreamed of now, when some of the man remained?

"Are you afraid of me?" he asked.

Elen didn't know how to respond. She searched her mind for a moment, wondering if he wished to be feared or not. Finally she answered, "Yes, my lord. I am much afraid of you."

"Good," he said, and the woman on the bed breathed again, assured that she had found the right answer.

Ciro lay atop Elen and pressed his body to hers. She did not know what to expect, since he was no longer hard and as a man had no more use for the body which was all she had to offer.

He kissed her throat, and tasted not only the blood beneath but the dimly lit soul. Usually it was here that he asked for permission. It was at this moment, with his mouth on the throat, that he asked, "Will you offer me body and soul?"

Today, he did not ask. Nor did he hurry. He felt the woman beneath him relax. Elen believed she was safe here. She had accepted him as master, and had agreed to do everything he required of her. She tried to reach between their bodies to caress him, to make him hard again, but he grabbed her wrist and moved her hand aside. "Not now," he said gruffly, his mouth still against her throat.

Could he do what needed to be done? Was she his for the taking, without the spoken permission?

Ciro bit into Elen's fine, slender throat, and she flinched. "Easy, my lord," she whispered.

"Easy," he replied. "Yes."

He bit fully into her throat, finding the vein and opening it, taking her blood and her soul into his body. What he took filled and satisfied him in a way the simple orgasm could not. The dim light of her soul filled him, fed him, made him stronger. In the back of his mind he realized that Elen struggled, but she was no match for him. He had surpassed human strength long ago.

There was much warmth in the taking of blood, and he had come to crave it as much as the soul which would not stay within him long enough before the Isen Demon took it away. They danced together, the soul and the blood, as he took them. He savored the taste of the blood and the remarkable sensation of a soul leaving one body and entering his. It was as if he had been completely empty before, and now . . . now he was fulfilled. There was power, even in a damaged soul like this one, and now that power belonged to him in all ways.

When the soul was entirely his, Elen stopped struggling. He continued to drink her blood, as it, too, nourished him and he did not wish to waste even a drop. As her soul danced within him, he knew Elen as no one else ever had. She was scared all the time, and had been since the age of fourteen, when she'd caught the eye of a rich man who'd purchased her, the first man who'd owned her body and soul. She'd had more than one disease in her short lifetime, and had serviced more men than she could remember in more ways than Ciro had known possible. She'd done murder, not once, but twice. And she'd gotten away with it both times.

She would've killed him if the opportunity had arisen.

Elen was seventeen years old.

When the blood had been drained from her body, Ciro

rose off the dead woman and wiped the blood from his mouth. He was getting better at this. In the beginning, he had always made such a mess. Now there was not a drop of blood on the coverlet, and only a small amount had stained his mouth.

He'd call Fynnian to remove the body shortly, but first he needed the Panwyr.

A supply was always stored in the desk by the window, in the drawer to the far right. He reached inside, grabbed a vial, and poured a small amount onto his palm. He held his hand close to his nose and inhaled sharply. Panwyr went up his nostrils and immediately filled his body with a burst of sensation.

He knew the souls he took were not his to keep, and that's why they were never enough. That's why he was always so hungry. For this too-brief moment, he was all-powerful and completed sated. The soul, the blood, and the Panwyr completed him; made him strong and satisfied and, yes, invincible.

The Isen Demon which had taken control of his body and his mind danced around him, black and heavy and powerful. Ciro tasted Elen's soul one more time, and then it was gone, taken into the Isen Demon to join the others.

A part of the demon was always with him, sometimes dominant, sometimes subdued. There were moments when Ciro felt the full force of the demon, but those moments were rare. The Isen Demon was everywhere. It was huge and powerful and not easily contained. The full force of the demon came and went, taking souls and growing stronger and issuing orders only Ciro would hear.

The demon issued orders now, whispering in Ciro's head. Fynnian was not to know that Ciro could now take souls without permission. The old fool thought he was in control, but he was not. He had almost served his purpose, and it was time to draw away.

It was too soon to take a white soul, like Rayne's, but dark souls, damaged souls, they were now his to take, the demon promised. And take he would. This was just the beginning.

Still caught in the Panwyr euphoria, and missing the soul which had been his for too brief a time, Ciro parted the curtains and peeked outside. Rayne continued to work in the garden, oblivious to the fact that he watched.

When he made a son, she would be his mother. Rayne was untainted. Untouched. She was pure, so what better vessel for his child?

Rayne was to be his. She had been promised to him by Fynnian, and by the Isen Demon. One day her soul and his would be joined, before being fed to the demon, but not until she birthed his son.

Our son.

Our son, of course. Until that day she was his. As a man. As the fiend he had become. She *would* love him. She *would* be his companion.

She must be pure when you make our son.

Yes, of course.

Now was not the time to make Rayne his own, not in soul or in body, but Ciro knew without doubt that he didn't have much longer to wait.

6

ARIANA DIDN'T HAVE TO CALL ON HER EMPATHIC powers to know that something had changed while she and Sian had been down in Level Thirteen. For days, he'd been avoiding her. He sent teachers in his stead. Some taught her to fight. Others instructed her on simple magics.

It was as if Sian wanted her to be prepared for anything. One aging soldier showed her how to find drinkable water, and how to recognize edible plants and poisonous ones—something in which she had been well educated, though she listened carefully and did learn a few new tricks. Her lessons on swordplay were held daily, and again, it was an older sentinel who served as her teacher. He did not know why she required such lessons, and he had been a part of palace life long enough to know better than to ask. A palace witch who was talented with the casting of simple spells held one session, and again, while Ariana was already well versed, she did learn something new.

Just as telling as her empathic powers . . . perhaps more so . . . she was very aware that the enchanter hadn't looked her directly in the eye since they'd climbed out of Level Thirteen. More accurately, he had not looked her directly in the eye since she'd come out of nothingness to find his hands around her throat.

At least he allowed her to wear skirts as she went about her business. In fact, he had mentioned that she should not call attention to herself by dressing differently, though there would come a time when a different sort of clothing would be required. Odd, since he had been so insistent in the beginning that she wear men's trousers so she'd have freedom of movement and be able to fight. Even when the swordsman gave her lessons, she wore her skirts, and no instructions to the contrary reached her.

After several days of instruction in which he did not participate, Sian sent to her an older woman who was knowledgeable about herbs. The instruction was a waste of time. Ariana knew more about herbs than anyone in Columbyana, most likely. She certainly knew more than the doddering old woman Sian sent to her.

With the herbalist dismissed early, Ariana set out in search of Sian. He was not difficult to find, as he had been spending almost all his time in his quarters. Alone. The sentinels and ministers did not disturb him. She suspected they were afraid of the enchanter, and were well pleased when he was not in their way. Many of the ministers' wives had been known to dote on palace guests, feeding them too often and having silly parties at all times of the day. If that guest was an unmarried man, he would be introduced to the eligible daughters with match-making in mind. But they, too, left Sian alone. She suspected he was too dangerous for them, and for their daughters.

It was his eyes. He probably thought it was the odd shade of purple and the unusual shifting patterns there that put people off, that made people jump when they first saw them, but he'd be wrong. Sian Sayre Chamblyn had the eyes of a man who knew darkness. Ariana had quickly grown accustomed to the unusual color and the way they seemed to have a life of their own; she would never grow accustomed to the shadows that lurked there.

She knocked on his door, but as it was the middle of the day, she had no qualms about opening the door when she did not receive an immediate answer to her knock. Sian had told her very little about what he'd discovered in Level Thirteen, always promising "later," after he'd discovered more about the Isen Demon. Well, "later" was today. It was, in fact, right *now*.

The quarters the enchanter had been assigned consisted of one large room which held anything a man might desire. A massive bed. A chest for his clothing—which was apparently all black. A small table, for the meals he took here. A tub, which sat in one corner until it was time for it to be filled by a queue of servants bearing hot water.

Sian sat before a massive desk, which was littered with small books and loose papers. His head snapped around as the door opened. He was surprised to see her. So surprised, it took him a moment to gather his wits and say, "I did not call for you. Get out." With that, he returned to his study.

Ariana considered leaving the room, but not for long. Superior as he thought himself to be, Sian was here to help her. How could she prepare to fight when she did not know what she was up against?

She ignored his command and walked toward him. "What do you know about the Isen Demon?"

"Not enough," he answered sharply, not even bothering to rise from his hard-backed chair.

"I don't suppose you can flick your talented fingers and make him go away."

She did not realize the possible misunderstanding in the words "talented fingers" until Sian raised his eyebrows ever so slightly. Ariana felt the warmth of a blush on her cheeks. Beyond that, she showed no reaction.

"I have not found a spell to rid us of the demon, no," Sian answered, "but I have many more volumes of palace witches' ledgers still to study."

When Ariana made it clear she was not going away to leave him in peace, Sian grimaced. "I don't suppose you have heard of a crystal dagger?" he asked.

"No. Is there mention of one in the ledgers?"

"The prophesy my grandfather penned mentions such a weapon. He does not give details as to where it can be found or if it will defeat the demon. I thought perhaps you had heard of it."

"No." Ariana stepped closer to the desk, and to Sian. "May I see it?"

"See what?"

"The Prophesy of the Firstborn."

It seemed that Sian paled a little before turning back to his papers. "No. Not at this time."

"Why not? For all I know, you . . . made it all up."

"I am not in the habit of creating false prophesies for my amusement, or for yours. The prophesy is as I told you."

"But—"

"When the time is right, I will show it to you," he said sharply.

"When will the time be right?"

He sighed and turned to glare up at her as if she were a bothersome child. "When I say the time is right. Don't you have lessons to attend to?"

"No. I'm finished for the day."

"Surely you have something to study."

"Not really. My lessons have not been very challenging in the past few days. I thought you were going to teach me. I thought you were going to increase my magical abilities so I'll be better able to fight."

"I have much to do," Sian explained. "And you are not ready."

He was so dismissive, it would be easiest to turn and leave him alone. She did not.

Sian was an aggravating man, but also a fascinating one. He was powerful magically and physically, handsome in a manly way she had not recognized when she'd first seen him, self-assured . . . and that was an understatement. His nose was a bit large, but it suited his face somehow. And he tasted wonderful, with lips firm enough and soft enough . . .

Ariana blinked hard. She had no idea what Sian tasted like! He was so dismissive of her, she would likely never know such a thing, even if she were so inclined. And yet, she did know what he tasted like. Deep inside, she was so certain the memory called up his scent, his taste, the feel of him in her hand.

That unexpected and very real thought must be the result of a dream she had forgotten. She'd been dreaming about Sian, but not remembering the dreams. That was the only explanation. Like it or not, she was attracted to him. Just thinking about how he tasted and felt caused an unexpected reaction at her very core. A warmth. A calling. There had been times in the past two years when she'd considered taking a lover, but no man had ever called to her strongly enough to help her take that step. Sian could, if she allowed it. He could call to her very well.

Suddenly she felt a little dizzy, and to steady herself she gripped the back of Sian's chair. "What happened in Level Thirteen?"

"I told you what happened."

"You told me a fragment of a dark spirit entered my body and conversed with you, telling you about the Isen Demon."

"Yes."

"What else happened?"

"Nothing."

What she remembered, what she *knew* . . . it was too distinctive to be a remnant of a dream. "Then why do I know the taste of your mouth?" *Why do I want you the way a woman wants a lover?*

For a moment, Sian didn't answer. He was very still and quiet, and then he turned to look up at her. She searched his shadowed eyes for an answer, and found none.

HOW COULD HE POSSIBLY EXPLAIN THIS ONE AWAY? Sian was surprised that Ariana remembered anything of the kiss, but then she had been present, in a way. Diella had been in control, but Ariana had not been entirely absent.

While he tried to formulate an explanation, Ariana

reached out and caressed his face. The move was unexpected, and Sian found himself flinching. She did not withdraw.

"It's all right, you know," she whispered. "This is all very scary for me, and I like the fact that I'm not alone. Who else can I turn to for comfort, Sian? Who else can I hold when the fear grows too deep and too strong? Only you. No one else." She tilted her head to one side. "Are you afraid of me?"

"Of course not."

"Do you want me?" she whispered.

Should he be honest or prudent? Normally he would choose prudence in this situation, but with what was coming, Ariana deserved honesty. "Yes."

"Then why don't you take me?"

The offer was so bluntly spoken, Sian was again taken by surprise. Before he had a chance to respond, Ariana sat on his lap and wrapped her arms around his neck. Her voluminous skirts brushed the edge of the table and sent papers scattering to the floor, and when she laid her mouth on his throat, he dismissed all thoughts of ancient witches' ledgers and notes.

He had been a while without a woman. Long enough that it didn't take much in the way of seduction to drive everything else but this woman from his mind. War could wait. Demons could wait. Ariana wanted him.

She kissed his mouth, and he tasted desperation on her fine lips. She moaned a little as they kissed, making that maddening little sound deep in her throat, that sound women called upon to drive men wild. This was a woman who could possess him, who could touch him, who could ruin his life—if he allowed it to happen.

"Ariana, think about what you're doing."

"I don't want to think." She followed that statement with a wandering hand to prove to herself that he did indeed want her. She stroked and caressed and laughed.

When she laughed, Sian sighed. He should've known this was too good to be true. He should've immediately recognized the subtle change in her voice. He'd been blind not to see the signs. Women like Ariana didn't plop down in a man's lap and fondle him. She didn't offer herself so easily. She was a woman to be wooed and won, by the right man. He had never been the right man for any woman, least of all one like her.

Apparently he and Ariana had not escaped from Level Thirteen alone.

"Ariana, love," he said softly, "will you do something for me?"

"Anything, Sian, love," she answered.

He led her to the bed, glimpsing a smile that was Ariana's and yet not Ariana's. It was a wicked smile, without heart and without love. Not that he expected love from any woman, but Ariana Varden was not the kind to seek out a man without it.

"Sit here," he said, gesturing to the side of the bed. Ariana sat, and Sian went to the dresser where his clothing was stored. Arik had given him some hideous ceremonial robes for fine dinners with priests and ministers, and they each came with a length of fine soft fabric to encircle the waist. Sian grabbed two of the lengths, one crimson and one blue, and returned to the woman who had offered herself to him.

She had already removed a goodly portion of her gown. Things had been unfastened, and fabric had been shifted. The globes of her breasts were partially exposed, and her skirt rode high on her bare legs.

There was nothing he could do about that, not at the present time. "Your hands, Ariana, love."

"You deviant," she said with a widening smile, offering her hands.

Sian bound those hands together tightly, but not too tightly. "Lie back, Ariana, love."

She did so, falling back with a bounce that sent her skirts fluttering, offering Sian a very unladylike glimpse. "Is this a game?" she asked. "Ah, I believe I understand. I have played this game before. I will be your love slave, and you will command me. Is that the game, enchanter?"

"Yes, that is the game." He caught her legs in his arms, and she laughed lightly. When he began to bind her ankles, she protested minimally. "That binding might turn out to be rather inconvenient, enchanter."

"I command you," he said sharply. "Have you already forgotten?"

"No. I simply don't see how my body can be of any use to you tied thus."

"Let me worry about that, Ariana, love."

It soothed her when he called her "Ariana, love." He saw the satisfaction on her face, and in a slight, enticing ripple of her body. Sian shifted the partially undressed woman and made her more comfortable on his bed. There was a pillow beneath her head, a soft mattress beneath her body. He sat beside her and smoothed away a wayward strand of hair. "There, now, are you comfortable?"

"I'll be more comfortable when you're inside me, Sian, love."

Sian shook his head. "If I had not already known that you were not entirely Ariana, I would know it now. Love," he added belatedly. "How long have you been out, Diella?"

The smile died rapidly. "What gave me away?"

"I don't intend to tell you."

Diella sighed dramatically. "Any other man would've had his fun before revealing that he was aware of the charade. After all, this is the body you want. What difference does it make who possesses it?"

It makes a difference to me. "How did you make your way out of Level Thirteen?"

"I hitched a ride with your lover. She's wide open. Her empathic abilities work both ways, as you certainly understand. She can reach out and touch the unseen spirits, but we can also reach *in*."

"You've been inside her all this time."

"Sleeping," she said softly. "Resting. Growing stronger. I'm not as resilient as I once was." Diella glared at him. "If you don't release me, I will roll off the edge of the bed and bruise this body. I will scream at the top of my lungs, and tell everyone who comes to my rescue that you raped me."

"Thanks for the warning." Sian waved his hand over Diella, and she floated up so that she drifted a few inches above the coverlet. With no mattress to give her purchase, she was unable to roll. Another wave of his hand, and she was unable to speak. "Not particularly bright, are you?"

She could not speak, but that last comment made her angry. Her green eyes—Ariana's green eyes—blazed with cold fire.

Sian left her that way, bound ankles and wrists, floating above his bed, unable to speak. He turned his chair to face her, and sat down to watch. "You will leave Ariana, and you will not return."

Diella tried to respond, but the spell that made it impossible for her to speak also made it impossible for her to spit.

He sat back, relaxed, and studied the vision floating above his bed. Perhaps he should've refastened the hooks and eyes that had been unfastened and now allowed him a very good view of Ariana's breasts, but he was, after all, a man, and the view was quite nice. Ariana would be angry when she awoke and found herself in such disarray, but her state of dress would convince her that something had to be done about Diella.

Diella opened and closed her mouth, trying to speak. She attempted to gesture with bound hands, which was quite comical—or might've been if not for the circumstances. Finally Sian said, "I will allow you to speak, if you promise not to scream." After all, there was surely more she could tell him about the Isen Demon, and the more he knew, the better able Ariana would be to fight. "I will make you very sorry if you disappoint me."

After a moment's hesitation, she nodded reluctantly. Sian waved his hand, and a moment later she began to speak.

"If you won't fuck this body, I'll find someone else who can. This palace is filled with men who would be more than happy to have a tumble with a pretty girl." Her grin widened. "How do you know I haven't already had half the sentinels in my bed?"

"Because you lie badly," Sian said calmly. There was more, but he did not want to explore it at the moment. Ariana was still in there. At the moment, she and Diella shared a body. If Ariana was entirely opposed to what Diella wanted . . . but now was not the time to pursue that subject. "Tell me about the Isen Demon."

"I want Panwyr."

"You're not getting any."

"If I can't have anything I want, then why should I speak to you?" Diella snapped.

"You might not get the sex or the drug you desire, but you do have one thing you want which will very soon be gone."

"What's that?"

"Life."

Diella paled.

"Yes, you have made it this far, but you won't last. You're weak from the effort of rising to control, and with Ariana's help I will dismiss you. Permanently. For now, you can breathe. You can feel anger, and satisfaction, and hate. When all that is gone, what will you have? Nothing. You've had nothing for a very long time, haven't you, Diella?"

"Yes," she whispered.

"As long as you give me what I want, you will be allowed these few moments of life."

"You could not want that which every other man—"

"I am not every other man, Diella."

"You should address me as Empress Diella." She pouted, like a spoiled little girl who was not getting her way.

"You haven't been an empress for a very long time. You're nothing now. Less than nothing."

Her eyes narrowed.

"Leave that body," he ordered.

"You can't order me out of Ariana."

"Who can?"

Her refusal to answer made him feel certain that *someone* could order her from the body she possessed. Ariana herself? Her brother? A palace wizard or witch? The emperor? What power was necessary?

"A real man would take advantage of this situation," Diella argued. "It's not too late, Sian, love," she said. "Untie my ankles, and lower this body to your bed, and . . ."

Sian lifted his hand.

"Wait!" Real fear colored Diella's face. Ariana's face. "Don't hurt me, please. I can offer information you might be able to use, if only you will allow me to stay awhile longer."

"What sort of information?"

"Like me, the Isen Demon needs a body to possess in order to have an effect on earthly matters. In Level Thirteen, the demon collected the souls of the dead, souls addicted to Panwyr and lost forever. It grew stronger over the years, but after Level Thirteen was closed, it also grew hungrier. The demon still needs to feed on souls."

"What body did the demon possess?"

Diella smiled. "Not yet. Once you have all you need to know, you'll immobilize me, as you did down below, and then I won't feel. It's terrible, not to feel anything at all."

"I imagine it is."

"This one, she feels everything deeply. It's nice to rest inside her for a while. I had forgotten warmth, and the chill of a breeze. I had forgotten the power of anticipation, and excitement, and even fear. Love. Comfort. Desire. Even caring, which was never my strong suit in life."

"I can't imagine," Sian said dryly.

"I wish you had made love to me," she whispered. "It's not too late."

He shook his head.

"For her, it will be love, when it comes. Do you think I can convince her she loves that sentinel with the black curly hair and brown eyes? Now, he looks like a man who would not refuse—"

Sian lifted his hand.

"If I tell you, will you give me a few more minutes?"

He lowered his hand. "A few."

Diella licked her lips. "I saw it happen, a few months ago. A wizard came, and lured the boy into Level Thirteen. It wasn't difficult. The boy was given to wandering where he should not."

Sian had a sinking feeling that he knew the boy of whom she spoke. He did hope he was wrong. "Names?"

"You'll spoil the telling," she snapped. "Show some patience, enchanter." She shook back Ariana's fair curls and began again. "The wizard lured the boy into Level Thirteen, after casting a spell to send the guards above to sleep for a while. There, in the darkness, the wizard offered the boy power. Endless, unimaginable power. He offered the boy everything he'd ever wanted. The boy didn't consider the proposition for very long. He wanted what the wizard offered, and while he knew power of a sort would eventually come to him, he was tired of waiting. Like you, he was impatient." She smiled. "He was also weak. Weak of spirit and mind, weak of heart. The wizard cast a mighty spell, and the Isen Demon took the boy. The boy actually grew a bit larger, taller and wider, and right there, right then, the demon took his soul."

"But not his life."

"No, not his life," Diella whispered. "The boy lives. It was amazing, to watch the demon take the boy as it did. Darkness in the form of gray mists and black stars surrounded the boy, and then it was all sucked inside. A few bits of darkness could not find their way in, so they sank into the dirt beneath his feet and grew until I could feel them everywhere. Having the body makes it stronger. Not just that which lives inside the boy, but also that which lives without. It's all connected, as if with an enormous spiderweb, and when one grows stronger, the other grows as well. The Isen Demon grows every day. If you were connected to darkness instead of light, you would feel it, as I do."

"Names?" Sian prompted again.

Diella sighed. She knew her time was growing short. "The wizard's name is Fynnian."

"And the boy?"

She smiled. "Prince Ciro, he is called."

Sian had been expecting as much, but still, his heart sank. He did not want to be the one to tell Arik that his son, his only child, was dead. No, worse than dead.

"You hitched a ride out of Level Thirteen with Ariana. Why didn't you depart with Fynnian and Ciro?"

What was left of Diella's smile vanished. "Oh, no, I couldn't do that. They scared me. They scare me still."

7

ARIANA BEGAN TO PANIC, BECAUSE IT SEEMED THAT SHE was drowning. How was that possible? One moment she'd been standing behind Sian thinking unlikely and unwanted thoughts, and the next . . . she was drowning. She could not breathe. She could not see, for the murkiness of the water that threatened to drag her down.

She forcibly pushed her panic aside. This was a dream, nothing more. There was no water. She was not drowning. If she wished it, she *could* breathe.

Even though she continued to tread water, she took a deep breath. The murkiness of the water cleared a bit, so she could see what surrounded her.

She was not alone. Just a few feet away there floated another woman. A dark-haired, harshly attractive, very thin, grinning woman.

The woman mouthed words Ariana could not hear, and still she knew what was being said.

This ocean is mine. Drift deeper, witch. Leave it to me.

No, Ariana responded. She didn't know why, but her heart reacted fiercely to the woman's claim. *This place is mine.*

The evil grin faded, and the woman swam closer. With every stroke, Ariana felt the darkness that threatened to choke her grow stronger. *I can take you, witch, if I wish. I can take this life, this body, this man who thinks he can stop me. They will all be mine.*

It would be easy to convince herself that this was just a bad dream, but suddenly Ariana knew it was not a dream. Not at all.

This was her first battle. The first of many, if Sian's prophesy was correct.

Ariana called up every crumb of power that rested inside her. She called upon all her strengths, as well as the might of her ancestors. She drew from her family. Her mother's sunshine, her aunts' incredible abilities, her grandmother's force, her cousins' power. She called upon Duran's strength, even though he had never known a touch of magic. They all came to her. Her family, her blood, made her stronger. They made her strong enough.

This is my ocean. This is my life, and I will not step back and give it to you or anyone else. Ariana felt a surge of energy, a confidence that went well beyond anything she had ever known. *Get out.*

Enjoy what little is left of your pathetic life. The dark-haired woman didn't swim to the surface. She screamed in anger, and then she vanished. Ripples in the water drifted softly from the place where the woman had once stood.

Ariana swam to the surface in a leisurely manner. She was alone in the ocean—*her* ocean—once again, and the light above called to her. The light of the sun. The light of her life.

What little is left . . .

Ariana opened her eyes, and it took her a moment to orient herself. No wonder she had dreamed of swimming. She was floating on air. She glanced around and acquainted herself. Apparently she was floating above Sian's bed, and her clothing was not as it had been when she'd come to his room. She felt a cool breeze on the rise of her breasts, and a similar coolness on her bare legs.

"What have you done?" she snapped. When she tried to move, she discovered that she could not. Not only was she floating, but her hands and feet were bound. A moment ago she had felt so powerful, so strong. And now, she was helpless.

Sian sat nearby, watching her with an aloof air. Those cold eyes of his barely reacted to her awakening.

"What have you done to me?" Ariana snapped. "Release me this instant! When the emperor discovers what you've done, he will have you . . . he will have you . . ." Oh, she did not want to stumble over her words at this moment. "You will be sorry."

"Very good," he responded emotionlessly. "Almost believable. Do you really think I'm that gullible?"

"I think you have lost your mind."

"Perhaps, Ariana, love," he said with a sarcastic edge to his deep voice.

"How dare you call me . . ." Oh, what if he really had lost his mind? Was there anything more dangerous than an insane enchanter? "Sian Sayre Chamblyn, release me this instant!"

He stood slowly, studying her face. No, studying her

eyes, as if he could see beyond them. "Ariana, is that you?"

"Of course it's me, you . . . you . . ." She could not find a sufficient word for a man who would bind her, halfway undress her, and leave her floating above his bed.

"So, you no longer want a tumble?" With that, he reached out and caressed the globe of one mostly exposed breast and then the other, using the back of his hand and barely touching her. Deep inside she reacted, as a woman reacts to a man who touches her just so. She tried very hard not to show that she felt anything but revulsion.

"I most certainly do *not*."

He withdrew his hand. "So, you truly are Ariana."

"What gave me away?" she asked sharply as Sian began to untie her wrists.

"I suspect demons don't blush."

He unbound her hands and feet, and then, with a wave of his hand, gently lowered her to the bed. As soon as she was able, Ariana leapt up and sat on the edge of the mattress, quickly and efficiently fastening her bodice. "I don't understand what happened, but do you care to explain, before I go to the emperor, why you felt it necessary to undress me?"

Sian remained calm. "You are only partially undressed, and you did it yourself."

"I did no such . . ." Ariana stopped abruptly. The woman in the water . . . the ocean, her life . . . That had been no dream.

"Who was she?" Ariana left Sian's bed sharply, anxious to escape. Anxious not to appear too comfortable there.

"Empress Diella," Sian answered. "Apparently her dark soul was left behind in Level Thirteen, and she hitched a ride in you when we departed."

Ariana stepped away from Sian. "She's been with me for five days and I didn't know it?"

"Apparently she was gathering strength in order to take control."

Spine straight, Ariana did her best to appear unaffected. "I sent her away. I don't know if what I said or did was sufficient, but I don't feel her with me now. Of course, I didn't feel her presence for the past five days either." Was the thin, evil woman still lurking inside her somewhere? "She said my life would be short."

"She was trying to frighten you," Sian said gruffly.

Ariana didn't precisely believe her teacher's words. Yes, the demon had been trying to scare her, but she had sensed a touch of truth in the telling. "Do you think she's still here? With me?"

Sian sighed tiredly. "I don't know." He shook off the problem as if it were a small, pesky bug. "I did glean some useful information from her, concerning the Isen Demon."

Ariana was grateful for anything which would turn her mind from the position she had found herself in upon waking. "Then I suppose it was a worthwhile exercise."

"Can you keep a secret?"

"From whom?"

"From everyone."

Normally, she would say no. She hated to lie! She was like her mother in that respect. Neither of them had ever been good at card games where bluffing was a part of the strategy. "If I must, I will try."

"Eventually it will no longer be a secret, but until I decide how to proceed, secrecy is best."

"All right."

Sian watched her closely, as if he wasn't sure who she

was anymore. As if he wondered if Diella still lurked and listened. Finally he shared the news. "The Isen Demon has taken Prince Ciro. The emperor's son is lost."

SIAN WISHED HE COULD BE SURE THAT DIELLA WAS gone, but he could not. The demon spirit could do a lot of damage in a short period of time if allowed to rule Ariana's body unchecked.

Now that he knew more about the Isen Demon—even though he still had not found a way to stop it—he felt he could spend more time looking for a way to be completely and finally rid of Diella.

As he searched through yet another sheaf of papers from ancient ledgers, his mind went back to certain words Diella had spoken that afternoon. Something about a black-haired brown-eyed sentinel who would be glad to give her what Sian would not.

He should not care. If Diella made use of Ariana's body in such a way, it would not affect her ability to fight. Eventually they would find a way to be rid of the demon, and what happened between now and then was of little consequence if Diella's interests were simply sexual. And yet, he did care. Ariana had blushed mightily when he'd brushed the backs of his fingers over her breasts. They were nicely shaped breasts, very soft, and he was certain that no man had ever touched them the way he had this afternoon.

Like it or not, he could not allow Diella to rise up and make use of Ariana in order to fulfill her own need for physical sensation.

Most of the palace residents slept at this late hour. The sentinels who had the night watch remained alert, and there were a few residents about who preferred the late-night hours to daylight. But for the most part, the hall-ways were empty and eerily silent.

He would simply check on Ariana and assure himself that she was asleep. And alone.

Sian made his way down the stairwell at a brisk pace, and without making a sound. He was sending this girl, this *woman*, to her death, and it bothered him more than that death that she might end up lying with a sentinel, with her body under the control of a spirit other than her own. And if it was Ariana herself who chose the hand-some sentinel?

The thought still bothered him. He was allowing him-self to be drawn too close to the girl, in an entirely emotional way. He was not an emotional man, so the un-expected connection worried him. It would be best if he turned back now and returned to his research.

The hallway was deserted, and Ariana's door was locked. Locks had never been a problem for Sian. He touched the door handle, spoke a soft word, and the latch moved silently.

He opened the door and stepped into a dark room. There had been gently flaming lights in the hallways he'd traveled, so it took a moment for his eyes to adjust. Ari-ana slept beneath a soft, pale-colored coverlet, her blond curls stretching across her pillow, one arm thrown across her face as if she were hiding from a light that was not here.

She was alone.

Sian knew he should leave immediately. He had proven to himself that Ariana was all right, and alone, so there was no reason to stay. Of course, it was possible that in a sleeping state she was most vulnerable, and at any time during the night she might . . . Diella might . . . climb from that bed and leave in search of a willing man. Any willing man, if she had her way.

It was likely that this afternoon's exercise had weakened Diella, and if she still remained, it would be days again before she could rise to the surface.

Likely. Not certain.

Sian locked Ariana's door from the inside, and took a chair from her desk. Making not a sound, he placed that chair near the side of her bed, and sat. He could go without sleep, if necessary. He would watch over her because it was his calling, his destiny, just as this war to come was hers.

He hadn't been sitting there long when she dropped her arm, rolled over, and opened her eyes. She was surprised to find him there, but perhaps not as surprised as she should've been.

"Why are you here?" she asked, her voice filled with sleep and dreams he could not share.

"I was worried about you," he said simply.

All he could see was her face, since she had the covers pulled to her chin. Her smile seemed genuine enough. "Worried? You?"

"Until we can assure ourselves that Diella is gone, it's best if you're not left to your own devices for long periods of time."

"I suppose that's true, though I don't know what sort of damage she could do in the middle of the night."

Sian sighed. With all she knew, with all her powers, Ariana was still naïve. "She could poison the emperor, throw your body out the window, and seduce a sentinel for the fun of it. She could do all three before morning, though not necessarily in that order."

"I see your point." There was teasing in her voice when she added, "Would the sentinel be handsome, do you think, or one of the older and less-fit men?"

"This isn't funny," he snapped.

"I know. So, what are you going to do? Watch me day and night?"

"Until we know she's gone, I suppose I should."

"You have to sleep sometime."

How annoying. Why couldn't she just go back to sleep? He didn't want to examine his reasons for being here, and talking to her this way, lowered voices in the dark, only made him feel closer to her. That was a potential disaster.

He certainly didn't want her to suspect where his thoughts had taken him. "I can go without sleep for a long while. You should learn to remain alert through sleepless nights as well. Once you're on the road, there might be many nights when there is no opportunity for rest."

Sian did not want to think of what might befall Ariana after she left this palace. Battles, split-second decisions, uncertainty. Death. He did not know when or how that death would come, but he did know the Land of the Dead was waiting for her. In the beginning, he had accepted that as an unfortunate circumstance, but one he could not change. But now he wondered . . . Was it in his hands to change that part of the prophesy? Could he alter the destiny his grandfather had foretold?

He had planned to return home as Ariana began her journey to battle, but now he wondered if he could.

She snuggled beneath the covers, but did not close her eyes and return to sleep. "Today, when I was fighting Diella, I gathered the strength of my family to me. I felt them, so close, and they gave me the courage and the power to do what had to be done."

"That's good. We will work on harnessing that power tomorrow. You might be able to—"

"Let me finish," she interrupted without anger in her voice. "They gave me strength, but now they're gone again, and I just feel empty. Empty and lonely. It's as if I am no longer complete. It's as if I was offered a glimpse of something exquisite, and then it was stripped away. I have been frightened of what is to come, but now, now that I feel so unbearably alone, I'm terrified."

He could tell her not to be afraid, but in truth she should be terrified of what was coming. Any intelligent warrior would be.

"I don't want to be alone, Sian," she continued. "I'm so very tired of being alone."

"You are not alone," he argued. "You have your family, even when you do not sense them so closely. When you leave here, you will have all the soldiers you desire at your command. You will command an army, Ariana."

"That is a man's dream, not a woman's. I could have command of all of Columbyana, and I would still be alone." She drew the covers down and sat up. Her nightdress was modest, white and plain and just barely thin enough for him to see through.

"When I was seventeen, I fell in love," she began.

It sounded like the beginning of a conversation he wanted no part of. "This is none of my—"

"None of your concern, I know," she said sharply. "Listen anyway. I can't tell this tale to anyone else."

"All right." Sian leaned back in his chair, relaxing as much as he could for a man who was confused and hard. Heaven above, he could see her womanly shape through that gown, the tempting curve of her hips and the swell of her breasts.

"You don't know what it's like to be the eldest daughter of a beautiful woman who retained her beauty long after other women of her age had lost theirs. To be compared all your life to a woman who caused men to stop in their tracks and lose their tongues and stumble over their own feet with no more than a glance or a smile. My mother is a fertility goddess, Sian, and a true beauty. I have always suffered by comparison."

"I could disagree with that statement," he said in a lowered voice.

"And I would thank you, but you have never met my mother."

"True enough."

"When I was seventeen, I fell in love," she said again. "At that age, love is like all else. Intense. All-consuming. That love quickly became the center of my life, and it was as if nothing else mattered. Pryam said he loved me, too, and I believed him. In my mind, our future was set. I would be his wife, and he would be my husband. We would love one another forever, just as my mother and father have done and will continue to do. One thing led to another, as it often does, and we . . ."

"You had sex with Pryam," Sian said when she stuttered.

She sighed, perhaps in relief that she did not have to say the words aloud. More proof that Diella was not present tonight. Diella was never shy. "My mother always told her daughters, when they reached a certain age, how wonderful the physical act of love could be when there was true love between a man and a woman. We were advised to wait, to choose wisely, but there was never any doubt that what awaited us would be wonderful." Again, she sighed. "What happened to me by the riverbank was not wonderful," she said. "There was pain and sweat and it was messy, and . . . I just wanted the whole thing to be over. It wasn't all terrible. Afterward he held me, and I was so sure that I was pregnant. After all, my mother is—"

"Yes, yes, I know," Sian interrupted. The picture she painted was much too clear to him.

"We tried again the next day, and Pryam told me it would be better this time. It didn't hurt as much, but I didn't experience any of the beauty and pleasure my mother had told me about. Again, it was fast and clumsy. While he was . . . occupied, I thought of the babies we would have. I didn't want so many as my parents had had, but one or two would be nice, I thought.

"The affair, if it can be called even that, lasted for two weeks. I kept expecting more, but there was no more. I did not get pregnant, which was a relief to Pryam, but was an unexpected disappointment to me. It crossed my mind that perhaps I didn't love him after all. Mama had said beauty came with true love, and there was no beauty in what Pryam and I had. Not for me."

"You ended the affair."

"Yes. He was very angry. My family's land adjoined his, and his father had promised him a nice reward if he married one of the Varden girls. Hearing that cut me to the very heart, even though I had already convinced myself that I didn't love him after all. The love I had imagined had never existed, not for me or for him. I warned my sisters to steer clear of him. I told them what he wanted from us. Land. All for land."

"How many lovers have you taken since then?" Sian asked.

"None." Ariana shuddered. If he had not been watching closely, he would've missed it entirely. "I don't want children now, not like I did when I was seventeen. I have a good life here in the palace. Well, I *had* a good life here, before you and your prophesy ruined it for me."

"Sorry."

"It's not your fault." Ariana squirmed a little, and his eyes were drawn to her not as a teacher, but as a man. "It's just that . . . I always thought I had time. Time to fall in love and try again. Time to find the beauty my mother promised me. Time, Sian. It's slipping away."

Again, he wondered why the firstborn Fyne child couldn't have been a man. He would not feel torn inside if that were the case. He would not be here at all if the chosen one was male. He would never have felt the need to protect a man so. It would be best if he did his duty as a teacher and maintained a respectable distance. "I could fashion a love spell and send the sentinel or minister of your choice to your room for an evening. Would that help?"

She laughed, and again he knew Diella was not present. They might on occasion share the same body, but there was soul in a real laugh. The two women were nothing alike. "No. I do not wish false love, not even for one night."

Though he could wish he was wrong, Sian knew what she wanted. "True love is not necessary for the beauty your mother promised. That's the way it came to her, but many people enjoy pleasure without love. Can you accept and embrace that?"

"I don't know." Her voice was so low, he almost couldn't hear her. For a long moment she was silent, and then she added, "I think I would like to find out."

Sian stood. He understood what Ariana needed, perhaps more completely than she did. He could leave her, collect a suitable sentinel, cast a spell, and walk away. Love was not an issue here, only physical connection. Togetherness. Physical pleasure. She did not want to be alone.

But Ariana was his in a way he had not expected. He could not bring himself to lead another man to her bed. He did not want any other man to show her all she had missed. From a distance, he directed her coverlet down to the end of the bed so that her entire nightgown-clad body was exposed. He threw a circle of wizard's light around the bed, so he could better see her.

"No magic," she whispered. The words were not a command but a request, one he was willing to comply with. The wizard's light died, and his hands fell to his side. In the near-dark he could still see Ariana pat the mattress beside her in invitation.

She was chosen. To fight, to lead, to die. He did not want to care for her more than he already did, because allowing her to fulfill the prophesy would be beyond painful. Diella had promised him he would live a long life. Long enough to watch everyone and everything he loved die.

But tonight was not about prophesies and battle. It was about a woman's need for beauty, and nothing more.

SIAN JOINED HER ON THE BED, AFTER SITTING ON THE edge of the mattress and removing his boots. Nothing else. Perhaps he intended to leave most of his clothes on during the act. Too bad, as she had rather looked forward to seeing him naked.

She reached down and cupped his erection with her hand, and began to fumble with the buttons there.

He uttered a tsking sound and grabbed her wrist, guiding her hand gently upward. "There is no need to rush, Ariana."

"But . . ."

He ended her protest with a kiss. A nice, deep kiss that made her feel as if she were melting. The kiss did not end quickly, but went on and on. She fell back to the mattress and he came with her, mouths fused, tongues gently exploring. The kissing stole her breath away and made her heart beat in a new and different rhythm. She had never known such a kiss was possible, and she did not want it to end.

This was much more than an attempt at casting aside her loneliness. She couldn't put a name to it, but the kissing was very, very right and good.

When Sian took his mouth from hers, she sighed and began to hitch her nightgown up. Again, he grabbed her wrist and put a stop to her efforts.

"Why are you in such a rush?" he asked.

She could barely catch her breath after that kiss. "I'm trying to help."

He lowered his head and kissed her throat. "Do not help," he rumbled against her skin. "From this moment on, you do nothing unless I instruct you. Understood?"

"Understood." She melted into the mattress and enjoyed the way his mouth felt on her throat, the way his tongue teased. Deep in her belly she felt a stirring that was new and full of promise.

Ariana wanted to realize the beauty her mother had promised, and deep inside she knew Sian was the man to show her what she had missed. She wasn't sure why. Perhaps what had happened while Diella had been in control of her body had set something into motion that could not be easily ended. Perhaps she simply felt safe with Sian. They already shared more than one secret, after all. What was one more?

Soon she dismissed all her wonderings about why, and lost herself in the physical sensations he elicited.

Sian spent a few wonderful moments kissing the skin beneath her ear. Ariana found herself winding her fingers through his hair and pulling him closer. Tighter. She did not feel the touch of his mouth only on her skin, but experienced a rush of longing and pleasure throughout her body.

Her mind worked differently, it seemed, or else did not work at all. She hadn't realized that he'd worked the buttons of her nightgown until his hand slipped inside to caress her breasts. She lurched at the unexpected sensation of his palm brushing against her nipple. That sensation shot through her, filling her. Enticing her.

It seemed that she was racing toward something unknown, but Sian was in no rush. He did not race. He was amazingly languid, as if they had all the time in the world for this. As if nothing else mattered. She enjoyed believing that to be true, even if the illusion didn't last.

He was so incredibly warm. That heat radiated out and infused her with a shared warmth that was unlike anything she had ever known. Two long fingers tweaked her nipple, and before her gasp was complete, his mouth was there, sucking, drawing her in.

Everything else went away. Ariana closed her eyes and was lost in wonder and a growing hunger. She no longer questioned any movement Sian made. She was his, at least for this moment. Her body was his. Her body and her mind were his to mold.

Sian finally removed her nightgown. He did not lift the

hem to her waist, which was all she had expected and all
that was necessary, but gently drew the nightgown across
her hips and over her head, disposing of it with a flick of
his wrist. There was no wizard's light to illuminate them,
but she saw Sian well enough. He studied her as he
touched and caressed. He liked what he saw.

She had felt a moment of shyness when she'd first
broached the subject of making love, but there was no
shyness within her now. He could look upon her naked to
his heart's desire, and she would not mind. She felt different. Alive, in an entirely new way.

She felt like a woman.

"Now can I touch you?" she whispered.

"If you wish."

She unfastened the buttons of his shirt and drew the
garment over his head. She'd already felt the muscles
which were revealed, but the sight of them was still quite
lovely. He did not have the body of a man who spent
hours poring over old papers and moving objects magically. There was no fat here, no sign that he was on occasion sedentary. He was lean without being thin, muscled
without being burly. Perfect. He was absolutely perfect.
Her hands traced those muscles, and then brushed against
his small, hard nipples. She lowered her head and tasted
him there, brushing her tongue across his flat nipples and
tasting the salt and maleness of his skin.

Unfastening his trousers was more of an effort, but she
managed, and he was patient with her. It was not necessary that she do more than free his erection, but she
wanted him to be as naked as she was. She wanted nothing in this bed but their bodies when they came together.

When his clothing was shed, she took a moment to
study him, as he had studied her. She cupped and teased

him, she stroked while she kissed the curve where neck became shoulder. And as she did so, Sian slipped his hand between her legs and stroked her, his thumb finding the nub at her entrance and teasing it with small, circular strokes.

Her hips began to move, as if they danced. Her eyes drifted closed, and she felt nothing but Sian. Nothing else mattered, but this.

It was beautiful. It was primal and powerful and *good*.

She was on the edge of something powerful when he took his hand away. A small sound of frustration escaped from her throat, but Sian did not allow her to remain frustrated for very long. He shifted his body and hers, and then his head was between her legs, and . . . oh, my, his tongue took the place of his talented hands, and the wonder escalated.

She wanted to hold him, but had to clutch at the sheets instead. Her body swayed to meet his mouth, and when he slipped a finger into her trembling warmth, she was swept into a firestorm of release. Her body jerked and trembled, and the climax she had only dreamed of whipped through her body. She cried out, and clutched the sheet even harder with her hands, as if she needed purchase to remain earthbound.

Slowly, languidly, she returned to herself. Her body seemed momentarily worthless. Drained and heavy and wonderfully warm.

Now would come the less pleasant part of the act. If memory served, it would not take long. She remembered the actual experience of having a man inside her as being uncomfortable and unnatural, but somehow, at this extraordinary moment, she thought it might not be so with Sian.

Instead of driving into her, he kissed her inner thigh,

then rose up to kiss her still-trembling belly. She threaded her fingers through his hair. He had wonderful hair, long and silky and black as night.

"Satisfied?" he asked, his mouth against her skin.

"Yes," Ariana sighed, unable to speak plainly. She could feel her heart pounding, and her breath had not returned to normal. "Very."

And yet, she still felt alone, in a way she had not expected. Sian held her. He had brought her to unexpected heights of pleasure. She suspected that until he was inside her, a real and true part of her, she would continue to feel an aching emptiness.

Unexpectedly, he rolled away from her and left the bed.

"Where are you going?" she asked, rising up onto her elbows.

"Back to my room." Sian reached for his discarded clothes.

But they weren't finished. She knew Sian wanted her, at least physically. He was wonderfully erect, and even though she had just experienced a flood of release, she wanted him.

She wanted him.

"Why? Why are you returning to your room *now*?"

He stood by the side of the bed, apparently unconcerned that he was naked and aroused. There was visible tension throughout his entire body. She saw that tension in the set of his mouth, the tautness of his muscles, the trembling of his hands.

"Do you wish to conceive a child on this night?"

"No, but it's unlikely that I would conceive." After all, she'd not gotten pregnant in the two weeks when she'd imagined herself in love with Pryam. One night was surely not too much of a risk.

"Unlikely and impossible are very far apart, Ariana."

"But—"

"It's a chance I won't take."

Fine. He wasn't going to stay. He'd done as she'd asked, in a way, and now he was done with her. No, he was too aroused to be truly *done* with her, but still, he was leaving.

Sian dressed quickly, bowed to her with a new and formal crispness, and then he left the room. He did not slam the door, but closed it almost gently. The lock fastened itself, bidden by a magical hand on the other side of the doorway.

Ariana huddled naked beneath the coverlet. Somehow, she felt more alone than she had before she'd awakened to find Sian in her room. The warmth he had brought to her bed was gone. She felt his touch everywhere, on her skin and deep inside, and still . . . the loneliness was acute.

She heard the scuff of a shoe outside her doorway, and then another. A mild curse, barely audible, followed, and then there was a gentle thunk at her door. In the dark, Ariana smiled. The enchanter had not returned to his room. He was standing guard at her doorway.

Maybe she was not completely alone after all.

8

"MAGIC IS NOTHING MORE THAN THE MANIPULATION of energies," Sian said crisply. One hand rested casually on Ariana's shoulder. "As you already have the advantage of being able to see energy better than most, when aided by my touch, this should be simple." His voice grew cold. "Apparently it is not."

Ariana glared at him. She'd been trying all morning to move a small bowl they had placed upon the long table which sported the inlaid map of Columbyana. In the beginning he had hoped to see her move the bowl from one end of the table to the other. At the moment, he would be satisfied with a twitch.

"Perhaps that which comes easily to you is not as simple as you believe," she said, her voice tired and terse.

"Am I asking too much of you?" he asked sharply. "Is the task of moving a small, lightweight object too difficult?" He should not take his frustration out on her. After

all, it was not her fault that he hurt. It was not her fault
that he'd passed three nights without sleep and had been
hard most of that time. It was not her fault that the simple
contact of his hand to her shoulder was maddening. Oh,
wait. It *was* her fault. "I shudder to think that the fate of
this world rests in the hands of a girl who cannot learn the
simplest lesson . . ."

Ariana snapped her hand, and the bowl spun off the
table and through the air. Toward his head. He deflected
the crockery with his free hand, and it clattered to the
floor. One piece chipped off the rim and rolled away,
landing against the edge of the rug.

His pupil was surprised. "Oh, I'm sorry," she said, raising one hand to her mouth in horror. "I didn't mean . . ."

"Do not apologize. You are an empath, after all. It
makes sense that your abilities are tied to your emotions.
This is a valuable lesson, one we must take to heart."

She turned to him and he withdrew his fingers from
her shoulder. "Did the bowl hurt your hand when you deflected it? Oh, it did, didn't it?"

"No," Sian answered crisply. "My hand is fine."

"Let me see," she insisted.

"That's not . . ." Before he could say "necessary," Ariana had taken his hand in hers and was intently studying
the small red mark there.

"It might bruise. I can make a poultice that will—"

"I do not need a poultice," Sian said, taking his hand
from hers with some force. "And you must stop worrying
yourself over every small injury in your path. What will
you do when soldiers fall around you? What will you do
when you are surrounded by the blood of your comrades,
and the fighting continues? You cannot turn your back on
an enemy to mourn the dead or see to the wounded. If you

are distracted, if you let your need to care for others blind you, then you will die."

He wanted to rile her, to make her understand what she was up against. Instead of taking the bait, she sighed. "You have been in a foul mood these past few days."

Was it any wonder? "I have been my usual cheerful self," he argued.

She smiled widely at that claim. "I am no fool, Sian. I know why you are uneasy. We did not finish what we started."

He took her chin in his hand and stared into her eyes. Was Diella gone? Sleeping? Or here?

Ariana sighed. "I know what you're thinking when you look at me that way. Can Diella talk of beauty and love and pleasure in the same breath, or does she only speak of her physical desires? Can Diella speak of her family with warmth of heart and unending love, or is her every thought centered on her own self?"

"I know what you're attempting to do, Ariana," he said. "It won't work."

She cocked her head, appearing to be truly confused. "What am I trying to do?"

"You wouldn't be the first woman to attempt to bind a man to her through sex. And the very possibility of creating a child . . . you know no man would send the woman bearing his son or daughter into battle, and if he had no choice, he would not allow her to go alone. It is still my intention to return home when your training is done. You will not change my mind in this way or any other."

Not that he hadn't already realized that leaving her to her calling would be extremely difficult.

"I'm not trying to trick you, Sian, and like you, I do

not enjoy the idea of creating a child and then running off
to war not knowing what the future will bring."

"Then why do you torture me?"

And though she might not intend it, having her stand
this close was torture.

"I feel time slipping away from me," Ariana said gently. "I have so much to learn, and I know that even if I
spent years as your student, I would not be proficient
enough to face what I have been chosen to face. We don't
have years. I'm afraid I won't ever see my family again.
Duran, yes, but I suspect I will be gone before my sister
Sibyl arrives, and my parents and other siblings are so far
away, and . . . and you are all I have. No one else under-
stands what awaits me. No one else, Sian. So if I wish for
a particularly close togetherness in the time we have remaining, does that make me a scheming woman intent on
tricking you?"

"Of course not, but . . ."

Ariana reached into her pocket and withdrew a small
vial. "I am a healer and an herbalist. Do you think I do
not know how to make sure I won't conceive a child?"

The erection that had grown the moment she'd touched
his hand responded by growing harder and throbbing
slightly. "You have taken this formula?"

Ariana smiled. "It is not for me, enchanter. It is for *you*."

DURAN WAS A FINE SOLDIER, AND WHEN HE LEARNED
that she would be leaving here with an army, he would insist on being beside her. No, he would insist on being in
front of her, protecting her from all she was meant to fight.

And he would die.

Ariana didn't know what was intended for her beyond

the coming battle, but she could and would protect those she loved most from the war that was meant to be hers.

It was late in the afternoon when she found the opportunity to call on the emperor. She had turned some of his care over to other, less talented healers, and they followed her instructions. They would continue to offer care until Sibyl arrived. On this day the emperor's health was no worse, and no better. He always seemed to be slipping away, fading into nothingness. It was for that reason that she and Sian had chosen not to tell him that the monster she was going to fight was his son. The news would destroy him.

When she was finished with her examination and the administering of some potent herbs, Ariana stood before the emperor and adopted a subservient pose. Hands clasped, head bowed, she curtsyed gently.

"My lord, I have a favor to ask of you."

"Anything."

No one but the emperor, Sian, and she knew of the prophesy and what was to come. There was no other way. No one beyond those necessary could know until the time of battle was upon them.

"I suspect I will likely be leaving the palace in a matter of days. A week or two, perhaps. No more. The enchanter has not suggested to me the date of departure, but I feel it is impending."

Arik nodded his head once.

"I do not want my brother Duran with me."

The emperor's eyebrows lifted slightly in surprise. "Duran Varden is a fine soldier, one of the best. Why do you wish to leave him behind?"

"If he goes with me, he will be determined to protect me. I know Duran, my lord. He will throw himself between me and whatever comes my way, and he will die. This is not his calling, it is mine."

"How do you propose leaving him behind when the time comes?"

Ariana drew a folded sheet of paper from her pocket. "I have penned this letter to my cousin Lyr, explaining what I know of the prophesy and our part in it. It's my intention to head toward the Anwyn mountains and speak to Keelia personally, which leaves no time for traveling to Tryfyn. In my letter I ask Lyr to meet us there.

"The letter must be closed with your seal, one Duran would not dare to break. By the time he delivers the letter, I will be well on my way to the mountains."

"Sian approves this plan?"

"The enchanter does not know of this letter, or of my plans to travel to the mountains of the Anwyn."

"But—"

"He is my teacher, and a fine one," Ariana interrupted. "But the war to come is mine, is it not?"

"Yes, it is," Arik answered calmly as he took the letter from her hands.

"Then some of the decisions must be mine as well."

Arik agreed with her, and she left him resting, still clutching her letter in his aging hands. She was not surprised to find Sian waiting for her in the hallway. He was still concerned that Diella might rise to the surface once again. Ariana believed that the dark spirit of the evil empress was gone, had been gone since the moment she had told the demon to get out of her ocean, but Sian was not convinced.

"How is he?" Sian asked, distant and cool for the sentinels who stood nearby and listened closely.

"The same." They walked away from the emperor's

quarters, side by side, Sian's pace shortened to match Ariana's.

"His care must be left in the hands of others. You must learn to delegate."

"Delegate, not abandon," she argued. She could tell Sian of the letter, she supposed, but as he did not intend to leave the palace with her when the time came, the knowledge was not necessary. He said she was to be a leader. A general, of sorts. It was best that she start to act like one, rather than asking her teacher for constant advice and approval.

She could feel the time of her leaving creeping up on her, coming toward her faster than she had imagined it would.

"For now, you must return to your studies," Sian said. "We made great progress this morning."

Yes, learning that her magical abilities were tied to her emotions had been an important step. If only she could tap into those emotions at will, perhaps she'd be able to manage a few more of Sian's tricks.

He was a good teacher, but an aggravating man. When she'd given him the concoction she'd devised, he'd slipped it into his pocket and turned away from her. She supposed that was better than refusing to accept the vial, or laughing at her offering. Not much better, but some.

Heavens, she hoped he didn't try to ingest the mixture. Not that it would harm him, but it would surely taste horrendous.

Enclosed in the space that had become their classroom, Sian immediately began the lessons once again. He had already lined up several objects of varying size and heaviness on the table. One of the objects was a small knife.

Ariana lifted the knife and hefted the weight of it in

her palm. "I sent the bowl hurtling toward your head, and you select a knife for the next lesson?"

He smiled. "You must learn control."

"Must I? Now?"

"Yes."

Ariana turned her attentions to the array of objects. The manipulation of energy she needed to master was tied to her emotions. Goodness knows she was a bundle of emotions at the moment. Duran would soon be departing for Tryfyn. Sian would not leave the palace with her when the time came. When she led her army away from Arthes, she would be more alone than she had ever been.

Sian knew she still needed his power added to hers, so she was not surprised when she felt his hand at the small of her back. One touch from the powerful enchanter, and her magic was greater than before.

She saw the energy rise on the palm of her hand. It swirled and danced and sparkled, white and blue with touches of purple the color of Sian's eyes. Holding her breath, she threw the energy toward a book Sian had placed at one end of the table. The book opened, and the pages fluttered.

"Good," he whispered. "Very good."

Ariana turned her attentions to a small cup filled with water. She thought of nothing else but that cup, and with a wave of her hand she was able to lift it from the table. The cup floated in the air for a moment, and then she separated the cup from the water inside, so that the water floated on air.

"Wonderful." Sian's voice was deep and soft, a rumble that almost caressed her skin.

Ariana's energy began to fade. A few droplets of water fell to the table, and her focus faltered.

"Emotion," Sian said. "Always emotion."

The cup began to tremble, as if it was preparing to fall.

"Think of pain if you must," Sian instructed, his voice growing sharper as he sensed she was about to let the cup fall. He pressed his hand more firmly to her back. "Think of your long-ago love, and the way you felt when you discovered it was false."

She had not expected him to turn their private moment into a part of her lesson! It was a kind of betrayal, and a rush of anger rose to the surface. The water returned quickly and neatly to the cup, and the cup lowered to the table with a snap. Ariana turned her attention to the small knife. In a flash, it rose from the table, turned on air, and flew toward the door, where it thunked solidly into the wood.

For a moment all was silent in the room, and then Sian muttered, "*Very* good."

"I didn't send it anywhere near you, so don't sound so worried."

"I'm not worried," Sian said, very unconvincingly, as he dropped his hand and stepped away from her.

There was a knock at the door, and a moment later it opened. Duran stepped into the room, a sealed note in his hand. He left the door open, so he did not see the knife. "Sorry to interrupt your lessons, Ariana, but I'm to leave the palace tonight."

So soon? Arik had wasted no time. "Oh." She tried to pretend innocence. "Where are you going?"

"I'm going to Tryfyn, with a message for cousin Lyr. Well, more rightly I have a message for the new Prince of Swords." He waved the note, then placed it in the inside pocket of his green sentinel's vest. "I hate to leave you here unprotected, but I won't be gone a moment longer than is necessary."

It would take weeks to travel to Tryfyn, deliver the note, and return. By the time Duran's chore was done, she'd be gone.

If he knew she had a hand in this, he would never forgive her. Ariana stepped calmly toward her brother and smiled. "Have a wonderful trip." She took his face in her hands and kissed his cheek. "Give Aunt Isadora and Uncle Lucan my love. Lyr, too."

"I will." Duran glared down at her. "Are you all right?"

"I'm very well." She hugged Duran close, and for a moment she infused him with a healer's health, a healer's protection. A sister's love.

Duran glared at Sian in an overly protective, brotherly manner, then once again said good-bye to Ariana. When the door closed behind him, she began to cry. She did not sob, but large tears ran silently down her cheeks. It was very likely that she would never see her brother again.

She turned to find the objects on the table dancing. The knife, which was still embedded in the door, quivered. Sian was not touching her, and still, the objects were affected. Ariana wanted no more lessons, but this moment only proved what Sian had told her to be true. Her emotions and her power were linked. Her ability to do what needed to be done depended on her ability to harness that emotion. With tears running down her face, she pulled the knife from the door. The hilt lay, cool and heavy, on the palm of her hand.

The objects on the table stilled as she focused her energy on the knife. Sian knew what she was trying to do, and he did not reach out for her. This was a test. Could she function without his added power? Were these lessons wasted when he was not with her? The knife spun on her palm and flew from her hand, speeding toward the opposite wall at her command. It once again imbedded itself in wood, this time directly over a picture frame which held the portrait of some long-departed emperor's daughter whose name had been forgotten.

"I am impressed," Sian said reverently.

"Don't be," Ariana said as she crossed the room to retrieve the knife. "I was aiming for the curtain's sash."

The sash in question was several feet away from the portrait, but what she'd accomplished was a start. A very good one.

HE NEEDED SLEEP. THREE SLEEPLESS NIGHTS HE COULD handle, but four? Yes, he needed sleep, but he could not allow Ariana out of his sight for more than a few minutes, even though he had seen no glimpse of Diella since the episode in his quarters.

Pacing outside Ariana's room, Sian reached into his pocket and fingered the vial of potion she had fashioned for him. There were other ways for a woman to trap a man than with a child. He already felt too connected to this witch he was sending to her death. He already felt tempted to accompany her into a battle that was not his to fight.

He had spent years in study, in order to make himself more than a man. In deepening his magic he had by necessity often separated himself from that which made him mortal. People were not as important as the honing of his skills. Emotion was not as important as knowledge. And yet here he was, feeling like nothing more than a man where Ariana Varden was concerned. She waited on the other side of this door, and she wanted him to join her. At this moment he cared only about what his body demanded. Ariana wanted more from him, he knew that. She wanted the comfort of being held, as well as the sex. It wasn't the physical pleasure that would bind him to her. No, it was the closeness and that comfort that would undo him.

That had already undone him.

He unlocked her door magically, and opened it in the same way. Using no magic at all, he closed the door behind him and rebolted it. The vial sat on the palm of his hand.

"How is this applied, and how long does it take to be effective?"

Ariana was awake. Given the excitement of the day, he was not surprised. What did surprise him was that beneath the coverlet that only partially concealed her body, she was naked.

She had known he could come. She had known he could not resist her.

Ariana sat up, and the coverlet fell to offer him a full and unobstructed view of her breasts. She reached out, offering one hand, palm up. "May I show you?"

Sian was not an overly trusting man, and with good reason. He had never before considered giving a potion of a witch's design to her hand for application of an unknown sort.

And yet, he laid the vial on Ariana's palm.

"You must remove your clothing," she instructed.

"I assumed as much," he said as he began to hastily disrobe.

"You could smile for me," she teased.

"Or I could not." This was, after all, a moment purely physical. He need not seduce her with smiles or sweet words. He need not pretend that the true love she had waited for had arrived. She was special, and he would not lie to her.

Not about this.

He joined her on the bed, and she uncapped the vial. Sitting before him, she poured a few grains of the powder onto her hand. "Smell," she whispered, moving her hand close to his nose.

He began to inhale deeply but she stopped him, moving her hand quickly away and laughing lightly. "You are not to take this up your nose, just enjoy the aroma."

Sian did not feel the need to enjoy the aroma of anything but Ariana's skin, but to appease her he sniffed at the concoction. It did smell nice. Perfumy, but not too sweet or flowery. Musky, but not too much so.

She laid her finger on the bridge of his nose and traced the length.

"I have a tremendous nose," he said. "Does it repulse you?"

"It's a fine, noble nose," she responded, "long and straight, perfectly shaped and impossible to ignore. And please be assured that nothing about you repulses me."

Ariana took the palm full of contraceptive powder and lowered it slowly. Her hand came to rest low on his belly, the backs of her fingers barely touching the erection that had driven him to this bed. She made small circles with her hand, rubbing the mixture into his skin and arousing him even further.

The scent grew stronger, and it, too, was arousing. Her hands grew warmer, and so did his skin.

"Are you certain this creation of yours will work?"

"Yes."

She sounded confident, which was good, since he no longer cared if her concoction would be effective or not. He no longer cared about anything but being inside this woman who was his in a way he had never expected. He was her teacher. He was the bearer of the foretelling of her death.

Tonight he was the man who had come to show her
that there was much more than she'd ever imagined between a woman and a man.

He would not take as much time preparing her as he had
on his first night in this bed, but he would not jump upon
her like the animal he felt himself to be. Remembering the
sweet taste of her breasts, he kissed her there and suckled
on her nipples. Her reaction was strong, and she arched her
back to bring herself closer to him, to urge him on.

His skin seemed to slide against hers. She was smooth
and overly warm. He was rough and burning. They were
very different, and yet they were the same. In strength, in
need, in surrender, they were much the same. While he
caressed her breasts, her hands wandered, tracing hills
and valleys, teasing and tweaking and stimulating. The
woman had lightning in her fingertips.

Ariana brought his mouth to hers, demanding a kiss.
Taking what she wanted from him because he had lost all
will to fight her. Had he ever thought her weak? Had he
ever believed her to be powerless? Her tongue teased his,
sweet and unbearably arousing. Her lips moved over his,
and her hands . . . her hands continued to study.

She draped one leg across his hip, while they were still
lying on their sides, and took the tip of his erection into
her body. Just the tip, nothing more. She swayed there,
teasing him and herself, telling him with little moans and
catches of her breath that she liked what she felt, that she
wanted more . . . but not yet.

Sian wanted to see more clearly the woman who was
wrapped around him, so he cast a small circle of wizard's
light over the bed. In this dim light her skin looked even
paler than before, as flawless as ever but ghostly. Lumi-
nous. She had asked for no magic on his first night here,

but tonight she did not seem to mind the light. Eyes opened, she watched him as she continued to move. While their eyes were locked, she took him an iota deeper, and the sensation was beyond any he had ever experienced.

He wondered if Diella would attempt to make an appearance. If she did, would he be able to stop? He saw only Ariana in the eyes that were locked to his. Diella could never fake the emotion he saw there. The warmth. The love that a woman like her gave when a man touched her in this way.

Not her true love, perhaps, but love just the same.

Unable to wait any longer, Sian rolled Ariana onto her back. He did not need to force her thighs apart in order to push inside her. She opened herself for him. She lifted her hips off the bed and swayed into him with a primal force that matched his own.

Their release was quick, powerful, and in harmony. Ariana's muscles milked him as the spasms of her release squeezed and fluttered along his length, and he climaxed while buried deep inside her. She did not scream, but instead whispered his name again and again, in a husky voice.

Movements slowed, breath came unevenly, and Sian became aware that the light he'd created for them had died. He had completely lost his focus. All of his power had been flowing into Ariana.

Perhaps he could not change her destiny, and he could not change the single-mindedness of her days. But the nights to come could be pleasurable. He could share with her the beauty she had been promised. As a woman. As a Fyne witch.

"How long is your potion effective?"

"Three days," she whispered. "Perhaps four, but three is safe. You can come back to me tomorrow night and—"

"Come back?" Already he was growing hard again, which was a surprise. Perhaps there was more to her concoction than preventing the creation of a child.

He did not have need of light to see her reaction. She was hurt. "You're not coming back tomorrow?"

"Coming back implies that at some point I will be leaving." He moved inside her, and she felt his growing length. "I'm not going anywhere, Ariana, unless you send me away. Unless you ask it of me, I won't leave you alone."

ARIANA DRAPED HER BODY ACROSS SIAN'S, SATED AND happy. Happy, when the world was threatened and her life was not her own. Happy, when her future was more uncertain than it had ever been. Neither of them slept, but they were silent in an easy and companionable way, and had been for a while. Now and then Sian's hand would caress her in an almost absent manner, palm raking across her hip or her thigh. More than once she had brushed her fingers across his chest, or down his side.

Dawn was coming when Sian said, "I have an idea."

Ariana rose up and smiled down at him. "Another one?"

"Yes, another one." He sat up and left the bed, heading for her chest of drawers.

Ariana watched this beautiful naked man who seemed so at home in her room. She admired the shape of his body and the way he moved with such masculine grace and confidence. For now he was hers, and he did belong here, in this room, with her. And when she left? Well, she chose not to think about that any more than she had to.

He opened her top drawer and rummaged there.

"What are you looking for?" she asked.

"Rope, ribbon . . . a length of something sturdy."

Ariana slipped from the bed, as naked as Sian and as unconcerned by her state of undress as he seemed to be. She went to the opposite corner of the room, where her sewing kit was stored, and grabbed her basket of supplies. She was quite an accomplished seamstress, and passed many hours on one project or another. She placed the basket on the bed, and Sian joined her as she delved inside.

"I have ribbon." She snagged lengths of red and white ribbon from the basket, and placed them on the bed in a jumble. "Did you say rope?" Beneath a few decorative pieces, she had a tangled length of a rough twine.

Sian studied the ribbon and the twine, but when she pulled the last offering from the basket, he smiled.

He took the leather cord from her hand and hefted it. "This is perfect. Sturdy and soft." He shook out the cord, which was a good length.

Ariana took a step away from him. "You're not going to tie me up again, are you?"

"Not unless you ask me to," he responded, a hint of teasing in his usually serious voice.

"Then why do you need that leather cord?"

Sian ran the length of the cord through his hands, making sure there were no tangles. No knots. When that was done, he took the two ends in his hand and tossed the cord over her head, circling her waist and pulling her gently toward him.

"What are you doing?" she asked. "Oh, when you said you had an idea, I should've inquired as to what sort of idea you spoke of."

His expression was entirely serious now. "Your strength has grown, Ariana, but you are still stronger when I touch you."

"I know," she whispered.

"And yet I cannot be with you all the time."

His words stole a portion of her happiness. "I know that, too."

Sian lifted the cord so that it was caught behind her neck, trapping her hair. He then wrapped the cord around his neck, binding them together. Ariana grabbed one end and reached around his back, and he did the same. It wasn't long before they were closely and completely bound together by the thin leather cord.

"We have been one in body," he said, "and with a few spoken words we can be one in spirit as well. We can meld our energies, Ariana. You can invite a piece of me into you, through this simple cord and a few words, and in that way I will always be with you. Do you consent?"

"Yes." There was no hesitation in her voice, or in her heart.

As the sun rose, Sian spoke words she did not entirely understand. She caught a few familiar words, but she was not proficient in the language of the wizards. He spoke, and she felt the words as if they had a life of their own. She saw the energies his spell created, and they were beautiful . . . unlike anything she had ever seen before. Blue and pink and lavender, the energies swirled around them, separating them from the rest of the world and making them both stronger. Then the energies were not only around them, they were inside. Inside Sian and inside her, linking them together.

What they shared was as intimate as the moment he had entered her body, as precious and powerful as the release they had enjoyed. She closed her eyes and felt Sian join with her in an entirely new and different way. They shared one space, one heart, one soul.

He held out one hand and snapped another word, and the dagger he had left on her dresser flew across the room. The handle smacked neatly into his palm. With precision, he cut the cord that bound them together. Ariana wanted to stop him, because she was immediately and unexpectedly bereft at losing the connection.

When the cord had been cut, Sian tossed the dagger to the bed and began to gather the ends together. He wrapped the cord loosely around her neck three times, and tied the ends in a secure knot. When that was done, he directed her to do the same to the cord which was draped around his neck. They stood there in a shaft of warmth from the rising sun, naked but for the bits of leather cord around their throats.

Ariana touched the three strands of cord at her throat. "I don't feel you the way I did, when you said the words."

"No, but that doesn't mean I'm not there."

With this connection, perhaps she could become more proficient at the magic which had once required the touch of his hand and which was now sporadic at best.

"This doesn't mean I don't need you," she said briskly.

"You don't *need* me, Ariana. You never did."

He sounded and looked serious, but she knew without doubt that he was wrong. She needed Sian, and while she took comfort in the bit of cord that was wrapped around her throat, it was a poor substitute for the man she had come to love.

9

"WHEN WILL MY LEGION BE READY?" CIRO ASKED, HIS voice suitably cool.

The boy was beginning to make Fynnian nervous. He'd taken to dining alone, and just yesterday he had helped himself to one of Fynnian's own servants, which was quite annoying. There was a new, unreadable gleam in the prince's pale eyes. He was hungry in an entirely new way. "Soon."

Ciro paced. Had he grown again? Perhaps a bit wider, perhaps a bit taller. The prince had been a rather small fellow when the Isen Demon had first entered him and taken his soul, and an immediate spurt of growth had followed. Was he growing again?

"How soon?"

"The task I have set for myself is not an easy one, Prince Ciro."

Ciro turned his head slowly, and cold, pale blue eyes

burrowed into Fynnian until he could feel the burn of that glare. "If the task is too arduous for you, perhaps I should place a more powerful wizard at my side."

"There is none more powerful than I," Fynnian said arrogantly.

"That is not what I hear." There was an unexpected confidence in Ciro's voice, an unexpected assurance.

"What do you hear?" And from whom? The boy was purposely isolated. A prisoner. Fynnian's prisoner.

"I hear many things now," Ciro said. "Day and night, I hear constant whispers and screams. I hear promises. And I hear truth, through the demon who serves me."

Ciro apparently believed that the demon served him, rather than the other way around. He'd find out soon enough who was in charge. It was disturbing that the demon had been communicating directly with its vessel, though he should have known that day was coming. Fynnian did not like being left out of those conversations. After all, he had discovered the demon, and he had chosen Ciro as its host. He should be privy to everything.

"What truth did you hear?"

"There is a wizard more powerful than you, and he'll soon be traveling this way. He is not dark, as you are. As we know, that can be rectified."

Fynnian thought the claim to be a lie, but to play along he asked, "Does this wizard have a name?"

"Chamblyn," Ciro answered easily. "His name is Chamblyn, I am told. Do you think he might ready my legion in a more timely manner than you have done? Do you think he might provide more suitable and regular feedings than you have done?"

"I do my best, my prince."

Ciro turned away and looked out the window. This late

at night, with no moon, there was little to see beyond the glass. "Your best is no longer enough. I have been forced to assemble my own soldiers."

"How is that possible?" Fynnian asked. Ciro had not left this house or communicated with anyone other than Fynnian himself in months. No, that was not entirely true. Apparently he was communicating quite well with the Isen Demon. How strong had the demon grown?

"How such is possible is not your worry," Ciro said coldly. "They will come, and they will serve me, but they cannot accomplish all that is required alone. I need more soldiers, I need a legion which will serve me, and the assembling of that legion is your mission. If you do not have my army prepared to march by the next full moon, I will take your soul and drink your blood and toss what is left of you down the mountainside."

Fynnian felt a flush of fear. There were a mere fifteen days until the next full moon! "I will not give you permission to take my soul."

Only Ciro's head turned, and the boy cast a thoroughly evil smile Fynnian's way.

The monster standing in his study no longer needed permission, not for the taking of a soul as tainted as the one which Fynnian possessed.

"If you kill me, what of Rayne?" Fynnian asked desperately. "She will never forgive you. She will never willingly be yours if you destroy the father she loves."

"That is why you have until the next full moon to deliver my legion, old man. Do not think my desire for your daughter will buy you more time than that. I can take her if it appears there is no other way. I can bind your beautiful daughter to me in a thousand ways, none of them pleasant for her, I imagine."

Ciro had not yet gained the strength to take a pure soul like the one Rayne possessed, but when he did, when he grew that powerful, there would be no stopping him.

"It takes time to build an army such as the one I have planned for you."

"You have had time, old man."

Fynnian's fists tightened. When had he lost control? Even a few days ago he'd believed himself to be in complete control. Now Ciro was in command.

No, it was the Isen Demon which had infected Ciro that had control of the situation. The same demon which had infected this land, which had spread its darkness into gray corners of the earth and taken control of those who already danced on the edge of evil.

If the Isen Demon had grown so strong, then those dark corners of the earth were already active . . . perhaps more active than anyone yet realized.

A SLEEPING MAN WAS OVERTAKEN BY A DARK MIST which rose from the floor beneath his bed. Deep within her own sleep, Keelia shuddered. She knew this was a dream, and yet like so many dreams which had come before, it was more. It was prophesy, enlightenment, and truth. A horrible, ugly truth.

The man awoke and sat up, turning his attention to the woman at his side. His wife of many years slept peacefully, blissful and unaware. The sleepy man ran a hand through hair almost as red as Keelia's. His hair was duller, and streaked with gray, and wiry in many places. But it was also very red.

The red-haired man's marriage had not been a particularly happy one, but neither had it been disastrous. He and his wife had made five healthy children, all of them grown now and living on their own. Whatever love they'd known had died a long time ago, but they did not always hate one another. Not every day. There were some good days when they laughed together.

There were more bad days. The husband was not faithful, and had not been for a very long time. He was sometimes fond of inflicting pain on his partners. He took more joy in their screams of terror than he did in their screams of pleasure, but that was a dark, secret part of himself. It was hidden from all, most especially from this woman.

He looked at his wife for a long while, the hate within him growing stronger with every breath he took. Each breath fed the hate, each exhalation of that breath expelled the lingering affection and the civility which had kept him in check for so many years. After a while the husband left the bed and headed to the kitchen. There he grabbed a piece of bread which was left over from supper, and he nibbled on it calmly and slowly, his mind swirling. When the bread was done, the crumbs brushed almost daintily from his nightshirt and his gray-streaked red beard, he grabbed his wife's best kitchen knife and hefted it in his hand. The knife had a sharp, wide blade, and a well-used wooden handle the color of a butternut.

Keelia knew what was going to happen. Panic welled up in her heart and she attempted to shout a warning, but she was a silent observer, unable to touch the husband or warn the wife. All she could do was watch.

The husband returned to his bed, knife in hand. It would be so simple to plunge the blade into his wife's heart and have done with it, but that would not satisfy him. He wanted to see the woman he had shared his life with suffer. He wanted to watch her die.

The man with the knife straddled his wife's sleeping body. She woke suddenly, at first angry with her husband and then, when she saw the knife, afraid. With fear and indignation, she ordered him to get off her, but he did not move. The tip of the knife touched her nose, and then her throat. The man grinned . . . and that was when Keelia realized that there was very little of the husband remaining in the man with the knife. A fiend had moved in and taken over. A fiend held that knife above the frightened woman.

He began to make small cuts, on her face and on her throat. With each cut, the man's physical appearance changed. His arms grew longer, his hands larger. Knots rose up on his face and his neck, and his mouth . . . his evil grin . . . grew impossibly wide. When the wife tried to scream, the changing man clamped one hand over her mouth and moved the knife to her breasts. Again he changed, until his distorted face was no longer recognizable as that of the man she had once loved. The transformation was not complete. Killing her was going to take all night . . .

Keelia came awake and sat up briskly. She was in her own bedroom, alone and safe.

As Queen of the Anwyn, Keelia was given all that she desired, and more. She lacked for nothing she asked for . . . but for one request which went unanswered.

She wanted these dreadful dreams to stop.

She'd been suffering with these dreams, as well as continuing visions of darkness, for months now. Her mother advised that if she'd marry and give in to her natural Anwyn urges, the dreams would abate. She believed the visions were tied to Keelia's female urges—the strong urges of an Anwyn Queen which were meant to ensure the survival of their species. Queen Mother Juliet believed the visions her daughter had been suffering of late to be metaphorical, rather than factual.

A few misinterpretations in the past year or so, and suddenly every vision was called into question, at least by her family. Keelia knew that if her mother had been having the same sort of visions, there would be no doubt that something was wrong, but Juliet's dreams had been of the peaceful sort.

Keelia's visions were not always easy to interpret. She knew the man she had dreamed about tonight had not actually transformed into a monster as he'd murdered his wife, not on the outside at least. The physical changes she'd seen in her dream represented the darkening of his soul, not an actual transformation which would make him easy to note in a crowd.

If her mother were here now, Keelia would insist again that some darkness was rising, that the dreams of shadows were real, even if they had received no word of such horrors, even though Juliet herself had not suffered the same unpleasant visions. The darkness that made these actions possible also kept the news from those who would rise up against it—perhaps even blocked Juliet's powers, as well as the powers of those like the former Queen.

Keelia was different. Her mother had been telling her all her life that she was *different*. In this case, that was true. Whatever force protected those with psychic gifts from these visions had not protected her.

Somewhere in this world tonight, a husband was cutting up his wife and enjoying every moment of it, as he transformed from an ordinary man to an unimaginable fiend, and Keelia believed that if her mother were here, she might be able to convince her it was real this time.

But her mother was not here. Keelia's parents had

taken to the mountains. They took frequent long trips so they could be alone, so they could run in their wolf form unfettered by their responsibilities. They would not make that transformation until the next full moon, which was fifteen days away, but they seemed to enjoy these journeys which took them to places no other human, and very few Anwyn, had ever seen. These trips came more often now that all their children were of an age where they no longer needed parental supervision. Their youngest child, their only other daughter, had turned fifteen a few months earlier. Giulia had her own suite of rooms in the palace, and basked in the attentions lavished on the Queen's sister.

Juliet insisted that she and her husband, Ryn, needed these trips now, since as soon as Keelia produced grandchildren, the regal grandmother would be required more often here in the Palace of the Anwyn Queen.

There would be no grandchildren unless Keelia gave in to the urges of an Anwyn Queen and took a lover or a husband.

It was her duty to reproduce, to make princes and princesses to fill this palace. Her mother reminded her often of her responsibilities, as did the priestesses. Keelia was adamant that she did not want a lover simply for the sake of servicing her body. She did not require a man to still the longing. She wanted her mate, the one who was meant to be her own, and he had not yet come.

Her heat grew stronger with each onset, as if protesting her denial of her Anwyn urges, but there were ways to still the longing without taking a man inside her body to create a child. Many ways.

Keelia's powers were legendary, and unsurpassed. Her shifting to wolf form was not guided by the cycles of the moon, as other Anwyn peoples were. She could change at will, and could even shift only a part of her body if she so desired. She would never have need of a weapon when her claws were only a heartbeat away. These powers did not help her with what she craved most. Why could she see so much of the world, and yet she could not see her mate? Was she destined to live her life as a virgin Queen, possessing powers beyond those of any other Queen, and yet lacking what she most desired?

She dismissed the ancient legend that said the red-haired Queen would take a Caradon lover and in doing so bring peace to her people. First of all, it was ridiculous to imagine that she would bed a lowly Caradon. The cat-people were not civilized, as the Anwyn were. They did not have a queen or a king. They were solitary beasts, whether in the form of man or cat, living from one day to the next with no thought but of their next meal, their next kill, their next comfort. Second, her people were already at peace. Yes, there was the occasional Caradon scare, when two or more of them who had a functioning brain got together and thought to attack, but the attacks were rare and never successful, so how would sleeping with one of the creatures bring peace if there was already peace?

Something unwanted whispered in her ear. If the darkness she dreamt of came to her mountain, would there still be peace?

Keelia left the bed, knowing there would be no more sleep on this night. Standing at the window looking down on The City, she wondered where the people she had dreamt of were at this moment. Did they live in one of the villages at the foot of the mountain she commanded, or were they far, far away?

And then, with a clarity that came to her often . . . whether she wanted it or not . . . she knew that the violence of which she'd dreamed was taking place in more than one village, with more than one husband and wife. Child and parent. Slave and master. Woman and lover. Tonight there was violence and death and a wicked transformation for those who had danced on the edge of evil and now passed beyond that edge. The darkness she did not yet understand was growing stronger, and for all her powers, for all her knowledge, she did not know how it could be stopped.

The newly formed monsters would gravitate to one another, and when they were legion, they would be a plague upon all those who were in their path.

After a few moments, she managed a gentle breath of relief. Dark visions were often followed by something warmer. Something soothing. If not for the more pleasant visions, she might not have survived these twenty-five years, so she always embraced them. She opened her heart and took them in.

Someone she loved was coming her way soon. Someone who loved her would soon be here, in this isolated palace.

Keelia placed one hand over her heart. *Ariana.*

TIME, WHICH HAD ONCE MOVED SO SLOWLY, RACED PAST. With every breath that Ariana took, with every word she spoke, time rushed by. She felt the coming of her calling as acutely as she felt the pain of her failures, and the warmth of Sian's touch.

She did not regret taking him as a lover, not when he offered her such pleasure—as well as a welcomed respite from the constant knowledge that she'd soon be leaving the palace with her own army, headed for a war she did not yet understand.

As she had learned to tap into her emotions as well as

the power of her ancestors and family, her magical skills improved each day. The ceremony Sian had performed at dawn, linking them in some magical way with the three strands of leather cord which remained at her throat always, also fed her gifts. She would never be as talented as Sian, who'd had a lifetime to hone his skills, and her aim went askew now and then. But she was better able to manipulate objects than she had been on that day when she'd almost impaled the portrait of a long-ago imperial daughter, and her own healing power was as sharp as it had ever been. And still—Arik did not improve.

In the confines of a secluded room, with no one but her teacher and lover watching, she could manipulate objects. When she found herself in battle, with distractions all around her and Sian many miles away, would she still be able to concentrate enough to call upon these new gifts? Or would she be helpless as a kitten?

Ariana had told the emperor of her plans, and she'd shared with him the date of her departure. Her army would march on the morning before the next full moon. She had not yet shared that date with Sian. She didn't want that creeping deadline to come between them.

Now that the date was a mere two days away, she knew it was time to tell him she was leaving. Best to save the news for tonight, when they were lying in bed side by side.

She was going to miss him so much.

Before she left, she would like to have a look at the written Prophesy of the Firstborn Sian protected so fiercely. He said there were words and meanings still to decipher, and dismissed her offers of help. As he was her lover and teacher, she knew his expressions well. Even though he was stoic, his expressions minimal, she saw the light of fear in his eyes. There was something in the prophesy he did not want her to see.

A knock at the doorway interrupted their lessons, just as Ariana was perfecting—or so she hoped—the casting of a field of protective energy around her body. Sian seemed quite excited by the prospect of her making use of this magical armor, and in truth it eased her mind considerably. Not that anything would protect her entirely, but every edge she could find would be helpful.

She dropped the shield, answered the knock with an ordinary, "Enter," and it opened on one of her brother's best friends.

Merin was like Duran, in that he was charming, dedicated, and quite popular with the ladies of the palace. He had curling dark hair, nicely shaped dark eyes, and very tanned skin. While he was not as tall as Sian, or as well built, he was definitely a fine example of the male species.

"You asked for me," Merin said as he closed the door behind him. He cast a suspicious glance at the enchanter. Not only was he, like many of the soldiers, wary of excessive magic, but he was also Duran's good friend. As a good friend, he was obviously experiencing a moment of protective ire.

Did the residents of the palace gossip about Ariana's relationship with Sian? Once she might've cared, but today she had more on her mind than propriety and overly protective friends.

"Yes," she responded. "I did ask for you. Thank you for coming." She glanced over her shoulder to catch a glimpse of Sian. "Enchanter, would you leave us?"

Sian did not hesitate before responding calmly, "No."

"This does not concern you," she argued.

His only answer was an imperious lift of his eyebrows.

"Fine." She had hoped to tell him later, when they were alone, but as he insisted on remaining where he was not needed . . . now would have to do, she supposed. It wasn't as if he didn't know she would be leaving soon.

She faced the sentinel, and gathered to her every speck of confidence she had built in the time Sian had been her teacher. "I have been called to fight a war with a darkness I do not yet understand. In two days, I will leave the palace with an army. We—"

"Two days?" Sian thundered. "We have not discussed this. It is too soon."

She looked at her lover. "This is why I asked you to wait outside."

Merin momentarily glanced at the floor. To hide a smile? Or in an embarrassed attempt to completely ignore the exchange? If the sentinel did not already know there was more between Ariana and her teacher than lessons, he knew now.

Sian crossed his arms over his chest and his jaw went hard. His lips thinned. His eyes sparked.

She ignored him, and returned her attentions to Merin. "I will take an army with me when I go. My army, Merin. If you are agreeable, I would like you to lead the men."

"But . . . but . . ." It was out of character for Merin to stammer, but he did so. "I am no general, and . . . and what of Duran?"

"Duran will not return from his journey until I am well gone, and I want no generals. I want seasoned warriors who will answer the command of a woman. I want good men who will fight evil, no matter what form it presents to us. I trust you, Merin. Will you join me?" She knew it was a request no self-respecting sentinel would refuse. "Will you follow the command of a woman?"

He bowed crisply. "I am at your service."

She sighed in relief. Next to Duran, she trusted Merin above all other men in the palace. But for Sian, of course, who was no soldier and who had promised more than once that when she left here, he would not be with her.

"Your first task is to raise forty of the best warriors to fight with me."

"Forty?" Merin asked. "In two days?"

"Yes," Ariana said confidently. "Forty men, in addition to yourself. Is that task beyond your capabilities?"

"No, of course not," he answered arrogantly. "What of the emperor? Will he allow me to take his best sentinels for your army?"

"He has promised me anything I need for this journey."

Merin nodded. "I must proceed immediately if I am to gather together all you need in two days."

He left the room, his step a bit lighter than it had been when he'd entered. A true soldier loved nothing more than a good fight. Good heavens, what was she asking of Merin and the men he would collect?

"Why the pretty boy?" Sian asked softly, his lips very near her ear.

She laughed at his description of Merin. "He's Duran's friend, and I trust him."

"So you said." A long, strong finger raked across her shoulder. "I'm surprised you would choose someone so young as the leader of your militia. Doesn't he rather remind you of a puppy, with those lavish curls and those wide, dark eyes? I believe the Minister of Finance's wife has just such a puppy. Or is it his mistress?"

Ariana spun to face Sian, a smile spreading across her face. "You're *jealous*."

"I am not."

"You are." Did he forget that she was an empath? That she could feel what he felt?

"I suppose a woman as passionate as you are will require a suitable young companion for your journey," he said. As he spoke, he touched her in a possessive way, lightly fondling her breasts as only a man who truly knows a woman can. Her nipples peaked in response, and her inner muscles clenched. "Your trusted friend certainly seems sturdy enough."

"Do you think me so needy that I would choose a new lover while the old one is still in my bed?"

"As you remind me so often, time is running out. Life is short, and we must make the best of every moment."

"Yes, we must," she said. Ariana slipped out of Sian's grasp too easily, and hopped up on the table so that her rear end touched the edge of the inlaid map of Columbyana. Without taking his eyes from hers, Sian flicked his fingers in the direction of the door, and the latch fell into place.

His purple eyes flashed. Ariana had seen shadows and darkness there, but on occasion she also saw fire. She saw fire now, and he moved toward her, his every step graceful and masculine and strong.

Was it worth a call to battle if that was the only way she could know these days? In the beginning, knowing what was to come had filled her with dread and a certainty that she would not survive, but Sian gave her hope. He walked to the edge of the table, and she wrapped her thighs around him. "When this war is over, how will I find you?"

The length of his body twitched very slightly. "Let's not speak of what's to come. Not now."

"I will find you," she said, reaching down to caress his erection through the plain black trousers he wore. "I'm a witch, you know," she teased. "A very powerful one."

"I'm very well aware."

"You cannot hide from me."

"What man would be so foolish as to try?"

He eased her back onto the table, followed her, and pushed up her skirts. Until now, they had cleanly separated the two parts of their relationship. This room, the hours of their days, was strictly for lessons and preparation for war. Her bedroom, the hours of nighttime, was for making love. For touching and laughing and sex.

But now time was truly short, and no opportunity should be wasted.

The table beneath her was hard and cold, unlike her bed, but the kiss Sian gave to her was as wonderful as any other, and when he teased her entrance with his fingers, the reaction was as acute as in any other encounter. Perhaps more so, as she was so very aware that time was slipping away.

This was not a slow seduction, but was instead a fierce act of possession and demand. If he could brand her as his, he would. And if she could brand him as hers and hers alone, she would not hesitate.

He was quickly inside her, and she was ready for him. Hungrily, impatiently ready. They mated on this table, not with practiced skill, as lovers who know one another well might, but as animals making their claim and taking what is theirs. Taking. Demanding. Reaching. They were more clothed than not, with only the necessary pieces of clothing moved aside for this connection, but she had never felt so naked and vulnerable before him.

She clutched at his hair and grasped him tight. Her hips rose to demand all of him, and he answered her demand. *Mine.*

Sweat shone on both of them, and their labored breathing changed dramatically. They were beyond control.

There was nothing else in this world but the places on their bodies where they were joined, and the demand for the completion that remained just out of reach.

She felt that completion tease her. *Not yet . . . not so soon.* And yet her body would not slow, would not draw back from its demand.

Sian grasped one of her trembling thighs and shifted it, lifting her leg higher so that he could bury himself inside and touch a new and sensitive place. Ribbons of pleasure unfurled and then burst, and she clutched at him even tighter, rising partway off the table and shuddering around him. He came with her, as if he had been waiting for her, as if he had been holding back and could wait no more.

They collapsed onto the table, sweating and breathing heavily, holding on to one another in the oddest ways. Ariana grasped a handful of Sian's long, black hair in one hand, and the other rested over his pounding heart. He had made a fist in her skirt, and his other hand rested possessively over one of her heaving breasts.

She could barely breathe, much less speak, and still she managed to say, punctuated with long, necessary gasps of air, "And you think . . . there is the slightest possibility . . . that I will not . . . find you . . . when my battle is done?"

For a long moment Sian was silent. He did not laugh, or kiss her, or—even better—tell her precisely where he lived. She was so close to him, it was impossible not to feel the sadness that radiated from him.

Sadness, at a time like this. True, sad moments were surely coming, but this was not one of them.

Sian rolled from the tabletop and straightened his trousers as he walked toward the door. He did not even turn to look at her as he said, "I have some research to do this afternoon. Please, forgive me." With that, he was gone.

Ariana rolled up slowly, still shaken and not nearly as satisfied as she had been before Sian had made his odd exit. Close as they had become, he was hiding something from her. She knew it.

She leapt from the table, and something made her turn to look at the stone map on which she and her lover had engaged in wildly out-of-control sex.

She started in surprise, and tentatively laid one palm over the stone.

Portions of the map of stone and gems glowed, as if the table had somehow drawn in the power she and Sian had just shared. When she had first touched the table, it had been cold. Horribly cold. Now it was warm to the touch, as if it had somehow come alive. Very clearly she saw the outline of a road, a path from the palace to the mountains of the Anwyn. Not very far from the foot of the mountain, where she knew of a village too small to be indicated on the important map, a swirling dot glowed red. It was red, and then black, and then red again.

Her heart hitched. Was her battle to take place there, before she even reached Keelia? Instinctively she touched the cord at her throat.

The unnatural markings on the map vanished quickly. It was as if she blinked and they were gone. The stone beneath her hands grew cold once again. If not for everything else that had happened of late, she might be able to convince herself that what she'd seen had been delusion. No, what she'd seen had been real. Was it a warning or a promise? Was she being guided or warned?

Should she avoid the village of the red-and-black markings—those cryptic symbols which had already disappeared—or should she race toward it?

IO

SIAN WAS NOT AN INDECISIVE MAN. THE RIGHT PATH was always clear to him, and he never hesitated in taking it, no matter what the cost.

Until now. If he told Ariana that the prophesy foretold her death, would it increase her strength and will or would she cower with fear and thus make herself more vulnerable? Like it or not, he could not think only of her. She was necessary in this coming war. Something she was to do in the coming months—or perhaps in the coming years—would make a significant difference in the battle which was hers to fight.

So, should he warn her of all that awaited her? Or should he allow her the blissfulness of false hope? He didn't have much time left in which to decide. Her army of forty men had been assembled by Merin. The sentinels had been told that they were going to fight in a battle like no other, that they would fight evil itself with a woman as their leader. Word had traveled through the palace quickly, as he had known it would. Men and women whispered in fear, and they stared at Ariana as if she were a stranger to them. Word of the battle to come was likely now traveling across the land, warning those who would be their adversaries that they would not be allowed to take what they wanted without a fight. It had begun.

In a matter of hours, Ariana and her army would leave Arthes.

She slept at Sian's side, and he allowed her to sleep. In the past two days, since he'd learned that she'd chosen her date of departure, there had been a strain between them. That strain did not keep him out of her bed, but there was no more laughter here. No more teasing and easy banter. Instead what was between them took on a desperate manner.

Perhaps Ariana didn't know that she was destined to pass into the Land of the Dead before the battle was over, but somewhere deep inside she realized that what she and Sian had would be over the moment she marched away from the palace. She was not coming back.

Was it Diella, lurking deep and whispering dark truths? The empress, if she remained, had been silent and still, but that did not mean she was gone. Sian could only imagine that more than a quarter of a century in Level Thirteen would make a few days or weeks of sleeping and waiting for the right moment to rise very easy, especially if those days or weeks were spent inside a woman like Ariana, who loved life and lived it well.

Sian drew her sleeping body to his, so that he might better feel the brush of her warm skin against his, so that he could drink in the utter and complete femaleness she wore so well. She was special in so many ways he could not begin to list and appreciate them all, and he knew with everything he possessed that she was not meant for war.

He desperately wanted to change the prophesy, but it took a magic much more powerful than his to do such a thing.

Ariana's eyes opened, and gentle fingers brushed away a strand of his hair, hair that had fallen across his cheek as he studied her. "You should sleep, enchanter," she said sleepily. At times like this, that simple word that described his powers sounded like an endearment, as meaningful as the "love" he had tossed so thoughtlessly at Diella.

"We need to talk."

"No." Her bare body shifted into his, and she was warm. Wonderfully warm and soft. "Our time for talk is done." She sighed. "Don't make me sad, Sian. Don't whisper revealing words that I will carry with me when I go. A soldier isn't supposed to cry."

He would argue that he had no revealing words to whisper, but she was an empath and surely knew better. "You need more study," he said, removing emotion from his voice. "I thought I might travel with you for a while."

She tipped her head back and looked him squarely in the eye. "No. Thank you, but no."

Sian bristled. He had not expected her to refuse. "You're not ready to go on alone."

"I am as ready as I will ever be."

"But—"

"And I'm not entirely alone." She caressed the cord at her throat.

"That's hardly sufficient—"

"Don't make me say it," she interrupted. "Don't make me tell you that I am leaving you behind for the same reason I sent Duran to Tryfyn."

Protection. Worry. Love.

She curled against him and didn't say another word. Neither did he. He held her close, and rubbed his hand up and down her back. It was the fine, sweet back of a woman, not a warrior.

After a while, he whispered, "If I could take your place, I would do so. If I could carry all your burdens, I would not hesitate."

The words she did not want to hear were wasted, as she had already fallen into an uneasy sleep.

Eventually Sian slept, too. When he woke, he saw that Ariana had awakened and left the bed without disturbing him. The sun was barely up, and yet she had begun to dress, pulling on a sentinel's green trousers and a sentinel's loose-sleeved green shirt. Her vest and weapons sat close by, but she had not yet donned them.

She was too busy reading the prophesy she'd plucked from his coat pocket.

ARIANA FELT LIKE SHE COULD MELT THROUGH THE floor. She had always known that death was possible, she had even often thought it was likely. But to see it written this way, not as a possibility but as a certainty . . .

Sian had known all along. He had purposely hidden the truth from her. He'd trained her, shared her bed, come to care for her . . . and all that time he'd been lying to her.

"Ariana."

Her head snapped up when he called her name so softly. He remained there in her bed, naked and maddeningly calm. "Why didn't you tell me?"

"To what end?" Sian asked as he left the bed. He moved toward her, but she backed away two short steps. She did not want him to touch her. Not now.

"Must there be an *end* to the truth? Must every word that leaves your mouth be weighed and calculated and . . . and . . . cold?" she finished. "Calculated and cold, that's what you are."

Sian reached for his trousers . . . trousers that had been hanging on a chair near the coat she had been drawn to as she'd dressed. It was as if a little voice in the back of her head had whispered, *You know the prophesy is there. You know you want to read it before you leave.*

And so she had. Now she wished she had ignored the impulse that had driven her to read this prophesy which doomed her.

Sian pulled on his trousers quickly. "I have been studying the witches' journals from Level Seven, trying to find a way back from the Land of the Dead as I searched for more information on the Isen Demon."

"There is no way back from the Land of the Dead," she snapped as she threw the prophesy at him.

"How do you know? Perhaps there is something we don't know of which can change this prophesy. A spell or a potion or an amulet . . ."

"Stop it," Ariana ordered in a lowered voice. She raised her chin, and even though everything that meant anything to her was currently falling apart, she did not cry. She did not even whimper.

Not everything in her heart was gone. She still had the love of her family, and the knowledge that her actions could save many people much pain. What she'd lost was Sian, and in truth, he had never been hers. If he had been hers in the ways she had imagined, he would not have lied to her.

"You're dismissed," she said calmly. "I hope your journey home is a pleasant one." Words caught in her throat, but she did not let the reaction show. "No wonder you never told me where you lived. You knew all along that I would not be looking for you when the battle was done, because when the battle is done, I'll be dead."

He reached for her.

"Don't, Sian." She tilted her head slightly and studied the face of the man she'd thought she knew so well. "Does every man lie when it suits him? Is any man capable of speaking the truth even when it is painful to him, even when that truth gets in the way of what he wants? Will a man lie simply because it is *convenient*? I think perhaps that is the case. No wonder a woman is destined to lead this army. Truth is necessary, Sian, even when it's unpleasant."

"You need more men," he said sharply, completely ignoring her argument.

"Not yet," she responded with confidence. "Right now I need Keelia and Lyr and their people. Once we're assembled, then I'll decide how many more men I need."

He was clearly frustrated as he folded the prophesy and stuffed it into his pocket. "You have Merin and his forty. Why not make it forty-one?" he asked gruffly. "I can fight, you know. And my magic would be helpful, in battle and in travel."

Since she'd discovered the extent of the prophesy and Sian's lies, Ariana had stepped away from him, keeping her distance. Now she moved toward him. She reached up and took his face in her hands, her palms resting against cheeks rough with a morning's stubble, and then she went up on her toes and kissed him. It was a cold kiss, unlike any other they had shared. When she pulled her mouth from his and dropped down, she said, "I love you, Sian, and I thank you for everything you have taught me. I love you, but I do not trust you. I don't want a man I can't trust in my army."

She handed him his shirt, then stepped past him and opened the door. "Good-bye, enchanter. I wish you a long and happy life."

Frustrated, he stepped into the hallway. She slammed the door behind him, and then, without pause, crossed the room to continue preparing for the day. She would wear an outfit very much like that of any soldier as she marched away from Arthes. Her fingers trembled as she fastened the buttons of her vest, and she tried to dismiss the reaction by retreating into her own thoughts.

He's not worth a moment's heartache.

I know that.

There are other men in the world, men who would be more than happy to take his place. You will soon discover that one man is very much like another.

But I don't want another man. And even if I did, I'm going to die, probably soon.

Death is not so bad . . .

THE SOLDIERS FYNNIAN HAD ASSEMBLED LOOKED fiercer and more prepared than those who had come at Ciro's silent command. They were certainly better armed. Still, the prince knew that when the time to fight was upon them, none would be fiercer than those who had answered his call.

Men and women, young and old, armed with whatever weapons they could steal or fashion, they were a ragged-looking army. Ragged but hungry for blood and unfettered by morals.

He kept to himself the belief that his legion could

easily decimate Fynnian's soldiers if he commanded it. Fynnian didn't need to know, and besides . . . they were *all* his soldiers.

Under the light of a full moon, Ciro studied his legion. Fynnian had provided a fine, large, white horse for Ciro to ride upon. His army consisted of more foot soldiers than horsemen, but in time that would change. As they marched across the country, they would take what they needed, including horses.

When they marched through a village, they would leave nothing behind. They would take what they wanted and destroy all else.

He spoke loudly enough that all could hear them, even though the men stretched partway down the mountainside, and more continued to come. He could see them coming, trudging forward lit by moonlight and determined to be one of his Own.

"Are you hungry?" he asked.

The answers were shouted and whispered and silent. He heard them all.

"Will you follow me wherever I lead you?"

Again he heard every answer, and those responses fed him almost as well as a soul and a mouthful of blood. These soldiers were not just his to command, they were a part of him. An extension of his power. An extension of the demon itself.

"Will you live and die at my command?" This time he shouted, and every answer, every one, was shouted aloud. The mountain shuddered, and he smiled.

"Do you love me?"

The answer was tremendous, and unshakably affirmative.

They would soon march down the mountainside, but not yet. Ciro had business to attend to first.

An anxious Fynnian followed Ciro into the house.

"This is not necessary," Fynnian argued. "The servants know to keep Rayne isolated and safe, and—"

"I did not ask for your counsel," Ciro snapped. "And if you think you are still in command, I will be glad to prove that you are not." He glanced back at the old man who followed him. Fynnian remained useful and might be so for a while. As long as he didn't get in Ciro's way, he would continue to live. If he faltered, however, there would be no hesitation.

Inside the house, Ciro made his way to a plain door that looked as if it might open onto a storage room or a pantry. Instead beyond the door there were narrow, steep stairs that led down to a cool cellar. The house had been built to accommodate the mountain, and this part of the dwelling was on the side of the mountain. Below the floors were the rock of the mountain itself, and one high, small window would allow a hint of light to touch the room each afternoon. Rayne would like that. She would enjoy the fleeting warmth of sunlight each day.

He heard her pathetic pleading before he reached the bottom of the stairs. She was begging one of the servants who had been assigned to keep watch to release her.

Ciro began to speak before Rayne or the servant could see him. "The man knows better than to release you, my beloved, as I would know of his betrayal immediately and would return here in a moment's time to eat his soul and drink every drop of his bitter blood."

The servant in question shuddered, knowing Ciro's claim to be true.

Ciro stopped in the center of the well-lit cellar to admire his future bride. His betrothed. The flames from many oil lamps and candles flickered, so that light seemed to dance over Rayne and the old man who had her keeping.

He would not be cruel where his bride was concerned. Rayne had all the comforts she might desire here in this cellar. A small but comfortable bed. A padded chair. A stack of books. Paper and pen. The servant he had arranged to care for her would see that she was well fed. Tonight she was dressed in one of her favorite gowns, a pale blue frock that was girlish and spoke of propriety and decorum.

The chains which shackled her to the stone wall allowed her to move to all of the comforts he had provided for her, so he could not understand why she cried and pleaded.

"Sir," she said, her eyes wide and beseeching. "Please release me. I will tell no one what's happened here. I'm sure this is simply an unfortunate misunderstanding."

He grinned at his future bride. The purity of her soul shone around her. That purity called to him, but it also kept him from her. Still he grinned, because he knew that when he returned, he would have the power to take what he wanted, and she would be here waiting for him.

"I'm going off to war, my beloved." He ignored her pleas and walked toward her. She backed away as far as she could, but had nowhere to go, thanks to the shackles and the cold stone wall behind her. "Think of me while I'm away." He caught up with Rayne when she had moved as far as her bonds would allow. He touched her chin with one finger and lowered his mouth to hers. He could not take her soul, and it was not time to take her body, but he could take a kiss.

When his lips were almost on hers, she turned her head away.

Angry, Ciro clutched her face in one hand and held her fast. This time when he took his mouth to hers, she could not move.

He opened his mouth wide, and though she fought him, he forced her to do the same. She was very warm and she tasted good, as he had known she would. Ciro was vaguely aware that his beloved was beating against him with her small fists. The chains that hung from those fists clanged. Her tears dampened the kiss, and they tasted salty and good. She pushed against his arms and his chest, she even tried to pull his hair. He paid no mind to her efforts and the keening noise she made. No mind at all.

He thrust his tongue into her mouth and she tried to squeal and push him away, but he held fast and moved his tongue in and out of her mouth, mimicking the act she was so afraid he would force upon her now.

She had no need to fear. Not today. The time was wrong for the making of his son, but when he returned, the time would be right.

When he returned, Rayne wouldn't fight him this way. When he returned, he would be strong enough to make her do anything he wanted. She wouldn't dare fight him after he returned to her victorious.

Just to make her squeal, he cupped her breast and gave the nipple a tweak. Her entire body shuddered, not with anticipation but with fear.

He liked it, so he bit her lip lightly and tasted a drop of her sweet blood.

Ciro finally released Rayne and backed away. She was so beautiful with terror in her damp eyes and one small drop of blood on her bottom lip. He wanted another taste, but the blood of others would soon enough satisfy that need. He wanted souls to sate the hunger, but for now tainted souls would do, and there were plenty of tainted souls awaiting him.

"Good-bye, beloved," he said. "When I return, we'll be married."

Rayne shook her head in denial, but said nothing.

"We will be married," Ciro said. "There will be a priest of my choosing in attendance, and we will have a few witnesses as our guests. And if you do not happily agree in front of them all to be my wife, I will kill them one at a time until you do." He continued to smile. "I'll start with your father, if he lives that long." Ciro cast a glance at a cowering Fynnian, who had wisely remained silent throughout the exchange. "And then I'll continue with the kitchen help, and perhaps that one mousy maid you like so much."

Rayne managed to force out one hoarse word. "Why?"

Ah, she was so naive. "Because I love you, of course."

SIAN PACED IN FRONT OF THE EMPEROR. HE HAD BUN-gled everything, hadn't he? The news about Ciro, the truth of the prophesy, giving in to his desire for Ariana . . . he had bungled it all.

Arik waved a hand at the pacing enchanter. "Sit."

"No, thank you. I really must be going."

Ariana's army was gathering at the gates at this very moment, preparing to march. Ariana's army. If there were any words more ridiculous, he had never heard them.

"Stay a few days," Arik said. "I've missed you. I've missed your entire family. Did I ever tell you about the time your father and I ventured into the village where your mother lived? It was long before you were born, of course. Your mother was just a girl, and was already a celebrated witch in her village."

"I'm very sorry, but I can't stay," Sian said. "I must go." *Now.*

Arik looked disappointed. "I'm sorry to hear that. It seems as though you've been here no time at all, and you were so busy, we had little time for visiting." He nodded slightly. "I wish you well on your journey."

Now was the time to nod in return, to wish the emperor well, and to depart. If only it were so simple.

"There's something I must tell you first," Sian said. "I do not wish to tell you, I would do anything not to tell you, but recent events have taught me that secrecy between friends is not beneficial, even if it seems as though it might be."

"You have bad news."

"Yes," Sian said simply.

"Is it . . . Ciro?"

At that moment, Sian realized that Arik already knew his son was not coming home. The emperor did not know why or how, and he did still hope, but he possessed a father's intuition that told him all was not well.

"Yes, I'm afraid it is."

Sian knew no way but the blunt truth, and so he told it, from the meeting in Level Thirteen to the second appearance of Diella in his chambers. The light in Arik's eyes dimmed significantly as Sian told what he knew, as the last of his hope was snatched away.

Finally, he knelt before the old man's chair and took two trembling hands in his own. "I'm sorry," he said softly. "If I could change this for you, I would."

"I know," Arik whispered.

"If Ciro comes here, do not let him into the palace. He is no longer Ciro, but a monster without a soul. He might look like Ciro, but what lurks beneath the skin is not your son."

"Perhaps something of Ciro remains, and I can—"

"*Nothing* of your son remains," Sian said, boldly interrupting the emperor in a way few dared to do. "Do not allow him to fool you into believing that he can be saved. He can't."

The emperor sighed, downhearted. "This changes everything," he whispered.

"I know. I'm so sorry to be the one to bring you this news."

"I will always grieve for my son, and I would like to remain here and convince myself that you are wrong and he can be saved. My responsibilities demand more of me. I cannot die without an heir," Arik said in a low voice. "The resulting struggle for power would tear this country apart."

"Then you must get well," Sian said. "You must marry again, and have more sons." He did not think it was possible that Arik would recover to that extent, but if the battle against darkness was won, and the darkness that had infected the emperor was gone, then it was possible.

If Ciro and the demon who had taken him were destroyed, then Arik might live to produce another heir. He was still young. Many previous emperors had produced children well into their seventies, and when he recovered, Arik could do the same.

But if that opportunity did not arise, the country would be, as the emperor said, torn apart. "In order to allay the confusion that would arise if something were to happen to you . . ."

"If I were to die," Arik said bluntly.

"If you were to die, then," Sian repeated calmly. "You must name another heir or a trusted comrade to follow you. A relative or a minister, perhaps."

Arik's pain showed all too clearly in his eyes and in the tremble of his once-strong hands, but his voice remained relatively calm. "Even if I name a minister to follow me, there will still be war. Another will claim the throne, and sides will be chosen, and in the midst of this unholy war of yours, a struggle entirely human will also take place. There must be blood for the successor to be accepted. In the past, bastard sons have been named emperor."

"I am aware." In fact, Arik had been a bastard child who took the throne from a legitimate son who had been a vengeful and unworthy leader.

"Do you believe my ministers and priests, the people of this country, would think less of me, or of him, if I revealed at this late date that I have a son by a woman I never married? A son I never claimed, as I did not want him to suffer the heartbreak I suffered as a child who was always looked down upon as less than one who was legitimate?"

Sian experienced a shiver of surprise. Arik, who had always been so upright and truthful, had a hidden illegitimate son? "Is he worthy?"

"Oh, yes."

"Is he old enough to assume the throne?"

"Yes," Arik whispered. Tears filled his eyes. "I did not want him ever to know," he said. "It might seem cruel, but in my own way I only wanted to protect him. He had a good life, I made sure of that. He had everything he ever needed, including a loving family and a name not my own. My son had a good life," Arik insisted again. "And now, in the name of Columbyana, I must strip from him everything he holds dear. Will I be forgiven, Sian? Do you think me a terrible person, a terrible father, for keeping this secret so long?"

Sian was dismayed by the way the emperor held his hand so desperately. His health could not take this kind of strain.

"My lord, you do not need my approval or forgiveness. When the time comes, you might need to ask those things from your son, but—"

With a surprisingly strong hand, Arik gripped Sian's chin. "But I am doing just that. Do you?" he asked. "Can you forgive me?"

II

IN HER LIFETIME, ARIANA HAD TRAVELED MUCH MORE often than most females of her age. More than most females of any age, thanks to her family's need for frequent reunions and their fondness for adventure. Her experience was not limited to the long journey from her home to the capital city of Arthes. Protective as her father was, he had never hesitated to take his daughters as well as his sons on hunting trips or simply away from home for a few days of exploration. She had never cared for hunting, which was a shame since it would have prepared her in some ways for what was to come, but she had loved the journeys to the seashore or to unexplored places high on a mountain.

Those journeys had prepared her for this one in many ways. She did not mind long hours on a horse's back, eating sparsely, or sleeping on the ground.

Merin's most trusted sentinels, and Merin himself,

surrounded her as they traveled along the road which would take them to that village at the foot of the Mountains of the North. The horses were sturdy, and so were the men. The soldiers Merin had chosen were protective of her in some ways simply because she was a woman, but more staunchly because she was Duran's sister. Before this journey was over, she would have to cure them of that. If they were too intent on protecting her, they would not protect themselves well enough.

All were silent as they led their horses down the road at an easy pace. Some soldiers spoke to one another in lowered voices, but most rode silently, their thoughts churning with the possibilities of what might lie ahead. Most of them were dedicated, but she sensed a few were already questioning their decision to rush toward an unknown enemy.

This was their first day, and they had a long way to travel. They had no choice but to treat the horses, and themselves, well. As this battle they were heading toward was promised to be momentous, she imagined the silent soldiers were thinking of what was ahead of them . . . or what they'd left behind.

Ariana thought of what she'd left behind, while absently fingering the thrice-wrapped cord at her throat. If only she hadn't followed her impulse to peek at the prophesy Sian had kept secret from her. If only she had left the palace with the hope that one day she would return, and what had begun between her and Sian would be allowed to continue, and even perhaps to grow into something more.

No wonder he had been so insistent that she not conceive a child. She'd thought him to be cautious. She'd believed him to be determined not to tie himself to her in any way other than the sexual. Now she knew the truth.

He did not want to send his unborn child to a certain death.

Do not mourn that one. He is not worthy.

True.

There are other men who would be glad to take his place. Many of them surround you now.

I do not want another man.

The one called Merin, he is quite handsome, and on a cold, dark night he would serve you well, if you asked it of him. Cut that unattractive rope from your throat and cut the last of your ties with that unworthy enchanter. Merin would do quite nicely.

Ariana started slightly. Where had that thought come from? She liked Merin, and she trusted him. But she had never been attracted to him in that way. He was her brother's friend, and in many ways felt to her like yet another brother.

He is not your brother.

I don't love him.

Love is not necessary.

Again, Ariana twitched. For her, love was necessary. Perhaps not the grand love her mother had spoken of, but at the very least a special affection. She was not an animal content to sate her urges with any available man. What she'd had with Sian was special and she was grateful that she'd known those days and nights. That did not mean she was willing to try to re-create them with just any man.

Time is slipping away . . .

I need love.

You'll be sorry . . .

No, I won't. Ariana pushed the odd thoughts down, and after a momentary struggle, they faded. If she had not been so horribly disappointed by Sian's lies, her mind would not wander so.

Sunset was upon them when Merin pulled his horse alongside hers. "There is a comfortable campsite just ahead, with flat ground that is not overly rocky, and a small lake of drinkable water. We could travel for a few more hours, as the moon will be full tonight, but I suggest we stop there for the night."

"I agree," Ariana said. "We have more than enough harsh traveling days ahead of us. If there is a suitable place for us to camp, then we should make use of it."

Merin nodded, and glanced back at the line of sentinels who filled the narrow road. Ariana took a moment to study his profile.

He is handsome, is he not? What a lover he would be.

The idea came from nowhere, and Ariana suddenly wondered if the thoughts she'd been fighting were her own.

It couldn't be Diella. Both times that Diella had taken over, Ariana herself had known nothing of what was happening to her.

But what if that had changed? What if she and the mad empress now shared mind and body?

IN ORDER TO LEAVE THE PALACE UNESCORTED, SIAN had been forced to braid his long hair, as he often did for travel, and don clothing that was unlike his own. He had even tucked the telling black braid beneath the back of the vest he wore, in case anyone looked at him too closely. Without an explanation as to why, the palace sentinels had been told that Sian was not to leave the palace unaccompanied, so the disguise had been necessary.

Arik apparently thought Sian would be tempted to run

from this new and surprising development. More specifically, the father was anxious to make sure his newly claimed bastard son didn't run away.

Sian had been thinking about the revelation all day, which was only natural, he supposed. He barely remembered his father . . . rather, the man he had always believed to be his father . . . who had passed away before Sian reached the age of eight. But he did remember moments when the man looked at his son as if he found the child to be strikingly odd. Sian had always thought that odd expression existed thanks to the magic the ordinary man did not share with his son. Now he wondered if the man he'd called father had hated him. He wondered if those looks that had appeared to a child to be wonder had indeed been hate. What man wants to raise another man's son as his own? Were he and his mother simply sacrifices made to ensure the success of the revolution, and nothing more?

No matter how the man who had raised him might've felt, Sian did not want him to be disrespected now, so long after his death. He didn't want his mother whispered about in unsavory tones either. They were good people, and he did not want their memories tarnished by gossip and supposition.

Sian was, in many ways, very much like his mother. He had inherited her magic, her eyes, the shape of her strong chin. He even had her nose, though his was much larger than hers had been. The long and prominent shape was much the same. As far as he could tell, there was nothing in him of his father . . . of either of his fathers.

He quickly moved away from the palace. For a while he had tried to convince himself that Arik had panicked and quickly concocted a tale to produce the heir he so desperately needed. But the detailed story that had followed—the story of one night with a woman, of a revolution he could not abandon for his own contentment, of discovering one day that the woman he had loved so briefly had birthed him a son. It was a story of a loyal friend who had willingly offered to give the woman a husband and the child a father, when his wounds made him no longer suitable for fighting the revolution they both desperately believed in, at a time when a family would've hindered Arik.

Gareth Chamblyn had walked with a severe limp. It was that injury to his hip that had made it impossible for him to fight as a soldier. Apparently he had sacrificed in the only other way presented to him. To the outside world, the child and the woman were his. No one would know that the bastard son who claimed the throne had produced his own bastard son. A son who could be used against Arik if his enemies found their way to the small village. A woman he loved dearly, who could also be used if his enemies knew of her existence.

So Arik had ridden away from them and left them in the care of his friend. A woman and child were luxuries he could not afford at that time.

All others worries aside, Sian did not want to be emperor, and so he had spent the day riding and wracking his brain for a solution. Could Ciro be saved? No. That was impossible. Was there another possible heir, someone more suitable for emperor, someone who would be willing to take Arik's place when the time came? Perhaps the emperor really could improve his health and make another child before it was too late.

With this argument, Sian had been able to convince the emperor not to share the news. Not just yet. Arik had written the story of Sian's birth in a shaky but legible hand, and he added to it his wish that his illegitimate son take the throne when he was dead. He'd hidden these papers in a place where they would be discovered should he die, but would remain safe should he cling to life for a while longer.

It wasn't that Sian thought himself completely unsuitable to be leader of Columbyana. He could make the decisions that needed to be made. He was well acquainted with reason and logic, and did not allow his decisions to be colored by emotion. No, he would have no trouble making decisions.

But there was more to being emperor than leading. As night crept upon him and he led his horse down the road, Sian actually grimaced. Emperors were expected to host palace guests, to throw parties and dinners for decorated ministers and ambassadors and even visiting royalty. In the name of being *cordial*, they were expected to speak endlessly of things that meant nothing. There was talk that a shipman who'd sailed from a port off the southernmost point of the Southern Province had reached a country that was farther from Columbyana than any man had ever been, and he'd returned to tell the tale. If there were new countries recently reached and still to be reached, there would be an endless stream of people in and out of the palace. Ambassadors. Kings or queens or emperors. There would be new political relations to forge, smiles to cast, allies to woo.

Sian was not very good at wooing. Not at all.

Worst of all, if he were emperor, he would be obligated to marry and produce at least one heir. He'd spent most of his adult life avoiding such social obligations, and here they were, thrown into his lap without a hint of warning.

Had his grandfather seen this coming? Had the old man known? If Sian had been born before the soldier had returned to marry his daughter, the wizard must've known something. Unless, of course, he had been convinced that this wounded rebel was the man who'd impregnated his daughter.

Even seers and prophets could be fooled at times. They didn't see everything. Perhaps his grandfather had not known that when he sent Sian to the emperor with the prophesy, he was also sending his grandson to confront his father. His real father.

Sian did not feel a great obligation to return to Arthes and take up his place as heir. It was a position he did not want, and if war resulted from the lack of a clear heir, then that was not his concern. Unless this battle with evil was won, a civil war would not matter in the least.

No, his obligation was not to Arik. Not now. His obligation rode well ahead of him, at the front of a column of solemn sentinels. Sian rotated his head slightly. This damn green vest was made of the cheapest, roughest fabric that had ever touched his body, and the trousers were not much better. He wore a hat with a wide brim which shadowed his face, and his braid remained tucked down the back of his vest. For now he had no choice but to wear the uniform, as the other sentinels did. More suitable clothing was packed in his saddlebag, in case the opportunity arose to shed this costume and confront Ariana with his presence.

She and Merin led forty-one soldiers, not forty, and if Arik's tale of Sian's birth was true, they were headed toward a battle with his own half-brother.

*   *   *

MERIN OFFERED TO CONSTRUCT A TENT FOR ARIANA'S use, but she declined. The night was warm enough so that sleeping under the stars would not be detrimental to her health. Besides, she would not demand comforts others in her party would not enjoy. That was not the way to build loyalty, and she would need the loyalty of each of these men before the battle was over.

Ariana informed Merin that she'd be happy to sleep on the ground like everyone else, and he reluctantly agreed that was best. Finding a private place to empty her bladder was not quite as easy, since she didn't want to be one of the men in every way, but she managed. The area just beyond their camp was thickly wooded.

Some soldiers slept, while others were taking the first watch. Merin paced by the fire, waiting for Ariana as she emerged from the woods. She knew he was waiting for her by the tension in his body and by the way he watched her so intently as she strode toward him.

A fine figure of a man . . .

"Go away," Ariana whispered, and the thoughts that were not her own faded. She didn't like to admit as much, but apparently Diella was not entirely gone. Without Sian to watch over her, how would she maintain control? What if Diella regained enough strength to take over, so that all that was left of Ariana was the faint rumbling of thoughts which were easily ignored?

"A word, my lady," Merin said as she came into the light of the fire.

Ariana smiled. "My lady? I have always been Ariana to you, Merin. There is no need to be formal."

He sighed deeply before answering. "Ariana is my friend's sister. My Lady Varden is my leader. Our leader."

Ariana sat on the ground, near enough to enjoy the fire

without taking on too much warmth, far enough away to feel the faint chill of the night on her back. She invited Merin to sit beside her, and after a momentary hesitation he did so.

"I'm still Duran's sister," she said softly.

Seated on the ground beside her, Merin twitched with apparent unease. He stared into the fire for a moment, and then turned to her. "The situation is unprecedented. The men are here because they know they're needed, and they will fight for you, Ariana. But tonight there are rumblings of confusion, I'm afraid. Confusion and fear. Many of them say they agreed too quickly, getting caught up in the call to duty without knowing what might lie ahead. Some, a few, have even spoken of turning back. They all heard rumors before leaving Arthes, rumors about what sort of war this might be. We have no general to lead us, no imperial edict to obey. We have been told that this battle is necessary and that it is a battle against evil itself, but . . . I must admit, I'm confused as well. What awaits us at the end of this journey?"

She could not argue with him. "I wish I knew more clearly what awaits us. I'm as confused and afraid as any man here. The prophesy speaks of monsters, but gives no details. If I could give the men more, I would." Looking into the flame of the hearty fire, she sighed. "I wish I knew what waits for us, but I don't. If anyone wants to turn back, they should do so now."

"There are just a few men who're grumbling." Merin said defensively.

"I'll speak to them in the morning, before we ride out. I'll give any man who feels it's best the opportunity to leave. At least then we'll know who's with us and who is not."

Merin nodded, and shifted his position in readying to stand. Ariana stopped him with a hand on his wrist. "One moment, please. I have a favor to ask of you."

"Of course." He resumed his seated position, and yet he still seemed to be at attention. Every muscle in his body was tense.

She could not explain Diella, not to Merin or anyone else here. Only Sian would understand. Still, she could not allow the empress to rise to the surface and take command. "If at any point I begin to behave oddly, I want you to restrain me. Use whatever means necessary. Chains, if you have them. A sturdily tied rope if you do not."

Merin had been looking into the fire, not at her, but his head snapped around and he glared. "I cannot!"

"*If* I begin to behave oddly," she said again in clarification. "It is a necessary precaution, believe me."

Merin leaned back on his hands. "Oddly how?"

How could she tell him that if she began to ask the soldiers . . . him, more specifically . . . to lie with her, it would be most certainly odd? "You will know," she said. "I promise, you will know." From everything Sian had told her of his encounters with Diella, she and the empress behaved nothing alike. Merin would realize something was wrong.

At least, she certainly hoped so.

Ariana waited for a stray thought about what she was missing in denying the idea of quickly taking another lover. She expected a few observations about how Merin or this soldier or that one would do in Sian's stead. The thoughts did not come.

Maybe Diella did continue to lurk inside her somehow, but Ariana was in control. She made the decisions, and if she had to fight constantly to retain control, she would do so.

Pity. Your life is so dull.

Ariana began to laugh. Dull? She wished with all her heart for dull at this moment. She wished for ordinary, dreary, boring days. She had experienced many of those days in the past. She suspected she had none ahead of her. Not even one.

"Ariana?" Merin asked, concern in his deep voice. "Are you all right?" He studied her face as she laughed. "Is this . . . odd?"

"No, no." Ariana lifted a stilling hand to him as her laughter stopped. "It's just been a very long day." From awakening to discover the truth of the prophesy, to leading an army of her own away from the capital city and toward an unspeakable darkness. Yes, she believed this qualified as a *very* long day.

SIAN SLEPT A FEW HOURS, ONLY BECAUSE HE DID NOT know when the opportunity for sleep would come again. He took his turn at watch when ordered. Luckily these men Merin had gathered had come from different assignments and were not all acquainted with one another. No one was shocked to see a sentinel they did not know in their ranks. They simply assumed that he had been assigned elsewhere before taking on this duty. He gave his name as Sayre, which was true enough as it was his middle name, to the one sentinel who had bothered to ask.

The sentinels varied widely in age and experience. A few were mere boys, some were scarred veterans with weathered skin. Some were thin and lanky, others sported bellies that marked them as well fed. All were well armed.

It was bothersome that a stranger—like him—could so easily join them, but Sian was not overly concerned.

Ariana, if she used her empathy correctly, if she concentrated as he had taught her, would've been able to spot a dark intruder at the outset.

A less-than-cheerful sentinel tossed Sian a biscuit and some dried meat. The offering was unappetizing, but he took it anyway. With a wave of his hand, he could make the simple food appear to be a feast, for him and for the somber soldiers around him. They needed a bit of cheering up. But such an act of enchantment would give him away. He wasn't ready for that to happen. More truthfully, Ariana was not ready to see him. Not yet.

Soldiers rolled up their bedrolls and ate their meager breakfast, Sian among them. He had been so tempted to move closer to Ariana last night, to look upon her simply to assure himself that she was well.

That was a lie. He knew she was well. Her most trusted soldiers surrounded her, and the night had remained quiet and still. To move closer just to look at her, and in doing so taking the chance of giving away his presence, would be foolish.

So he had done so only twice.

He watched Ariana step into the forest with a bundle in her hands. She should enjoy her moments of privacy now, while she could. When they reached the mountains, there would be no convenient stands of trees for cover, not for long stretches at a time. When the battle was more certainly upon them, he would not allow her to secret herself even for modesty's sake.

He knew she was safe now, and still he waited anxiously for her to reappear. When she did, stepping almost haughtily through the same space in the trees where she had exited the camp, Sian cursed.

Fool woman. What was she thinking? She might as

well ride along this road alone with a target painted on her back. She might as well ride headlong into the fray, shouting, "Here I am!"

Ariana was no longer dressed exactly as the sentinels were. No more rough green uniform for their leader, no. She had surely made the outrageous outfit herself, but when? Early on, before he took to sleeping in her bed? During those hours while he'd been lost in his research? While he slept? He did not know, and in truth it did not matter.

She wore white trousers—*white!*—and pale brown boots. Her blouse was loose and feminine, and allowed freedom of movement. The blouse was also white. The vest she wore was made much like a sentinel's with pockets in the front and plain buttons for fastening. This vest, which was also *white*, was adorned with ornamental *sparkly* things, as if she were headed to a blasted party. Her hair was loose, blond curls falling over her shoulders and down her back, wild and untamed as if she had just risen from his bed. She wore no hat, though he would not be surprised if there was one waiting nearby. If so, it would probably sport a tremendous white feather or a silken rose.

Sian took a step forward, but he forced himself to stop. If he revealed himself now, Ariana would send him away. Probably not alone. Had any of these sentinels heard that the wizard Sian was not to leave the palace unescorted? Unlikely, but not impossible. It was a chance he could not take.

Ariana stepped into the stirrup of her horse—which thank the heavens was not snow white but was instead an ordinary gray—and looked over the men, her soldiers who watched her so closely. She had to know what a spectacle she was making of herself. She had to know that if she rode into battle dressed like this, she would not last long. Every enemy combatant would be guided to her simply by the uniform she wore.

She rode forward gently, until she and her horse were positioned in the middle of the camp. Men surrounded her. Sian pulled the brim of his hat down so she could not see his face when she glanced in his direction.

"Many of you are asking what it is we go to fight," she said in a voice that was clear and loud enough to be heard by everyone. "You're afraid, and I can't say that I blame you. I'm afraid, too."

Heaven above, she did not look at all afraid.

"I will not lie to you," she continued. "I have never lied to you. There are monsters waiting for us at the end of this road. For all I know they are lurking along every step of this trail we travel. I do not know what form they will take. I don't know if they will look like monsters or if they will look very much like you and me." Morning sunshine glimmered on her blond curls and her glittering vest, making her look as if she were more than human. She was a blazingly white angel, come down to earth to lead these men to their deaths.

Every man in the camp was captivated by her, in a way they had not been on the day before.

"I have been told that I'm going to die in this war." She did not shake in sharing this news. She did not shed a tear or tremble, but the way she mindlessly caressed the cord at her throat told him she was not unaffected. She reached for that connection when she needed comfort, he had discovered.

A few soldiers whispered "no." Some shouted. She ignored them all. "Perhaps that is true. Perhaps not. Only time will tell. I plan to fight very hard, and if it is my time to die I will take with me as many of the monsters as I can." There was a harshness in that promise that touched Sian to the bone.

"I do not know if you are meant to die as well," she said, her voice less soft. "I do know that every man here is destined for this battle, just as I am." Her horse nickered, danced on nervous hooves, and turned about. "Every man here is a hero, or soon will be! If darkness wants to take this land and the good people who live upon it, if they want your friends, your families, your loved ones, then they will have to come through *us* to take it!"

A shout went up from many of the soldiers. Sian felt a shiver pass down his spine.

"No, my brothers, I do not know what form these monsters will take, so I tell you this. In the days to come, you must learn to see not only with your eyes but with your hearts. You must learn to see the evil in those we face before they choose to show it to you. And you must pray for God to be with us," she added in a lowered voice that still carried quite well, as if her whisper were carried on the wind to every ear.

"I won't think less of any man who chooses to leave us now," Ariana said, her voice rising once again. "All we know of what lies ahead is frightening and uncertain. It is the stuff of nightmares." A few men mumbled at that statement, but no one made a move to escape.

"But I promise you this," Ariana said as her horse danced skittishly once again. "If you stay with me, if you ride into this battle at my side, I will fight for you as if you were my brother. From this moment on, you are my brothers, each and every one of you, as if we shared blood. Come with me and together we'll make history."

Merin appeared at her side, and he handed Ariana a hat. A fucking *white* hat. At least there was no feather. Or rose. She slapped the hat on her head, took control of the reins, and spurred her horse onto the road. She raced away, and the soldiers . . . each and every one of them . . . scrambled to follow. Not one man headed back toward Arthes. Not one.

Sian was among those who scrambled, and as he did so, he felt an unexpected pride. Had he ever criticized Ariana as being too weak for this destiny? Had he ever called her a mere girl who was unfit for the prophesy which named her?

She was a general as fine as any other, and the men who followed this general would die for her if need be. They loved her, each and every one of them. They would be legend before this war was over. Whether they lived or died, whether they won or lost, they *would* be legend.

White hat and all.

12

IT WAS DAYS BEFORE THEY REACHED THE FIRST VILLAGE, and by then the soldiers were more than ready for combat. Ciro rode his horse down the center of a narrow, dusty street, and watched. This could not rightly be called combat, he supposed. His soldiers were, well, his soldiers. The villagers made for poor opponents.

What Ciro observed was rather like watching an unfair sporting event. His legion consisted of armed hunters; the villagers were the helpless prey. His soldiers were wrestlers of bears; the villagers were large, helpless, drugged rabbits. There was no hunger to compare to that of a man without a soul. Ciro knew that hunger, but at least he had a way to assuage it for a spell. His legion did not. They possessed the hunger, but not the ability to take another soul. They tried to quench the maddening appetite with the screams of those they terrorized, with blood, with the fear they created and enjoyed so well.

Fynnian's soldiers were ruthless, but they did not possess the hunger of Ciro's Own. Did he even need Fynnian's men? Perhaps eventually he would need their numbers, but those he called his Own were special. They alone could terrorize all of Columbyana.

The screams of the villagers did not affect Ciro at all, though he noticed that the man who rode at his side, his spineless wizard Fynnian, occasionally flinched. He did not mind watching one of his soldiers cut off the head of a screaming villager, but when one of Ciro's Own decided to take a taste of a kill, Fynnian turned his head away.

Fynnian was a fool. He thought Ciro didn't know what he'd done, and why, but through the Isen Demon, Ciro knew everything. He knew that Fynnian had chosen him because he thought him weak, and also because an infected prince would offer access to the highest position of power in Columbyana. He knew that Fynnian had used his beautiful daughter to bind the future emperor to him. Perhaps his trickery had been effective in the early days. Perhaps it had even been necessary. Now that Ciro had his army, he no longer needed a wizard who planned for the rise of darkness and then did not have the stomach for it.

Ciro's eyes were drawn to a public inn. They were drawn there by a light he recognized very well, a light which shone so brightly it overpowered the lamplight and the flames from many torches. His stomach rumbled, and he smiled. There. It was there, awaiting him.

He stopped before the inn and dismounted easily, leaving Fynnian to see to both horses. The wizard did so quickly, and then he followed Ciro into a large public room, where several of those who had been infected by the Isen Demon had congregated.

Fynnian cringed as he realized what had happened.

Ciro's personally called soldiers had dragged many of the villagers here for the sole purpose of torture and eventual death. They enjoyed their work. They fed on the fear they created. It was a poor substitute for their lost souls, but it satisfied them for a while.

One older woman remained untouched. She trembled and cried and prayed—silently and aloud—and her eyes were closed tightly against the heinous scene before her. The soldiers had instinctively known that this one was meant for their leader. The demon himself had spoken to them, instructing that the old woman not be touched. Not only had they not harmed her with their blades or their teeth, but her prim white nightdress was not stained with even a drop of blood. She remained completely pure.

The light of her soul shone as brightly as Rayne's. This woman before him was no beauty, and she had lived many years, which showed on her face in wrinkles and sagging skin. Her scraggly hair was gray. Her bosoms drooped.

But Ciro didn't care about her appearance. He cared only about the light. Was he finally strong enough to take a pure soul? There was only one way to find out.

The woman he sought had been bound to a post at the foot of the stairway that led to the second floor. Her arms were trapped behind her back, and her legs were lashed to the rough wood of the pillar. Her head was down, her eyes squeezed shut.

Ciro walked toward her slowly. She did not know he was coming. She did not know that anything had changed until the noises that had filled the room began to fade. His soldiers watched. Their victims died or else enjoyed a moment's rest while the man or woman who tortured them turned their attention elsewhere. There was a touch of hope revealed as the old woman's head snapped up and her eyes opened wide, but when she saw Ciro coming toward her, she knew there was no hope. Not for her or anyone else in this village.

He grinned at the woman with the pure soul, but she was not soothed by his expression. Instead, she shuddered and screamed.

Ciro grabbed a handful of wiry gray hair, which was not yet entirely silver but working its way in that direction. Looking at her closely, he realized that this woman had probably once been beautiful, but her best years had passed long ago. All that remained of consequence was her soul, which was pure and white and strong. Very, very strong.

Could he take it?

He held the woman in place as he pulled her head back and touched his teeth to her neck. Her pulse was quick and strong, and the blood beneath would be as sweet as that of a child when he tasted it. But what he wanted most, what he craved, was her soul. It was *his*.

He bit into her, and blood filled his mouth. The soul he desired was so close he could almost taste it. So close he could almost *take* it. But she fought him. The soul did not flow into him as he wished. It only took a moment for Ciro to realize that he was not yet strong enough to take what he desired.

With renewed vigor, he tried again. He bit deeper, and reached for the woman's soul. It was right there, teasing him, flitting away from him, refusing to flow out of the old woman and into his empty body.

Ciro lifted his head and looked into the old woman's dying eyes. "Give me your soul, woman," he whispered. He wasn't yet strong enough to steal a white soul, but with permission, surely he could take it from her. He moved his mouth closer to her ear. "Offer it to me now."

She shook her head.

"I will make your death a quick one, if you offer me what I want." He spoke the words softly, into her ear. "Say it aloud. Say, 'I give you my soul, Prince Ciro.'"

Again she shook her head, and she whispered, "No."

Ciro sighed, and licked a few drops of blood from the tear in her throat. She didn't have much time left to live, which meant she didn't have much time left in which to offer him what he craved. She was not going to give him what she wanted, not to save herself.

He smiled at her, quite genuinely. "Give me your soul, and I will spare those in this village who are not already dead."

Her dying eyes flickered for a moment, and Ciro thought perhaps he had won. And then the old woman glanced beyond him to the bodies of the dead and dying which surrounded her. He saw the moment when she realized that it was too late to save anyone.

Her eyes met his, and surprisingly, she returned his smile. "Devil, man, beast . . . whatever you are, whatever you have become . . . you can take my life, but you cannot have my soul." She closed her eyes, and in spite of the horrors that surrounded her, in spite of the fact that she was dying, her expression transformed into one that was oddly peaceful. She tilted her head back and offered him what was left of her throat.

Angry, Ciro took it. He drank every drop of her sweet blood. He gnawed at her throat as he had in the early days, tasting flesh long after she was dead. Tasting flesh long after he felt the soul he craved slip away from her, and from him. He ate until his mouth and his stomach were filled, and yet he was still hungry.

He turned away from the dead woman to find his

soldiers, the ones who were tied to him and the demon, watching. Many of them were covered in the blood of their victims. Others wore no more than a splatter of blood here and there. He would have taken one of their souls to quench his thirst, but they had none left. The victims of their violence were either dead or nearly so, and he had no desire to touch their wounded bodies and take a battered soul.

He wanted so much more.

Ciro walked toward Fynnian.

"Did you?" the wizard asked breathlessly. He was curious and excited and afraid. Had the monster he'd created reached new heights? Was he powered by the ingestion of a pure soul? The others in this room knew of the failure, as they were connected, but Fynnian did not. He did not feel what Ciro, the Isen Demon, and those joined to them felt as one. "Did you take it?"

Without changing his footstep or his facial expression, Ciro grabbed Fynnian's shirtfront and pulled the old man to him. Without ceremony, without a word, he buried his teeth in the wizard's throat. Fynnian fought, but it was no use. He tried to plead, to beg for mercy, but Ciro barely heard the words. He took the tainted soul he needed into his own body, took enough blood to ensure that Fynnian would not survive the feeding, and when that was done, he dropped the wizard's almost-dead body onto the floor of the inn.

Ciro walked out of the building feeling somewhat better. Not as well as he would have if he'd been able to take the old woman's soul, but still . . . a bit better. He was stronger. He grew stronger with each passing day. The day would soon come when nothing could stop him.

Two of his most loyal soldiers followed him out of the inn. "Next time, leave a few children alive, at least for a while," Ciro said. If he'd had young ones to barter with, the old woman would've gladly offered her soul in exchange for their lives. It was not the same as taking that which was not offered, but it was a start. With the power of a pure soul added to those he had gathered over the past few months, he would be significantly stronger. He was certain of it. "We've taken everything we can from this village," he said as he mounted his horse. Beyond the partially opened door, he saw one of Fynnian's fingers twitch against the blood-spattered wooden floor. "Burn this building," Ciro said as he led his horse away. He surveyed what was left of the village, the site of his legion's first battle and the site of his latest defeat. He had so wanted to be able to take that soul for his own, but the night was not finished, and he had tasks yet to accomplish.

"Burn it all."

THE SENTINELS NO LONGER SEEMED DOWNHEARTED. Wisely, they were still afraid of what awaited them, but none had turned away from Ariana and her destiny.

They'd been traveling four days, and the closer they moved to the mountains that were their first destination, the more anxious Ariana became. Was it possible that they could reach Keelia and her people before coming face to face with the enemy? Was it possible that her army could be complete before she confronted what was left of Ciro?

It was hard to picture the spoiled prince as a monster, but thanks to Diella, she knew that to be true. Would she even recognize him when the time came? Would she live long enough to see what had become of the boy who'd been the Isen Demon's first victim?

First victim in this war, at least.

He's too strong for you.

Perhaps. Perhaps not.

You are destined to die, witch. Doesn't that certainty make you want to run from this battle? Doesn't it make you want to run into the arms of your lover?

Ariana glanced over her shoulder. Sian remained, as always, near the back of the column. Did he really think that she would not know he was near? He had underestimated her powers if he thought he could hide from her in such a way. Of course, he had underestimated her powers from the beginning.

I can't run from this.

Step aside and allow Ciro and his men to reign, and you might live a long life with your lover, hiding in the mountains perhaps, with a cave as your home. It would not be the fine life you have accustomed yourself to, but it would be life.

I thought Ciro scared you.

He did.

He does.

But so does the thought of disappearing into nothingness scare me.

Ariana rode gently down the road on the back of the gray horse that had become her friend and constant companion. Today she wore a green uniform, like those who surrounded her, with a wide-brimmed hat much like Sian's to keep the sun from her face. The white uniform she had made was dramatic, but it was not practical for every day. She would have need of it again, but not today. Perhaps not tomorrow, if she were lucky.

She understood Diella better than the dark soul had imagined was possible when she'd chosen to hitch a ride out of Level Thirteen. If what was left of the dead empress had been able to escape from Level Thirteen before

Ariana's arrival, she would have. It was the empathy that all but invited the dark spirit in. Diella could not jump from Ariana's body to another at will. She could not move unless she found another empath whose soul was dangerously open. And if she left now, without the walls of Level Thirteen to contain her, what would she become?

Nothing. Nothing at all.

When we go into battle, you will fight with me, won't you?

I have no choice, witch. You know very well that if you die before I find another resting place, I will be lost. I'm not ready to be lost.

Neither am I.

Sian would be shocked if he knew that not only was Diella still with her, but they carried on frequent conversations and had even come to an uneasy truce.

He would be horrified to realize that Ariana had decided she needed something of the murderous empress within her in order to do all that had to be done.

RAIN. WHY WAS HE NOT SURPRISED? SIAN HAD BECOME accustomed to bad food, uncomfortable clothing, long hours in the saddle, and less than intelligent conversation among the sentinels—who seemed able to speak for extended periods of time about two subjects: women and liquor, neither of which was available to them on this march.

Now there was a gentle but steady rain. His hat kept the droplets from pelting his face, but water ran off the brim in streams that landed on his shoulders and down the front of his sentinel's vest. Like the others, he made sure his sword was stored where it would be kept dry.

There was not a word of complaint about the weather as they continued on. Nightfall was near, but it was not yet time to rest. Perhaps the others were accustomed to traveling in such weather—and worse. War did not stop for a change in the weather.

Of course, few of these men had known true war. A handful of the veterans had fought in the revolution twenty-five years ago. In more recent years there had been skirmishes here and there, small battles to fight, but since the War of the Beckyts had ended, there had been no true battle, so the younger soldiers were all but untested.

Ariana was leading an inexperienced army.

Even though the woman who led this small army no longer wore white, Sian spotted her easily. Not only were her stature and shape unique in this delegation, but her blond hair was as unruly as ever. There were many long-haired sentinels, and a few of them had fair hair. But none caught his eye as Ariana's did.

Was it possible that she was ready to forgive him? Would she ever be?

They stopped for the night, and the rain continued. As it was no longer clear and warm, a number of tents were quickly constructed. Those who were assigned the first watch would not be able to enjoy the shelter, not for a while, but those who would watch over the camp at a later hour quickly made use of the rough tents.

Sian was one of those who had been assigned to take the first watch. That suited him, rain or no rain, as it gave him the opportunity to see that Ariana was safely settled for the night.

Merin and two others very quickly threw up Ariana's tent, which was larger and sturdier than the others, as befitted a leader such as she. Sian watched, but continued to

keep his distance. That was becoming increasingly difficult in a party of a mere forty-three. Ariana, Merin, her
forty soldiers, and Sian.

He watched as Ariana disappeared into the tent, and
breathed a sigh of relief. Two guards remained close to
that tent, their only duty to make sure that she remained
safe. The day would come when that task was beyond
their capabilities, but tonight . . . tonight it was not.

Ariana opened the tent flap and said something to one
of the guards, who nodded and immediately ran to
Merin's tent. He spoke to Ariana's first in command, and
Merin quickly exited. There was no urgency in his step,
so nothing was wrong, but still . . . why had Ariana called
to him? Sian's heart beat too hard. Was it Diella? Perhaps
Ariana herself called to the puppy-like man with curling
hair. Sian snorted softly as he took a few steps in the direction of Ariana's tent. Could he take the chance that
Diella had plans to seduce Merin tonight? It was the first
opportunity the party had had to make use of the tents,
which meant it was the first night which offered any opportunity for privacy.

He waited a moment, hoping that perhaps he was
wrong and they were speaking general to sentinel. Sister
to brother.

Not likely.

After a few torturous minutes, Sian began to step
briskly in that direction. If he made a fuss of some sort,
Merin would have to exit Ariana's tent. And then what?
He was not her keeper. He had no right to tell her what she
could and could not do. In fact, he was at *her* command.

So why was he so incensed at the very idea of Ariana—
or Diella—making use of Merin's body?

Before he moved too close, the tent flap moved and

Merin exited. Sian breathed a sigh of relief. His imagination had gotten out of hand; that was all. He felt himself responsible for Ariana; that was why he'd reacted so. He turned about to reclaim his post, so it was several moments before he realized that Merin was walking not to his tent, but directly toward Sian.

"Sayre, is it?" Merin called when he had almost caught up with Sian. The rain seemed to fall harder.

They had met in the palace, but it was dark in this corner of the camp, and with the hat shadowing his face, there was no way Merin would recognize the enchanter he had been introduced to once. When he was sure he stood in the blackest of shadows, Sian turned to face Merin.

"Yes, sir. Sayre it is."

Merin cocked his head to one side as if attempting to see into the shadows. "Our sister wishes to speak with you."

"Our sister," Sian repeated.

"Ariana," Merin snapped impatiently.

"I am the lowliest of soldiers," Sian argued. "Surely another—"

"She asked for you," Merin interrupted.

"She does not know me," Sian responded in a cutting voice.

Even in the dark, Sian could see Merin's smile. "Our sister sent me to fetch the purple-eyed, hawk-nosed, eagle-eyed wizard who lurks about and rides at the end of the column each and every day."

Sian sighed, not bothering to argue that he was not the one Ariana had asked for. "What gave me away?"

"She has known since the second day that you were with us." Merin's jaw tightened. "I wanted to send you back to Arthes immediately, but Ariana insisted that if you were here, then you were meant to be with us, just like all the rest."

"And yet she waited until now to ask for me," Sian said tightly.

"Yes."

"What does she want?"

"I have no idea."

That was untrue. Merin obviously knew that he and Ariana had been romantically involved. No, sexually involved. Sian did not care for romance, and never would. With that knowledge, it was apparent that Merin thought Ariana to be lonely tonight.

And there was that tent and the resulting privacy to be considered.

Sian seriously doubted that was the case. Ariana had been very angry with him when she'd discovered the truth of the prophesy. Whatever reason compelled her to ask for him, it had nothing to do with their previous relationship.

He followed Merin to Ariana's tent. The rain was beginning to let up, but the ground was already muddy and slippery, and the night's chill was touched with a dampness that cut to the bone.

One of the guards held the tent flap open, and Merin indicated that Sian should go first. If anyone but Ariana was in there, he would have to consider that it might be a trap. He crouched down and entered. There was no light to speak of in the tent that sheltered Ariana, but he could see her well enough. From a distance, he had not been able to see how very tired she was.

Merin made as if to return to his own tent, but Ariana called him and asked him to join her for a moment. The tent was barely large enough for three, but it was minimally sufficient.

Without even the most basic of greeting for him, Ariana began to speak. "It is ridiculous for a talented enchanter to hide himself among us when we could be making use of his magic."

"In what way?" Merin asked sharply.

Ariana sighed. "Light. Give us light, enchanter."

Sian was glad of the opportunity to illuminate the tent so he could see Ariana more clearly. Yes, she was under great strain, and that strain showed too clearly in her tired eyes. Merin was surprised by the light, but not shocked. He knew something of magical ways apparently.

Ariana locked her eyes to Sian's. "We also need full access to anything you have discovered pertaining to the prophesy. Have you learned anything about the crystal dagger? Have you found a way to defeat the Isen Demon?"

"I must answer no to both those questions."

"Some of what I saw scribbled onto the prophesy seemed to be nonsense. Can you interpret it for me?"

"Some," Sian admitted. "But much of what my grandfather penned on his death bed is a mystery to me, as well as to you."

"I see." Ariana breathed deeply. "I had hoped for better answers, but all I ask of you is the truth. From this night forward, I will expect only the truth from you."

"And you will have it."

Merin, who listened without comment, had no way of knowing how meaningful the conversation had become.

Ariana continued. "From this night forward, you will be my wizard, my counsel. You will ride beside me, and stop pretending to be something you are not." She sounded only slightly angry. "Given what lies ahead, we cannot afford to ignore any advantage. You are an advantage to us, Sian."

He nodded, but remained silent. Ariana continued to stare at him. "Merin, you may go."

Merin did so, not without some obvious trepidation.

Ariana was silent for a long while after Merin departed. She studied Sian closely. She cut him with the accusations in her eyes. No, she had not forgiven him. Not at all.

"Diella isn't gone," she said softly when she finally spoke.

It was one of his worst fears, that the empress would somehow rise up. Still, he knew it was Ariana who spoke at this moment. "I will find a way to be rid of her, once and for all. I promise you."

"I do not want promises from you," Ariana said sharply. No, she had most certainly not forgiven him. "And I do not want Diella gone. I want her under control." A touch of desperation touched Ariana's voice. "That is what I need from you, enchanter, control."

"I don't know that I can give it to you."

"Try."

He owed Ariana more than he could ever repay. He wasn't certain that Diella could be controlled, but the least he could do was, as Ariana requested, *try*.

"If you move yourself into the proper state where all your energy is under your command, you should be able to isolate Diella and rid yourself of her once and for all. I should've insisted that you do that before you left the palace, as a precaution, but I was certain she was already gone." He'd been so wrapped up in Ariana's body, he had neglected his calling. It was his fault that Diella remained.

Ariana sat straight and tall, close to him and yet very far away. "You were right when you said that I do not have it in me to kill. I am a healer, and always have been, and to watch men I have led and come to care for fall, to kill with a sharp blade without stopping to consider the wounds I inflict, to take a living being's life and then turn to take another without so much as watching the first fall, is not in me, and yet it's what I must be prepared to do. I can't. Diella can. Diella and I together can—"

"Let me fight for you," Sian offered, unable to listen any longer. "Let me do what you cannot, and let's send that dark spirit out of you once and for all. If she takes control, she would gladly slit the throat of every man you call brother. She would happily kill these men who have come to trust you. To *love* you."

"That is why I need you to help me take control. We can discuss the ways in which I can rid myself of her when the time is right, but as long as I can use her to do what has to be done . . . shouldn't I use her?" There was a hint of the girl he had first met in that uncertain voice.

"How long have you realized she's with you?"

"Days," Ariana admitted.

Sian uttered a low curse. "And why do you wait until now to tell me?"

Ariana hesitated before answering. "This afternoon, right after the rain began to fall, I lost myself for a few moments. I was drowning, and Diella was swimming to the surface. It was very much like that day in your chamber, only briefer and more intense. It took everything in me to pull her down and swim to the surface myself. The episode only lasted a few moments, but it scared me."

"As it should," Sian said through clenched teeth.

"I need to keep Diella," Ariana insisted. "But I also need to control her. That means I need you, much as it pains me to admit. I need you to help me keep her under control, and if I can't, I need you to restrain me. Restrain her. And if you can't restrain her, then you must kill her."

Sian's reaction was physical as well as emotional. His fingers jerked, and the light he created flickered. Kill Ariana? He could not. Would not.

She saw his reaction. "If it comes to that, I'll already be gone. You know that, and I know that if you have to kill me, it will be painless and quick. Since I now realize that I will soon be going into the Land of the Dead . . . dying at your hand seems preferable to the other possibilities."

"You ask a lot of me."

"These days I am forced to ask a lot of everyone," she admitted sadly. "Why should you be any different?"

He did not answer. How could she expect that he would actually kill her? How could she ask him for this?

"Promise me," she whispered.

"And if I can't?"

"Then I will ask someone else," she said sharply.

He could not allow her to do that either. "All right," he finally said. "I promise."

She sighed in what seemed to be relief. "Thank you."

"Tomorrow morning we will begin work on harnessing what remains of Diella," Sian said, his crisp voice that of a teacher. She might not want to hear it, but he would also be teaching her how to separate the dark soul from her own so she could be rid of it.

"If that is best."

"What's best would be for me to take you to my home and imprison you there until this war is over."

"You read the prophesy," she said. "If you take me away to some safe place, you condemn the entire country. The entire world. Maybe we could turn our backs on everything and everyone and have a few wonderful days, ignoring what was happening all around us, but it wouldn't last, and in the end we would be as much to blame for the destruction as Ciro. I appreciate the thought, I even understand it, but I'm not worth that kind of sacrifice. No one is."

The logic of war from a woman. Why could she not be the helpless girl he had once thought her to be? If that were the case, he could steal her away from this madness. His heart sank. Like Ariana, he knew that wasn't possible. Her logic was sound.

"Will you at least allow me to dry and warm you?" he asked. "You have begun to shiver with the cold."

"All right," she said tiredly.

Sian extended his hands until they were almost touching Ariana. He generated heat and a gentle white light from his palms. He held that heat and light close to her damp uniform, her chilled skin, her wet hair. She closed her eyes and basked in the light. Eventually her breathing changed. It eased as she released not only the dampness but the tension from her body.

At his instruction, Ariana lay back on the hard bedroll that would serve as her bed on this night. As her eyes were closed and she was drifting toward sleep, he took the opportunity to study her closely.

Ariana Varden was warrior and woman. Lover and student. Witch and sister to forty-one sentinels who would die for her. He had watched her laugh and seen her cry. He had heard her scream in horror and in pleasure.

It would be very easy to convince himself that he was in love with this remarkable woman. She certainly meant more to him than he had ever intended. Could he kill her if called to do so? Could he take her life if Diella took control?

"Sian?" Ariana called sleepily.

"Yes, love?" He ran his warming palms close to her lower belly, where some of the fabric of her uniform remained damp.

"We're very close to the darkness we seek. Very close."

"I know."

"I can feel it with every step my horse takes. I don't know what awaits us, still I don't know, but it's close."

"Don't think about that tonight, love," he said as he continued his work. She was almost completely dry now.

"How can I not?"

"I will think about it for you while you rest for a while. I will stay right here, and any troubles you have, any worries or uncertainties, any thoughts of darkness, they are mine while you sleep."

She sighed deeply. "Oh, that's very nice."

When Ariana woke, her troubles would be waiting for her. But for tonight, they were his.

He did not have Ariana's gift for protection, but he could share his power with her in hopes that it would strengthen her own abilities when she needed them most. In the days to come she would need tremendous strength to control Diella, and she would need much energy in order to shield herself when it was necessary. Sian projected his strength into the sleeping woman with a pulse of purple light that shimmered around her and then was absorbed. He shared with her all that he had, all that he was.

What he gave Ariana was more than illusion, more than a magician's well-practiced tricks. What he gave her was a piece of himself.

How could she believe that he would ever take her life? Even if Diella took control, he would never accept that there was no hope of bringing Ariana back and expelling the evil empress. To purposely kill this woman who had become so important to him was impossible, and yet he did understand her request. If Diella had un-controlled use of Ariana's body, how much damage could she do during this all-important battle?

He began to chant in a lowered voice that no one be-yond the tent would be able to hear. In the ancient lan-guage of the wizards he called for Ariana to be protected, to be strong, to be victorious. The Prophesy of the First-born doomed her, but that did not mean the days ahead were set in stone. With enough power . . . with enough light and love . . .

Sian's fingers trembled and his hands jerked, as words from that damned prophesy came into his mind.

Those who are called must choose between love and death, between heart and intellect, between victory of the sword and victory of the soul.

Wasn't that precisely what Ariana asked of him when she requested that he take her life if Diella took control? If these scribbled words were correct, then all those who had been called would face such a choice.

Did that mean Sian had been called to this war much as the firstborn had been, that he was, as Ariana had said more than once, meant to be here?

He draped his body over hers, as he felt his energy be-gin to wane. The choker at his throat burned, as the con-nection he and Ariana had forged deepened. He was inside her in a way he had never been before, as his light and hers merged. She did grow stronger, he felt it.

So did he.

13

WHEN THEY RODE INTO WHAT WAS LEFT OF THE VIL-
lage, Sian was at Ariana's side. He looked like himself
again, dressed entirely in black and no longer foolishly
attempting to hide his face from her. Even though she remained annoyed with the enchanter, she was very glad to
have him so close.

She couldn't afford to let the men who followed see
how grateful she was to be able to draw from Sian's
strength. They might think it a female weakness, and she
could not allow the sentinels to see any weakness from
her, female or otherwise. Since calling Sian to her side
she'd felt considerably stronger, and Diella had remained
silent. Perhaps the empress was afraid of the enchanter.

When she'd noted this small village indicated on the
stone map in the palace, glowing red and turning black
and becoming red again before disappearing, she'd had no
idea what the sign meant. Now, too late, she understood.

A battle of sorts had taken place here, perhaps the first battle in this war, but she and her army had arrived much too late to be of assistance. She'd led her sentinels here before taking the road to the Anwyn mountains, but she hadn't been fast enough.

Everything had been burned. Public buildings along the main thoroughfare, as well as homes which were spread just beyond, had been destroyed. Nothing had been spared the flame, but that was not what disturbed Ariana most as she rode down the center of the deserted street. She did not have the gift of sight, like Aunt Juliet or Keelia, so she could not see what had happened here. But as an empath, she could feel it.

Stark terror filled the air. The energy she had learned to feel—and sometimes see—reverberated with violence and fear and nightmarish screams. Men, women, even children . . . the innocent had suffered in the most horrible ways. The fire that had come at the end had been almost a relief for those who'd survived that long.

Beside and underneath that fear, there lurked another sort of energy, one that made Ariana tremble to her core. There was fiendish delight here, mingled with the thrill of a particularly nasty kill. There was hunger. Hunger of the most demonic sort. And power. Dark, wicked power.

The destruction of this village had happened very quickly. She felt that in the way the emotions that surrounded her blended and changed with fast precision. In a matter of hours the villagers had gone from innocently unaware to horrified to mercifully dead.

"Ariana," Sian said, and she suspected from the impatient and concerned tone of his voice that it was not the first time he'd called her name.

"Yes?" She turned to him as they stopped before one

of many buildings that had been burned to the ground. His expression might've been unreadable to the others, but not to her. He was worried. Not about what had happened here, and not about the battle still to come. Those were past and future, and Sian was very much in the present. He was worried about her. Only her.

"Ciro did this," he said. It was a statement and a question, one she was obligated to answer.

"Yes, but he was not alone."

"How many?"

"I don't know."

"More than our forty-three, I suspect."

"Perhaps."

Ariana's eyes were drawn to the building directly before her. She felt something different from this site. Fear and hopelessness almost overpowered the new sensation, but could not mask it completely. She dismounted and stepped toward the ruins.

"Someone fought him here," she said, a hint of hope in her voice. Maybe he was not yet invincible. Maybe Ciro could be defeated. "Someone did not . . ." She closed her eyes, trying to feel the energy as well as see it. "Someone did not succumb to his wishes. It was a small victory that took place here, to be sure, but it *was* victory."

Sian dismounted, and Ariana suppressed the urge to run to him and throw her arms around his neck. The sentinels likely already wondered what sort of relationship she had with the enchanter. They spent a lot of time together, much of it alone.

But today Sian was only her counsel, not her lover, and no self-respecting general would hug his wizard on discovering one tiny bit of good news. He placed one hand on her shoulder, feeding her power with his own so that she could see more clearly the energies that survived here. Even now, some darkness survived amid the devastation, as did more light than she had expected to find.

The sentinels who had followed her into the destroyed village studied the burned buildings with solemnity. Even though they did not feel what Ariana herself felt, they could see for themselves what had happened. Beyond some of the twisted and charred doorways of ruined buildings there lay twisted and charred bodies. It did not take empathic ability to understand what had transpired here.

Ariana walked away from Sian, and his hand dropped from her shoulder. She missed the connection, but she could not rely on him every moment of the day, much as she would like to do just that.

She smoothly mounted her horse, and rode into the center of the street. "This is the work of our enemy," she said, not shouting, but speaking loudly enough for all to hear. "We were called to this battle to stop atrocities such as *this*." A few of the men nodded. "Look around you," she ordered, as some of the sentinels, particularly the younger ones, were making an effort not to look too closely at the ruins. "Do not turn away. No one was spared here. Not women, not even children. We must stop them," she added, her voice trembling with emotion. "We cannot rest until—"

"One was spared."

Ariana spun her horse about so she could see the bearer of that news. Everyone turned to look, since the voice was decidedly female.

A slightly built woman with reddish brown hair stepped onto the street. Her clothes were ragged and torn. And bloody. Her face was pale and marked with one ragged cut and smeared, dried blood on her left cheek. Tear tracks across her ashen face also marked her as a victim.

As did the fear that radiated from her as she walked toward Ariana's army.

"I am looking for the woman in white," she said, steering clear of the men as if she were afraid of them . . . and she was. She was terrified.

Ariana was not wearing her white uniform today, but she dismounted and walked toward the girl. She had a hundred questions. When precisely had this happened? How many were the enemy? Why had they allowed this one to live? But to start, she asked, "Why are you looking for me?"

The girl shied away. "You are not dressed in white. He said I was to speak only with the woman in white. It's *very important.*"

Ariana nodded to Sian, and he understood her immediately. He dismounted, reached into Ariana's saddlebag, and drew out the neatly folded white vest. He did not care for her white outfit. He said it marked her too clearly for the enemy. But he brought the vest to her now, with nothing more than a slightly annoyed expression on his face as he handed the garment to her.

Ariana slipped the vest on over her green uniform, and apparently that was enough to satisfy the girl.

"He let me live so I could deliver this message to you." There was terror and a touch of strength in the girl's blue eyes as they caught and held Ariana's. She delivered the message, her voice almost dead as she repeated the words. "Turn back now, and he will let you live. Turn back now, and perhaps you will be spared a painful death at his hands. Turn back now, and your pathetic excuse of an army will not bleed into the battleground of his choosing, a battleground you will not see before you until the first head rolls. Turn back *now,* and your souls may be yours to keep."

"Who sends this message to me?" Ariana asked calmly.

The girl stumbled and almost fell, and Ariana instinctively reached out to steady her. Still, all she felt from the girl—who did not look to be yet twenty years old—was fear. Fear and pain and a bitter relief that she remained alive when all others were dead. "Prince Ciro, he said his name was," she whispered.

Ciro already knew of her and her army. She should not be surprised, but she had hoped that he was not yet aware of her part in this war.

Ariana continued to physically support the girl. "Do you have a place to go?"

She shook her head.

"Relatives in another village, perhaps."

The girl shook her head more fiercely. "I am alone now. All my family is dead. The man I was to marry in the summer . . . dead." Pale, slender fingers gripped Ariana's sleeve. "Take me with you. I heard you say you were going to fight the men who did this, and I want to be there. I want to take up a sword and . . . and kill the men who murdered everyone I love."

Ariana shook her head gently. "No. It's too dangerous."

"You're going to fight. Why can't I? I have nothing left, do you understand that? Nothing! I want to kill the brutes who did this to my home. I want to make them pay!"

The girl was no soldier, but Ariana couldn't very well leave her here in what was left of the village that had once been home. It was possible they would find a place for her down the road. If there was anything left down the road.

"What's your name?" Ariana asked.

"Lilia," the girl whispered. "Lilia Mindel, daughter of the village blacksmith." Her eyes filled with tears.

"How old are you?"

"Almost nineteen." She said the words as if being

closer to nineteen years than eighteen made her older and wiser.

"Well, Lilia, we will take you with us." Ariana put her arm around Lilia's shoulder and led the girl toward her own gray horse. "I cannot promise that you will get the opportunity to fight, but for now we will take care of you."

"I was bound, cut, terrorized, and forced to watch my entire family die in the most horrible manner," Lilia snapped, her voice harsh and her slender body tensing. "Everything I ever loved was destroyed in one night, and yet you tell me I do not have as much right as any man in this company to fight against those who wronged me?" Amid the fear there was now anger. Sharp, hot anger. "Who is in charge here? Who leads you? Surely he will see that I have the right to join you in every way."

"I lead," Ariana said simply. "I decide who joins us and who does not." Heaven above, she did not want to take this child into battle. But Lilia had a good point. She had been wronged, and had a right to fight. And if Lilia was with them now, did that mean that she was meant to be here?

Lilia cowered slightly. "I did not know a woman could lead an army."

"Neither did I." They did not have an extra horse, though it was likely one could be procured soon. Until then, Lilia would have to ride with another, and in order not to put too much strain on any one animal, she would have to switch horses often. Merin was closest. "Will you ride with my first in command?"

Lilia looked up at the solemn horseman and cowered. "Can't I ride with you?" she asked softly.

Ariana sighed. The girl was naturally afraid of men, after all that had happened to her. Still, she could not ride with any one horseman constantly. "If you truly wish to join this army, you cannot be afraid of the men who will fight alongside you. Ride with me, if you must, and we will take you to the closest farmhouse and leave you there."

A touch of fire flamed Lilia's blue eyes. She stepped away from Ariana and lifted a slender arm to Merin. He took that arm and easily drew her up, depositing her before him in a position that had to be uncomfortable for them both.

"There's nothing more to be done here," Ariana said as she once again climbed into her own saddle.

That little voice she had grown accustomed to, a voice that had been silent for days, whispered, *How can you trust one who survives such destruction?*

Ciro left her alive so she could deliver his message. That's why she survived.

You're so gullible.

You trust no one.

It's not a bad way to live. Trust no one, and you'll never be disappointed.

That's not who I am.

And see where it got you?

Ariana's eyes were drawn to a silent Sian, who rode beside her. Yes, she had once trusted him completely. With her training, her body, and her heart. And he had disappointed her.

And still, she would not trade what they'd shared for anything.

As I said. Gullible.

Ariana pushed the little voice deep. She and Sian had talked for many hours about controlling the demon inside her . . . the demon which scared him, the demon which she felt was necessary for facing Ciro. The enchanter had emphasized that Ariana could and must maintain control, so she effectively pushed Diella into a silent, powerless place.

Merin and Lilia rode just ahead. The girl held herself so as little as possible of her body touched the soldier, and her eyes remained on the road.

Sian surprised her by echoing Diella's warning in a lowered voice meant only for her ears. "Do not trust her entirely. Not yet."

"Her pain is very real, I see that clearly. Ciro hurt her. Why should I not trust her?"

"Because in a war like this one, there will be times when nothing is as it seems to be. Don't forget that, Ariana."

Ariana would like to believe that everything and everyone was exactly as they seemed to be. That was the way she'd lived her life, after all. Good was good, and evil was evil, and it was supposed to be easy to tell the difference. Luckily for her, or unluckily perhaps, Sian and Diella were always around to remind her that much of what she'd always believed was no longer true.

LILIA DREW INTO HERSELF—CONVENIENTLY SO, SIAN thought—when Merin and Ariana began to ask her specific questions about the destruction of her village. They had finally stopped for the night, and the camp's routine was followed as usual. Some sentinels ate, a few slept, others kept watch. By dawn, they'd be on the road again. Everyone realized now, more acutely than ever, that there was little time to spare for resting.

The girl they had found alive sat by the fire as she was questioned, her knees drawn to her chest, her head down. Aside from the cut on her face, she was pretty enough, as many of the sentinels had noticed, and there was a fragility about young Lilia that made them all want to protect her.

None who had been asked to share their mount with her during the day had complained.

It was entirely possible that every word of Lilia's story was true. Her face was cut, though not terribly deeply, and her clothes had been torn. There was blood on her skirt—blood she said was not her own, but was that of her sister.

"How many men were in the party that raided your village?" Ariana asked, not for the first time. Her voice remained gentle. Patient.

Lilia shook her head. "I don't know. I heard them outside the window, but I did not see them all. They sounded like . . . hundreds," she whispered. "So many . . ."

"How many did you see?" Merin asked, not quite as kindly as Ariana.

"Five . . . no . . . six. Six were in my house. We were sleeping, and they burst in all at once and—"

"You don't have to tell us what happened again," Ariana interrupted. They had heard the tale once. When Lilia had retired on that evening, her two parents, two sisters, and three brothers had lived. She'd had a large, happy family surrounding her all her life, and now she was alone. "We need to know what we're up against. If you wish to be a soldier, then you must think as a soldier, not as a victim."

Lilia lifted her head and looked squarely at Ariana. "Will you allow me to join you?"

"I have not decided."

The girl nodded, and seemed to pull herself together. She licked her lips as she reached inside herself for answers and tried to remain calm. "From what I heard beyond my home, I would say there were at least fifty. Perhaps more. Their arms were varied. Some carried fine swords like your sentinels, but others . . . others seemed to be armed with whatever they had found close at hand. Kitchen knives, scraps of wood sharpened to a point, metal chains." Her head tilted to one side as she searched her fractured mind, and a hank of dirty reddish hair fell past her marred cheek. "One of the men who came into my home brandished a fire iron he wielded as if it were a sword. It was brutal, the way they rushed into my home and . . . and . . ."

"So," Sian said skeptically, joining in the conversation for the first time. "They rushed into your home, dragged your family from their beds, brutally killed them all, and yet you were spared."

Lilia looked at Sian. She didn't care for him, he could tell. Of course, at the moment she did not care for any man.

"The one who dragged me from my bed said *he* would want me. I don't know how he knew, or why I was chosen, but there was no hesitation. I was for *him*, he said. So I was roughly bound and dragged down the stairs, and then those of my family who were not killed in their beds were dragged downstairs also, and I was forced to watch them die." Her gaze became strong. "You are not fighting one enemy, but two. There are soldiers among Ciro's army who attack as soldiers often do. They kill quickly and with precision and then turn to the next prey. But there is another type of soldier among them. They call themselves 'Ciro's Own,' and they do *not* kill quickly. They do not kill as a duty, but as a calling. They like what they do, and they never offer their victims death with any speed or mercy."

Sian's breath caught in his throat. Ciro's Own? *Beware Serrazone.* As with "Fyne" and "fine," his grandfather had heard the prophesy and misspelled it. In his own mind, Sian had been mispronouncing the word, but now it made sense. *Beware Ciro's Own.*

"The *he* you speak of in this tale is Ciro, I assume?" His voice betrayed none of the excitement that flowed through him. Another piece of the puzzle had fallen into place.

"Yes," she whispered.

"Why were you chosen?"

Her lower lip trembled, but her eyes remained strong. "Do you think I am one of them? Is that why you question me so?"

"I believe it is a possibility."

The honest answer made her angry. "The house was already on fire when he came. My family was dead. My mother's body was on *fire*, my father . . . my sisters . . ." She choked back the words she could not speak. "A man who looked almost normal to my eyes smiled at me as he stepped through flame and asked me if I would offer him my soul. I told him I would not. He threatened me, he promised to do horrible things to me if I did not give him what he wanted, but I continued to refuse. He said my soul was very white, but . . . I don't know what that means. You can't see a soul. It's just . . . there, isn't it?" She did not pause and wait for an answer. "He glanced around, at his soldiers and at what was left of my home, and bemoaned the fact that he had nothing with which to force me to offer my soul.

"And then he put his hands on me. He pinched and grabbed and . . . and poked at the most private parts of my body while his murderous soldiers watched and *laughed*, and that was when he gave me the message I was to deliver to the woman in white. Calmly, as if he were not hurting me as he said the words. He repeated the message slowly, again and again and again, so I would not forget a single word." She shuddered. "He also told me that he would not waste a perfectly good soul, that he would come back for me when he no longer needed my permission, and *take it*." She all but shouted the final words, and then she calmed visibly. "He said there was no place in the world I could hide from him when the time was right. He said he would be able to find me."

"Lilia," Ariana said softly, "did he rape you?"

Her fingers twitched. "No. I thought he would, I was terrified that he would, right up to the moment he turned away. I think I would've died if he had," she whispered. "I don't think he's . . . human."

In her righteous anger, Lilia had shared the most important bit of information yet. More important even than the words "Ciro's Own," which solved another mystery of the prophesy. Ciro was not yet able to take a pure soul without permission.

"Was it he who cut you?" Ariana asked, her voice, as always, kinder than Sian's.

"Yes," she whispered. "With his *teeth*. He scraped his teeth along my face, and licked the blood away with his tongue while he pinched me, so hard. I screamed, and then he . . . he grabbed me by the hair and dragged me out of my burning house, and left me in the street. Everything was on fire, and most of the invaders had gone. Only a few remained, and they . . . they laughed at my screams." A new anger sparked in her eyes and she shuddered.

If she was lying, she was very good at it.

Ariana was obviously touched. "Merin, I know the night is mild and we only have a few hours before we must move on, but would you have my tent erected for the night? I think Lilia needs some privacy, and so do I."

As Merin made to do as he'd been told, and Lilia turned her lost gaze into the fire, Sian led Ariana away from the girl. "You're not going to be alone with her all night."

"She cannot hurt me," Ariana said.

"You don't know that. Do you see anything in her besides fear and anger? Do you see any hint of goodness?"

Ariana remained calm. "Right now all is lost in the anger, as you certainly know. In time, I will be able to see more."

"Until you do, you should not be alone with her. Offer her the tent, if you must, but don't share it with her."

"What am I to do, sleep with you instead?" Ariana asked, her voice unusually tough and mocking.

"Yes," he said. "My bedroll is roomy enough."

"What would the men think?"

"I don't care what anyone thinks."

"I do."

Of course she did. "Fine. You may pass the night in my bedroll, alone. I don't need much sleep anyway. Never have. I will keep watch over you, and over the tent where Lilia sleeps."

"Do you really think that's necessary?" Ariana asked.

"If I didn't, I wouldn't mention it."

Ariana nodded. All sarcasm was gone when she said, "All right. If you think it's best."

Sian sighed in relief. "I think it's best that we deposit the girl at the first farmhouse or village we pass."

"You don't trust her, do you?"

"No."

"What if she's telling the truth?"

"What if she's not?"

Ariana sighed tiredly. "Let me see to Lilia. I'll get her settled for the night, and then I'll join you."

Sian stopped Ariana as she began to walk away from him. His hand fell on her shoulder, and she came to a quick and complete halt. He had not touched her often since joining her on the road, but when he did, he felt as if a jolt of lightning traveled through his blood. Did she feel it, too? Did she realize that what she tried so desperately to leave behind remained with them?

She was an empath, a very powerful one. Did she know that he sometimes thought he loved her, and that he would do anything in his power just to lie with her again? If so, she did not show it. Not to him, at least.

"The protective shield we worked on developing in Arthes," he said. "I think it's time you used it."

"The shield drains me," she argued. "It takes total concentration to maintain, and it isn't at all foolproof. I'll be worse off if I think I'm protected and it fails."

"True enough, but I'd like for you to try it again tonight," he said. "Consider it practice. Did you read all of the prophesy?" He hated to mention that which had torn them apart, but he needed to know.

She showed no emotion as she answered, "I did not read past the part which promises my death. I couldn't make myself read beyond that."

Sian nodded. "There is much I have not yet interpreted, but Lilia provided one answer for me. My grandfather wrote 'Beware Serrazone' in the margins of the prophesy." He spelled it for her, as it had been written. "I've searched everywhere for mention of Serrazone as a place or a person, but found nothing."

Since she'd heard the word instead of reading it, she immediately knew what Sian had discovered. "Beware Ciro's Own."

"Yes. Thanks to Lilia we know they're close, and we know what they're capable of. Use the shield if you can."

"I thought you didn't trust her word," Ariana said, throwing the words at him with some bitterness.

"In this case, I cannot afford to dismiss all that she says. Even if she's spinning a tale for us, there's bound to be some truth mixed in with the lies. Cast the shield," he said again.

It broke his hardened heart to see Ariana this way, embittered and accepting of the death that should not be hers. If there were a way to trade his life for hers, he would do so without question. He would do anything for her, and if he could not die in her place, he would die beside her, because there was no way he could stand back and allow it to happen without trying to place himself between her and the monsters she had been chosen to face.

Apparently he loved her, like it or not, convenient or not. Prophesy or no prophesy, he would not throw Ariana to Ciro or to Ciro's Own as a sacrifice to the greater good.

She nodded and walked away from him. As the time of her promised death grew near, did she have any regrets? Did she, perhaps, sometimes think herself in love with him?

As if in answer, she glanced over her shoulder and caught his eye.

An enchanter's heart was not supposed to be so easily influenced, but his lurched and clenched and broke a little more.

14

LONG AFTER DARKNESS FELL, CIRO WALKED AMONG HIS
men—and women—and studied them with the loving
care of a stern father. It amused him to scrutinize the
women who had answered his call. Females were often
viewed as being weaker than males, but in his experience
that was very often not the case. In battle, the few women
among his Own had fought as diligently as the men.

His army was exhausted after the razing of the village
that had been the site of their first battle. Days had passed,
and yet they seemed satisfied. Sated. His Own warriors
were not accustomed to the physical aspects of warfare.
They fought with vigor, but their bodies were not as
strong as they should be.

Strength would come, in time.

And so would *she*. The warrior woman in white was
coming his way. She was marching to him, as if he called to
her in a way she could not understand or deny. In dreams

he had seen the woman's face, thanks to the Isen Demon, and she looked familiar to him. The Ciro he had once been had known her, but apparently she had been of no real importance because whatever memories he carried of her were buried deep.

All had not gone exactly as he'd planned in the village, but he could not look back on that night without some hint of pride. His legion was brutal and merciless. They would do whatever he asked of them. All who faced them would feel utter terror, and rightly so.

Ciro knew he should take care not to allow his Own too much free rein. If they had their way, by the time winter arrived, there would be nothing of Columbyana left for him to rule.

With Fynnian gone, Ciro was forced to formulate his own plans. The warrior in white would be dealt with first, and then, when she was dead, he would march to Arthes and proceed with his father. It would not be difficult. The emperor was frail, infected with the Isen Demon's darkness just enough to make him weak.

In Arthes he would kill his father, and claim the throne that was rightfully his. When that was done, he would send someone to collect Rayne and have her delivered to him. Or else he would do the collecting himself. He had not decided. In either case, Rayne would be his empress, and she would give him a son. A son who would be more Isen Demon than human. A son who would be unlike any other the world had ever seen. Only utter darkness and unfailing light could produce such a child. He provided the darkness; Rayne provided the light.

Ciro hated to admit to such a human failing, but in many ways he missed the cranky old wizard who had been with him since the beginning of this journey. Fynnian had been bothersome and often did not know his place, but he was better company than these soulless creatures who called themselves Ciro's Own, and a much better conversationalist than the more ordinary soldiers who cared only for weaponry and tales of their victory and, on occasion, the souvenirs they took from the battleground.

If he grew very hungry as he waited for the woman in white to arrive, he'd feed on the soldiers Fynnian had organized. There was not an unmarked soul among them, which was understandable considering their mercenary calling, and while they would not offer the power and flavor of the white souls he craved, they would suffice in times of hunger. He did not experience the same possessive affection for them his Own elicited. They were necessary, for the time being, but in time they would become expendable.

From his position high on the rough cliffside, Ciro looked down on the winding road below. On the other side of the trail was a decently leafed stand of trees. With some men positioned there, others here where he stood, and still others stationed just to the west, the small army that thought to take him would march into a trap from which they would not be able to escape.

Ciro knew the warrior woman he almost recognized and the pathetic army she led would come this way. One of his Own was leading them here, just as she had promised she would.

The wizard Chamblyn was with the army. Not only did the Isen Demon tell him so, but the female who so easily led the army to this ambush also reached for Ciro in the night and whispered in his ear. They were connected, after all, as all his Own were. He was powerful, Chamblyn was, perhaps more powerful even than Fynnian had been. If he could be turned, he'd make a fine addition to Ciro's Own.

And if not, then his soul would feed Ciro and the Isen Demon well. Wizards, by their very nature, walked a fine line between light and dark. Chamblyn's soul might not be as tainted as Fynnian's had been, but he was not pure. No permission would be needed to feed upon his soul.

The soldier who was with the warrior woman whispered in the night, *I'm coming. I won't make you wait much longer. Remember what you promised me, my prince. Remember.*

I remember well.

Ciro smiled as he severed the connection. It was a fool who put stock in promises from one such as he had become.

SIAN CURSED UNDER HIS BREATH AS HE GLANCED AT ARiana. She had given Lilia her green uniform, since the girl's dress had been ruined beyond repair, and so she wore the only other clothing she had with her. The white. The white which made her shine like a beacon beneath the sun or the moon; the white which marked her as special and different; the white which would call every enemy directly to her. The fucking white.

If she were not so small, he would insist that someone in the party exchange clothes with her. Unfortunately, that was not an option.

"Why are you glaring at me?" she asked in a lowered voice. They rode side by side, with a few soldiers before them, and the rest behind. Since coming upon the destroyed village, they had all been restless and tense. There was less casual conversation, less chatter. Perhaps they all felt the weight of what they approached, as he did.

"I am not glaring," Sian insisted.

Ariana looked at him and smiled halfheartedly. "I have not been acquainted with you for a long time, enchanter, but I do know your glare well."

"Fine," he snapped. "White? What were you thinking? Whatever possessed you—"

"Interesting choice of words," she interrupted. "Whatever *possessed* me? Do you think Diella chose the white and I am unaware?"

"I don't know," he confessed. "It does have a dramatic flair, but it also makes you much too easy to identify in a sea of green."

Ariana smiled. "At first I thought a brilliant white uniform would be wonderfully symbolic. White light will be necessary to win this war, and we must embrace that light. I don't believe it actually brings power to us, but it reminds me of why I'm here." She shrugged as if her reasons were unimportant. "The white amid all the green also reminds me that I cannot hide from who I am."

"There's nothing wrong with hiding," he snapped. "There's also no reason to go out of your way to bring attention to your position of importance."

"It's done. I cannot go back and undo it."

She was maddeningly calm. Sian was no empath, and yet he felt the approach of darkness. He felt the coming of destiny, and he knew it would not be pretty. Monsters, the prophesy promised. After seeing what Ciro's men had done to the village, "monster" was a fitting term. Was that why the men remained so silent? Did they feel the approach of the battle they had been called to as surely as he did?

It was a warm day, making certain all knew that summer had arrived. They often traveled in the shade of ancient trees that lined the road, which kept them cool enough for some comfort. In the shade, the white was not so prominent as it was when the sun shone down, but even here it was bright and drew the eye.

All were silent as they made their way through another patch of shade.

"Do you feel it coming?" he asked, his voice again lowered so no one else could hear.

"Yes," Ariana answered.

"When?"

"Tonight," she said, her voice gentle and without fear. "Perhaps tomorrow night."

Sian tried to imagine this woman in battle with the men who had demolished an entire village, and he could not. No matter how grandly she led these men, she was a healer and a gentle woman, and when the battle she was being guided to fell upon her, she would die, just as the prophesy promised.

"Turn back," he said. "It isn't too late."

Ariana sighed, but she did not slow her horse. "I can't turn back." She looked at him, her green eyes scared but determined. "It was too late the moment the prophesy was written."

"I will take your place." Gladly, fiercely, if only he could know that she was safe.

"Thank you, but that's not possible."

"Anything is possible."

Sian had never suspected that he'd find himself in such a position. Ariana was right; she was necessary, and the fate of the world was in her hands. He would not sacrifice the world for her, or for any one person.

He also would not allow Ariana to face her destiny alone. When the time came he would fight with and for her, he would give his life for her if it was necessary. And if Diella rose to the surface and Ariana was gone . . . he could only hope that the strength he had shared with her made such an atrocity impossible.

"I don't think I can kill Ciro," Ariana confessed as they continued on their damned journey. "He's strong, and he has more men that I do. In anything resembling a fair fight, we will lose."

"Then why won't you turn back? Why won't you save yourself for another day and another battle?"

A few soldiers heard him that time. Heads turned. A few men whispered.

"Because whether or not we win, we will hurt him somehow," Ariana responded. "I don't know how, but if your grandfather's prophesy is correct then whatever we can do to hurt the enemy is essential. I don't want to see every village in the country decimated as Lilia's village was. I don't want to see whatever Ciro has become rule and destroy everything and everyone I love."

That was her weakness. She cared. Sian did not mind playing upon her weakness. "These men you call brothers will all die."

"Perhaps," she said calmly. "Perhaps not." Again she stared at him, and he saw the lover she had been, not the leader she had become. "You can turn back, if you'd like," she offered. "You are not obligated to follow me."

Sian made a sound of pure disgust. She didn't understand anything. He was obligated to her in more ways than he dared to admit.

NIGHT WOULD SOON BE UPON THEM, AND ARIANA FELT a growing sense of unease. With every step her horse took, she felt more trepidation. More fear.

Turn back, if you are too afraid to face Ciro.

I can't turn back.

No one really expects you to be a hero. You're a girl. A witch with insignificant healing powers.

You're no girl, and you're never afraid. When the time comes, you must lend me your strength. If I die, what becomes of you?

I disappear.

You don't want that to happen.

No, I don't.

It was odd and unexpected, this almost companionable truce with the dark spirit inside her. Perhaps Diella wasn't completely dark. After all, she had once been a woman, just like Ariana. She had loved, and fought for survival in what was perhaps the only way she knew how. The empress had not attempted to rise to the surface since Ariana had called Sian to her side. Perhaps she knew that the enchanter would kill her, would kill them both, if she was so bold.

What awaits me? Do you know?

Pain. Sorrow. Death.

You could lie and tell me that together we're strong enough to win.

Why would I lie to you?

Why, indeed?

The three sentinels who rode slightly ahead stopped at a fork in the road. They turned to her, and waited for her decision. After all, she had been this way once before, when traveling to see her Anwyn cousins. They were a mere two days from turning onto the only mountain road suitable for horses.

Ariana gestured to the trail to the left. "This is the way."

"Wait!" The sentinel carrying Lilia came forward, urged by the woman who shared his mount this evening. She pointed to the right. "This is a shortcut. There are places where the trail turns narrow, but it will save half a day."

Lilia had listened carefully to their travel plans, so she knew where they were headed. She knew the mountain trail which would take them to the Anwyn.

I don't think she can be trusted.

Her entire village was destroyed. Why would she lie?

Everyone lies, witch. Everyone. You're the empath, you're the healer. Do you trust her entirely? Do you think she's incapable of lying? How do you know she's actually from that village? How do you know she's not one of Ciro's soldiers?

I would see if that were true.

Would you?

Why would Lilia lead us down the wrong path?

Why, indeed?

Sian bit out her name, probably not for the first time. "Ariana!"

Her head snapped around and she found herself staring into familiar and oddly concerned purple eyes. The colors in those remarkable eyes swam, light and dark shades meeting and melding. She'd been so lost in her conversation with Diella that she had not heard a word that had been spoken.

"I'm thinking," she said sharply.

Whom should she trust? Whom could she trust? The woman they had saved; the demon who lived inside her; no one at all. At the moment, her magic seemed so insignificant. So useless.

In the end she made her decision about which road they would take, because she had no choice. The authority she did not want was her weight to carry, her place in this war that still felt as if it were coming soon but was not yet here.

This time she led the way, and Sian positioned himself directly beside her.

"It is not too late to turn back," he said, not for the first time today.

"Not for you, perhaps."

"I will not run from this fight or any other," he said tersely. "I only want you to be safe, and you make me feel as if that's a heinous crime."

"Not a crime, Sian, just . . . impossible."

He remained beside her, occasionally cursing beneath his breath as darkness fell. They traveled at a slow, steady pace, silent and tense. Ariana did not order her men to set up camp and rest for a few hours. Not tonight. Perhaps not tomorrow night, either.

If there was a tomorrow night for any of them.

THERE WAS A BRIGHT HALF MOON IN A CLEAR SKY, lighting the way well enough for soldiers who were accustomed to seeing in the dark. A steep cliff rose to the right, hinting at the harshness of the mountains they would soon be traveling into. Straight ahead that cliff turned into a steep, rocky hill, slanted sharply instead of shooting straight upward into the night. To the left, a stand of thickly leafed trees hid small scurrying creatures from their eyes, but not their ears. The view had been much the same for the past several hours.

In his gut, Sian felt the weight of what was about to happen. He cared little for his own life, when weighed against the dire possibilities that Ciro's reign would bring, but Ariana deserved better.

In the beginning he had been more than willing to sacrifice her to the greater good, but tonight he was certain the world would be a better place if Ariana Varden remained in it.

The enemy they had been waiting for appeared suddenly, but Ariana's army had been so alert that the surprise did not cost them an insurmountable amount of time. Sian's reaction was immediate. He drew his sword, as Ariana drew hers, and he placed himself between her and the men who rushed toward her.

Ciro's army was primarily on foot, which gave Ariana and her soldiers an advantage. Some of them were also strangely armed with weapons which did not stand a chance against expertly wielded weapons at the hands of trained sentinels. In that, at least, Lilia had been truthful. The attacking soldiers fell, and Sian saw that it was men, not monsters, who died on the narrow road. He watched one of Ariana's soldiers fall, and then another, but he did not even think to rush to their aide. No, his place was here, beside Ariana. To the death, if need be.

"Shield!" he shouted.

She either ignored him or was unable to erect a magical shield in the chaos of battle. Enemy soldiers continued to attack her, and he saw no evidence of any enchanted protection.

Even though she was unable to erect the shield, Ariana fought well. Sian wondered if it was Diella who wielded the sword which answered the assault of one ill-prepared soldier after another. Her lessons, practical and magical, had not been in vain. When she was attacked by three soldiers from two sides, she fought not only with the sword in her hand but with a knife she magically plucked from the body of a fallen enemy soldier and sent hurtling toward the neck of the man who tried to attack her from behind. He knew it wasn't at all easy to manipulate objects while fighting, but Ariana managed quite well.

Sian's fight was much the same. The enemy came, and they fell, and more came. Ariana's soldiers were reluctant to fight the women among Ciro's soldiers, until a female monster brutally gutted one of the younger sentinels, a boy who had hesitated when faced with a female combatant. Someone shouted loudly, reminding them of Ariana's words on that first morning. *See with your hearts.* After that, the others did not hesitate again.

It seemed that the enemy was trying to lead Sian away from Ariana, and he had to fight to remain close enough to be of any assistance to her. He was unhorsed by two men who grabbed him from behind and yanked him to the ground, where he landed hard and continued to fight without pause.

Slowly, surely, the oddly armed soldiers created a rough circle around Ariana, but most of them kept their distance, as if they were protecting her . . . or separating her. She was still atop her gray horse, and they were primarily on foot. Perhaps that was why they did not move in.

A slice of alarm crept into Sian's conscience. The soldiers, Ariana's army, were being drawn farther away from her. The enemy soldiers who died so quickly and so well were leading them into the trees, down the road, up the road, even onto the cliffside, when they were unhorsed. The fighting continued without pause. It seemed the enemy was inexhaustible, and when one fell, two more appeared to take his . . . or her . . . place.

Suddenly Sian realized that he and Ariana were all but alone, surrounded by the bodies of the fallen enemy, surrounded by soldiers who continued to attack. The sentinels had been led away from their leader, fighting endlessly and well. He looked for Merin, for other experienced soldiers, wanting to shout for them to return to protect their leader, their sister, but they were all engaged in deadly battle.

Ariana was tiring. She was no longer able to lift a knife magically, but was now forced to rely on her adequate but less-than-spectacular skills as a swordsman. More of the enemy encircled her, some on foot and some on horses of their own. She was visibly slowing, and the newly arrived adversaries were fresh and hungry.

One tall man reached up and grabbed Ariana's white trousers with a gnarly hand. He wrenched hard, and she tumbled from her horse, landing on the path hard, and with a cry of pain. Already tired, she let loose of her sword when she hit the ground. It flew, landing too far away to be of any use to her. Seven soldiers gathered around her, smiling and wielding their blades—and one heavy, sharpened stick—with delight.

Sian fought off the two who threatened him, trying to work his way toward Ariana, while they were doing their best to lead him away. Things had been happening too quickly and furiously for him to concentrate properly, but he tried to freeze the men who surrounded Ariana. He had never been able to affect more than one person at a time with his magic, but he had to try. Two became very still, but the others continued to threaten Ariana. He slowly worked his way toward her, swinging madly at the men who tried to stop him.

Ariana was lying on the ground, surrounded by those who meant to destroy her. Her head turned so that her eyes met Sian's. She mouthed the words "I love you," as if this were her last moment, her last statement.

They could not defeat all the men who fought them.

There were too many, and in the chaos his magic was not strong enough. But he would not stop, not until he reached Ariana. He would go into the Land of the Dead with her, if need be. He would kill as many of these soldiers as he could before they took his life.

The enemy soldiers could've ended Ariana's life quickly, once she was on the ground and unarmed, but they didn't. Instead they laughed and poked at her with their weapons, and one soldier held her in place with a dirty boot pressed into her white-clad belly. Sian used all his concentration to magically toss the sword aside when one enemy soldier moved the sharp tip too near Ariana's throat.

Since Sian's attention was on Ariana, he did not see the soldier wielding a rock approach from the rear until it was too late. The enemy swung, the rock collided with his head, and he dropped as his legs gave out from under him.

A deep, calm voice said, "Don't kill him. Not yet."

Woozy and weaving on his knees, Sian turned his head to see Ciro, his half-brother, walking down the sharp incline of the rocky hill. Ciro was not alone. He half carried, half dragged Lilia. Was she a willing companion who could not handle the hill as easily as Ciro did, or was she a prisoner?

No, if they had taken the shortcut Lilia had suggested instead of this road Ariana knew, they would not have ridden into this trap.

Sian's hands were quickly bound, and the rock-wielding soldier remained at his side. Without his hands, he was useless as a magician. The men he had frozen were no longer affected by his spell. If he could rise and loose the bonds . . .

As if the soldier knew what he was thinking, he kicked Sian to the ground and placed the toe of a dirty boot on his throat. A black dread washed over Sian. He was going to have to watch Ariana die, helpless and half dead and worthless to her and her cause.

He had never told her that he loved her. Never. Not because he didn't, but because he was a coward who did not want to lose again. Burying one wife had been harder than he'd ever allowed anyone to know. Burying a child had been even harder. Hope was a dreadful thing, because in the end it was always yanked away when you least expected it.

"I do love you," he said softly, wondering whether or not Ariana would hear him.

Perhaps she did. Restrained by seven of Ciro's soldiers—Ciro's Own, if he was correct—she smiled at him.

CIRO DRAGGED THE VILLAGE SLUT TOWARD THE WARrior in white, and his soldiers pulled the blonde to her feet. Her white uniform was no longer so purely white. It was stained with blood—hers and that of his Own—and dirt from the road she now lay upon.

Her soul was pure white, as he had suspected it would be. Perhaps he couldn't take her soul, but when the time was right, he could drink every drop of her blood.

He cast a glance at the enchanter, who lay on the road wounded and desperate and held in place by the boot of one of Ciro's Own. His soul was not entirely white, but was nowhere near as dark as Fynnian's had been. With time, he could be turned to darkness. Almost everyone could be turned, and many would be before this war was done.

Ciro held the girl from the village with one hand, which was fisted in her hair. She had come after him fiercely, as he had always imagined she would. It was amusing that she actually thought she could hurt him.

His soldiers held the warrior in white fast, so that she and the other one were face to face. Seeing her this way, so close and real, Ciro remembered more of her. Her name was Ariana, and she was a witch. Why was she here? She did not have the strength to stop him.

"My lord," one anxious soldier called to him. "Look."

Ciro lifted his head and found, to his dismay, that those soldiers he had directed to separate Ariana from her sentinels were losing. Some of her men had fallen, but more survived and fought on. Soon they would notice that their leader was in trouble . . . not that they could save her. They could be an annoyance, however.

The enchanter moved quickly, twisting his long legs up to wrap about one leg of the man who restrained him. Chamblyn easily flipped the soldier onto his back, and then he leapt to his feet. If he managed to free his hands, what Ciro needed to accomplish would become more difficult.

Chamblyn rushed toward him, shouting at the top of his lungs, "Dammit, Merin!" The enchanter threw his body at one of the men who restrained Ariana.

Ciro was annoyed. This would have to be done more quickly than he'd like.

While the enchanter wrestled with one of the soldiers, who dragged the wizard away from the scene without killing him, as he had been ordered to do, Ciro yanked the girl from the village around so that she stood before him. He smiled at her, and she shuddered. She knew what he wanted; what he was about to take.

"You . . . you don't have my permission," she said, her voice shaking.

"I don't need your permission." He lowered his head and nipped at her slender throat.

"But you said my soul was pure and you could not take it without—"

"I lied." He bit into her throat and immediately drained her of her gray soul. It filled him, satisfied him, alleviated his emptiness. Had she really thought herself pure? She'd stolen, she'd lied, she'd been unfaithful to the man she'd promised to marry. How could she have been so foolish as to believe that her soul was white?

Still reveling in the taste of her soul, he drank some of the girl's blood. He did not drain her, however; he simply tasted. With his teeth still attached to her throat, with her blood still filling his mouth, he drew the dagger which hung from his belt, flipped it in his hand, and drove it into Ariana's chest. He found her heart.

The enchanter shouted and freed himself from the two who restrained him. Over his shoulder, Ciro saw soldiers approaching, as well as Chamblyn. Some ran, while others remained on horseback. There were too many of them to take the chance of facing off here and now.

He had only a moment left.

At his direction, his soldiers dropped Ariana. She fell to the ground, motionless. The woman in his arms twitched and wrapped her arms around him. After a moment, she tried to pull away.

"Leave me some blood, you greedy pig." She slapped at his arms.

Ciro took his mouth from her throat and smiled down at the woman. Her face was much the same as it had been when he'd confronted her in the village, but the fear and naiveté had been replaced by cunning and delight. She closed her eyes and took a deep breath.

"Finally. Thank you, my prince."

He grabbed her arm and dragged her up the steep

hillside. His men followed. Some would fall behind, he knew, and they would die. They could be easily replaced when the time was right.

For now, he had what he'd come here for. The warrior in white was dead, and Diella, the first of his Own, had the body and the life she'd craved.

A sharp pain surprised him, halting his progress. He looked down to see that a long, sharp dagger was embedded low in his back. Ciro turned, and saw that the enchanter had managed to free his hands. It was the wizard who had sent the dagger flying such a distance to bury itself in Ciro's flesh.

Ciro very calmly removed the knife, studied the bloody blade, and then dropped it to the ground. Thanks to the power of the Isen Demon, the wound was already healing, already closing. It didn't even hurt, beyond that initial sting. He cast a smile to the enchanter and continued on his way.

At the top of the hill he turned back to survey the scene of his well-planned ambush. The enchanter did not attempt to follow. He was draped over the dead woman's body, and was no longer a threat. Not that he had ever been a real threat, not to Ciro himself. Pity there had been no time to imprison Chamblyn, or at the very least take his soul. Perhaps on another day. Some soldiers fought against Ciro's Own and Fynnian's soldiers, and many of his legion fell. Ciro felt no pity for the fallen. After all, those who fell were slow and ineffective. If they were better soldiers, he would have had more time with the warrior in white and the enchanter.

Most of his Own retreated, now that the mission had been accomplished. There were still many of them, and though they left the battlefield headed in many directions, they would soon be one again.

One green-clad sentinel slipped past Ciro's Own and charged up the hill, his eyes on Ciro himself. "I don't care who you are," the older man growled breathlessly. "You will pay for what you have done to our sister."

Ciro stopped his progress and allowed the pot-bellied man, who should not have the physical ability to climb this hill so fast, to reach him. The sentinel swung out wildly with his bloody sword, but he could not move fast enough . . . not that his weapon would do Ciro any harm.

Ciro knocked the sword aside, and grabbed the man by the throat. He enjoyed the terror in the man's old eyes, and squeezed so that the sentinel's eyes almost bulged.

"If you survive the fall, tell the enchanter that there is always a place for him in my court." With that he tossed the old man down the hill.

Ciro watched the sentinel take a rough ride over rocks and fallen bodies as he plummeted. He surveyed the destruction on the road and in the field and forest beyond. All had not gone as planned, but it had been a good night nonetheless.

The enchanter Chamblyn lifted his head from the body of the dead warrior. He glanced up the hill, and his gaze fell on Ciro and Diella.

"He will try to kill you now," Diella said coldly.

"Let him try," Ciro said as he moved Diella into the darkness. "Let him try."

15

SIAN DID NOT DOUBT THAT ARIANA WAS DEAD. AFTER
all, he had felt it when her heart had stopped, hadn't he?
Too far away, unable to assist her, his own heart had
stopped when hers had, as if the link he had fashioned
with a simple spell and a length of cord linked them not
only in this life, but in the next as well. It was as if he literally could not or would not live without her.

But his heart had resumed beating. Hers did not.

He threw his body over hers, too late protecting her
from Ciro's blade. He screamed at Ariana to come back,
even though he knew she could not. In a hoarse voice he
hardly recognized as his own, he ordered her to open
her eyes. He'd given her the strength to fight, he'd given
her all he had . . . and it had not been enough. The blood
on her blasted white uniform and the paleness of her
skin, the way her chest lay without movement, without
breath, the vacant stare of her eyes . . . they all spoke of

certain death, and he howled at the injustice and the unbearable agony that cut through him as if it could rip him in two. He felt the slice of pain in his heart as if Ciro's blade had found it as surely as it had found Ariana's.

Ariana's soldiers, her brothers, came. Sian didn't hear the others, he barely saw them out of the corner of his eye. Like him, they were too late. Too late to save the woman who led them, too late to protect her from the evil that threatened to take them all.

The sentinels who followed Ariana all loved her, Sian realized that, but none of them had loved her as he had . . . as he still did. None of them had failed her quite as spectacularly as he.

Sian tore his gaze from Ariana's face and looked up the hill to catch his half-brother's eye. The dagger he'd sent flying after Ciro had found its mark, and it should've caused a scream of pain. Ciro should've dropped to the ground, wounded, but he had not. He'd plucked the dagger from his flesh as if it were a splinter. This from a man who was not yet as strong as he would be in days to come.

No, not a man. Ciro was a monster, even though outwardly he appeared to be more man than beast. What was inside the body made him less than a man and more than an animal. Ciro was unspeakably evil, and Sian would not rest until he was dead. He would fight for Ariana, for all that she should've been, for all that he should've been for her.

And then Ciro and Lilia were gone, disappearing into the darkness with what remained of his army. Sian's eyes remained focused on the darkness, even as he held Ariana. He could not bear to look at her face again and see death there. Maybe her death had been foretold, but he had been the one to fail her. In so many ways, he had failed her . . .

ARIANA OPENED HER EYES TO FIND A NUMBER OF FACES peering down at her. Almost all were female. Some were vaguely familiar, some were not. When she shied away from them, all but one backed off.

"Welcome, Ariana. We have been waiting for you." The man who spoke looked a little like her father. Just a little.

"Who are you?"

"Duran Varden."

"As if I would not know my own brother," she snapped, sitting up to find herself on a cold stone slab in a very plain room. "What kind of a trick is this?"

"I am the first Duran Varden," he explained.

Her uncle. Ariana's heart sank. The dead rebel for whom her brother had been named.

Suddenly she remembered the feel of Ciro's knife cutting into her flesh, the odd slip as Diella left her body, the oddly weightless fall and then . . . "Is this the Land of the Dead?"

"Yes."

Death. She had known it was coming, but still she felt a deep sadness in facing the reality. Not for herself, but for those she'd left behind and all that she had left undone. She felt that sadness for Sian, who had not been able to admit his love for her until the end, and for her mother and father, who would be devastated when they learned how their eldest child had died.

She examined the plain room, which seemed to be constructed entirely of a pale blue-gray stone, and the people who waited patiently for her to join them. "I rather thought the Land of the Dead would be different."

Duran smiled. Oh, he did have her father's smile! "Beyond these walls there is a vast and peaceful paradise. It is waiting for you, should you decide to stay."

Ariana stood, leaving the cold stone slab behind. She wore the white uniform Sian hated, and it was unstained. There was no blood at all, and not even the smallest tear in her uniform, where Ciro's knife had cut into her. Even the embellishments she had foolishly sewn into the vest were intact. "What do you mean, if I decide to stay? I'm dead. How can there be such a choice?"

"You haven't been dead long," Duran assured her.

Ariana laughed sharply, and tears stung her eyes. "How long must one be dead in order for that death to be final?"

"Time is tricky, as your cousin Lyr can tell you. It moves at a different pace here than it does in your living world. Why, you've missed no more than one heartbeat while we've been chatting."

Chatting. With the dead. "What if I choose to return?"

Duran shrugged his shoulders. "Then you will live, for a time. We will be waiting for you to return to us when the time is right."

She studied the people who had moved away from her when she'd shown her fear. One woman had features much like her mother's. Another had Aunt Isadora's nose. They were ancestors. Fyne witches, like her. These were the women who had guided her and added to her strength when she'd searched for it in order to fight Diella. Why had she not reached for them more often?

Ah, because Diella had stopped her from doing just that. She'd been a fool to think she could control the demon.

"What happens if I stay here?"

Duran's smile faded. "I should not tell you . . ."

"How else am I to decide?"

"With your heart."

She closed her eyes and saw Sian leaning over her body. He was crying, a little, but he tried to hide his tears from the soldiers who ran to join them—too late. Ciro and Lilia . . . but it wasn't really Lilia, not anymore . . . made their escape, and all around them his remaining soldiers made haste to join them. This battle had not been about defeating her soldiers; it had never been about defeating her solders. That would come later, when Ciro and his army were both stronger. This battle had been about freeing Diella, about giving Diella the life she had craved for so long.

Beware Ciro's Own.

"I'm not ready to leave him," she said, her voice lowered. "We didn't have a chance to . . ." she sighed. "We didn't have a chance at all."

"Is love a proper reason to give up paradise?" her Uncle Duran asked.

"The best reason, I would think." She could not help but remember the prophesy. Had she done her part or was it still to come? "Will Ciro be defeated without me?"

Duran did not answer, but she saw the *no* in his eyes.

"What am I to do?" she asked sharply. How many more heartbeats had passed? How much longer did she have to make her decision? "I am no soldier. I proved that tonight."

"You fought well," Duran said halfheartedly. "But as you know, killing is not your gift. Healing is your gift. It is that healing which will be necessary for Ciro's defeat, should you decide to return and take up the fight once again."

"How?"

"I can't tell you that," Duran whispered. "It's time to choose."

The decision was easy. "I cannot choose paradise and leave all those I love to Ciro."

Duran nodded, and he did not seem surprised. Of course, he was a soldier, too, of a different sort. "Take care, Ariana. Next time you come to us, there will be no offered choice. Next time, you will stay." He directed her to lie down again, her back cold against the stone slab. He told her to close her eyes, and she did. Lying there, she felt the power of her ancestors washing over her. They infused her with strength. They fed her soul. She would not forget to draw from them when she needed strength, not ever again.

And then they were gone. She opened her eyes quickly, and found herself in yet another place. She was lost in a vast, blue nothingness, or so it seemed. A face swam close to hers. A desperate, pale face. Why did he look so familiar? Why did she feel as if she knew him? The creature which taunted her looked very much like a young Arik, which meant . . .

Sebestyen.

"Don't be afraid," he said. His image swam before her. "Listen carefully. I don't have much time. Ciro cannot be emperor."

"I know . . ."

"You must stop him. Given the chance, he will destroy everything. I swore I did not want this for them, but it's only right," he said desperately.

"You must explain," Ariana said. "I can't stay here for much longer." She felt that to her very soul. Here she was caught in between life and the Land of the Dead. Why?

Had Sebestyen somehow grabbed her and stopped her while she was on her way back to Sian? Time was precious. If she stayed too long, she might never escape.

"My sons," Sebestyen said. "They live."

Ariana experienced a deep chill. Perhaps Sebestyen did not see beyond this empty world in which he existed. "Your wife and son were murdered near the end of the revolution. There was no other son. Don't you remember—"

"Stupid girl," he said sharply. "Just like your mother, so naïve and trusting. Close your mouth and *listen*!"

She recoiled at the scolding from a long-dead and admittedly evil emperor.

"Liane gave me two sons. Twins. They live. If you do not believe me, ask your mother, or that irritating and meddlesome sister of hers. They know. They have always known the truth."

Ariana shook her head in confusion.

"I have watched them grow." His tone softened. "My sons have become good, honorable men, and they will fight for Columbyana if that's what is necessary. Either of them can be the emperor I never was. Either of them can rule with a dignity and decency I never possessed. I did not want this for them, but if fate has seen fit to lead them to you . . ." He grew dimmer. "Or you to them . . ."

Even though she knew she didn't have much time, Ariana was afraid Sebestyen would disappear before she learned more about the sons he claimed survived. "Where are they?"

"One is close, one is far. They will come to you or else you will find them."

"That's not helpful."

"It's all I have!" The air around her reverberated.

"Why are you still here?" Ariana asked as it seemed

that Sebestyen was about to disappear. "Why haven't you moved on?" To paradise or whatever hell awaited one such as this.

"I'm waiting," he said sadly.

"For what?"

"Liane," he whispered. "I am waiting for Liane. Maybe if I help you to defeat Ciro, I will be allowed to stay with her in this life. Do you think that is possible? Do you think by doing one last good deed I can . . . ?"

Ariana took a deep breath and her chest burned. Everything . . . everything burned! Sebestyen was gone. Duran and her ancestors were gone. She closed her eyes, thought of Sian, and reached for him.

And with a gasp of refreshing air, he was there.

WHILE SIAN STARED AT THE DARK PLACE WHERE HE had last seen Ciro, a hand gently touched his arm. He flinched, not wanting anyone's comfort at the moment. There was no comfort to be had, not anymore.

And then an exhalation of breath from the woman beneath him made him forget everything else. Even Ciro.

Ariana's face was still pale as death, but her eyes fluttered and opened. It was her hand on his arm, her comfort he had tried to ignore.

One sentinel, who also saw the dead woman open her eyes, said a quick and gruffly spoken prayer.

Another declared it a miracle.

One declared this unnatural resurrection the work of the devil they had been battling on this night.

The wounded sentinel Ciro had sent tumbling down the hill rose to his feet and said that the prince had offered the enchanter Chamblyn a place in his court. There was a hint of suspicion in his gruff voice, as if he himself had never entirely trusted Sian or his magic.

Sian would not take his gaze from Ariana's face, no matter what the men around him said, afraid that if he looked away, she would be dead again. She smiled at him. The effort was weak, but it was a smile.

Explanations flew from those soldiers around him. It was quickly decided that Ariana had not been dead at all; they had merely mistaken her for dead. The knife that had bitten into her had missed her heart, by some miracle.

Ariana remained silent. She did not try to sit or speak, but as Sian watched, life seemed to pour back into her. Her cheeks regained their color. Her breathing became deeper and more normal. Her heartbeat, which was oddly in rhythm with his own, became stronger. Steadier.

When she spoke, she asked, "How many of us are dead?"

"Six," Merin answered.

"Injured?"

"Fourteen have serious injuries. Most everyone has some small wound or two. Or ten."

Almost half were dead or seriously injured. Considering how badly they'd been outnumbered, that was not terrible news. Ariana, however, seemed to feel for every scratch. Of course she did. That was her power, after all. She felt.

When she attempted to sit up, Sian did his best to stop her. Perhaps Ariana had survived, but her wound was deep and serious.

She did not allow him to hinder her easily, and he could not bring himself to fight her too strongly. "I must see to the wounded. That's why I'm here, Sian. Not for killing. Not for leading. I am here to heal."

He placed his arm around her waist and walked beside her, lending his strength. His head hurt. His throat was raw and sore. And yet his wounds were nothing compared to those he saw around him.

Ariana stopped beside the first wounded sentinel she found lying on the grass. With Sian's help, she knelt beside him. The man was barely conscious, but he kept his eyes on Ariana.

"Do not bother with me, sister," he rasped. "I am beyond saving."

"Let me be the judge of that." His sentinel's vest was dark with blood. Wounds to the stomach were always the worst, it seemed, leading to prolonged suffering and certain death. Still, Ariana placed her hands on his stomach and closed her eyes. Sian felt the power draining from her, flowing through her hands into the wounded sentinel.

She had been a powerful healer before, but not like this. Never like this. He could actually see the energy she forced into the soldier. When she was done, Merin dropped to his knees and gently opened the sentinel's shirt. The wound which had soaked his shirt and vest with blood began to heal before their eyes.

Again, a frightened soldier began to pray.

Ariana glanced up at the men who surrounded her. "Don't be afraid of me," she said. "Please don't be afraid. You all know that I have magic, that I am, by birth, a witch."

"Yes," the praying man said. "But I have never seen the likes of that." He pointed to the healing gut of his comrade.

Ariana would not let their reticence stop her. She moved from one wounded sentinel to another, healing each one in the same fashion. In the dark of night, they sought out wounded sentinels. She could not save the dead, but those who were injured she healed with the touch of her hands and the power that had grown within her.

It was a mighty gift. The mightiest.

She was covered in her own blood, and the energy she expelled was great. And yet she did not falter. She did not hesitate or think of how she might be draining herself.

Dawn was upon them when she healed the last of the sentinels. None of the wounded were ready to do battle just yet, but even those who had been near death would be able to march on in a few days.

When the sentinels were healed or healing, Ariana's eyes were drawn to a wounded soldier who had fought for Ciro. He was a dirty, odorous, badly dressed red-haired man with an ordinary face and a kitchen knife clutched in one hand. Streaks of gray colored his wild hair and his beard, and his belly showed signs he'd been well fed.

As Ariana stopped beside the unconscious man, a sentinel snatched away the bloody knife.

Losing the weapon shocked the man to consciousness. "Give me that!" he commanded.

He had numerous wounds, and had lost a lot of blood. Ariana dropped to her haunches beside the enemy. "Do you see it?" she whispered.

"See what?" Sian asked, wishing he had the right to force her away from the enemy soldier who appeared to be harmless at the moment, but could be anything but harmless.

"This man has no soul," Ariana said, wonder in her voice. "No light at all. No dark, no white. Nothing. He is no better than a wild animal. I did not see it before when we were fighting, but now it's so clear to me."

Her trip to the Land of the Dead and back had infused

her with increased powers. She could heal in a miraculous way, and she could see that this creature had no soul. How else had she changed?

It was Merin who asked sharply, "You're not going to heal him, are you?"

"Don't," Sian said, adding his protest. He did not understand this new power Ariana had brought with her when she'd come back from the dead, but he did not want her energy to be mingled with that of a man who had no soul.

Ignoring him and Merin, Ariana laid her hands over the man's chest. She closed her eyes and concentrated until her entire body began to tremble. This was different from what had happened with the wounded sentinels. The soulless man's wounds did not begin to heal. There was no glow of health returned to his cheeks.

For a while it seemed that her efforts would not work on the soulless man, and then, both Ariana and the wounded enemy lurched.

Ariana dropped her hands and backed away quickly, ending up several feet away from the enemy soldier, sitting on her backside. Sian assisted her to her feet. The man on the ground looked confused, and then a light of understanding lit his dull eyes, "Oh," he whispered.

Merin stepped forward with his sword drawn. He brought it down swiftly and took the man's life.

Ariana did not protest. "Are there others of the enemy left alive?"

"Why?" Merin asked angrily. "Surely you would not gift them with this . . . this miracle."

Ariana smiled tiredly at her first in command. "Did you not feel it, Merin? Did you not feel the shift in this battle when his soul was returned to him?"

The sentinel stopped and stared at her. "No. How . . . what . . . ?"

"I'm not exactly sure how or what," Ariana admitted. "But I do know that when I returned that man's soul to him, dark and damaged thing that it was, the Isen Demon—Ciro himself—was weakened by the loss. Not considerably, mind you, but he was weakened. It's as if the Isen Demon is not a proper demon at all, but a chain of dark souls linked together. If I can snatch back other souls, if I can disrupt the chain . . ."

Merin needed no more explanation. "I will have the men search among the bodies to see if any others are left alive."

All night and into the morning, Ariana had shared her gift, and Sian had been beside her. Now that they were alone, she turned to him and smiled. "You will never believe what I saw," she whispered, and then she fainted into his arms. He caught her, lifted her, and carried her away from the carnage.

ARIANA WOKE TO FIND HERSELF AND SIAN IN A QUIET, secluded place. The place was heavily shaded, with thick bushes and trees on one side, and a tall rock wall on the other. She heard the trickle of a stream nearby, and the calm words of her adopted brothers in the near distance. She felt the cool wisp of a damp cloth on her body, and the rough rasp of a blanket at her back.

Sian was washing away the blood that had once soaked her uniform. Her blood. She did not open her eyes, not immediately. She lay there and reveled in the way he touched her. The way the damp cloth he wielded so gently cleaned her skin, the way he took such care around what was left of her healing wound. If she had ever doubted his love . . . all that doubt was now gone. She had never experienced such love as she now felt in his touch.

"You cannot fool me," he said roughly. "Open your eyes, woman."

Ariana smiled as she obeyed. *"Woman?"*

"You would prefer 'sister'?"

"Not from you," she admitted freely.

Sian bent over her, his long black hair loose and falling over his shoulders, hiding much of his face from her. She was completely naked, and a fire which was not necessary at midday burned nearby. She had but to glance in that direction to see that what remained of her white uniform burned there. Even her hat lay upon the ruins.

"Am I now to march into battle naked?" she asked lightly.

"You are not to march into battle at all," Sian said, his voice low and rough.

"Is that your decision to make?"

"Yes, I believe it is."

"How so?"

Sian pulled her into a seated position, so that her bare chest was resting against his black shirt, and her eyes were close to his. She saw purple flame there, as hot as the fire which consumed her white uniform. "You are mine to protect, and I will not allow you to risk your life so foolishly. You are a healer, Ariana, and that is the gift you must take to this blasted war."

"Yes, I know."

He sounded so angry, and yet the love was there. She took Sian's face in her hands and kissed him. Oh, she had missed kissing him. Her tongue teased his lightly, and then she caught his lower lip between her teeth. She pressed a hand against his chest and felt the steady thud of his heart.

His kiss turned hungry very quickly, and she felt his desperation and his love. She also felt his fear, not at anything Ciro could do to them, but at losing her again. At losing . . . more.

His hand caressed her back, stopping at her hip to hold her in place, to tease her curves. Curves he knew well.

All this time, he'd been so close and yet they'd remained separated. She wanted Sian to be her lover again. She wanted the pleasure and the closeness and that wonderful sense that she would never again be alone, because she carried a piece of him with her always. Surely he wanted that, too. After all, he had said he would watch over her, and she felt his love as surely as she felt her own.

She reached down to stroke him lightly. Yes, he was hard. Ready. He wanted her desperately. With great effort and regret, she took her mouth from his. "Did you bring the potion I gave you with you?"

"No." His voice near rumbled.

She sighed. Of course he had not. "Do we need it?"

Her entire body trembled for Sian. She wanted him inside her, she wanted the release, she wanted his body and hers joined, and yes, she wanted his child.

He rested his head on her shoulder. "I do not think I can bear to bury another child. Does that make me weak, Ariana? Does that make me a coward?"

"No, love," she whispered. "It does not."

"I do not wish to lose you either," he confessed. "Not again." He lifted his head and looked her in the eye. "You were truly dead, weren't you?"

"Yes."

"And yet you came back from that death. I did not know it was possible. How? More importantly, why?"

"I was given a choice. I came back for Ciro," she said, "and for my family." She stroked his hair gently. Should she tell him that she had also come back for him? For what they might have together? No, he wasn't ready to hear that, not now.

Sian had not asked for healing for himself, even though there was a large lump on his head and his throat was damaged and raw. Ariana placed one hand on his head, and drew out the pain. Beneath her palm, the knot eased and shrank. She laid her other hand over his throat when that was done. This injury pained him more than he had admitted, and she quickly eased that pain. She discovered a small cut on his forearm, and healed that as well.

Returning the dark soul to Ciro's soldier had drained her, but healing . . . no matter how horrible the wounds she treated were, healing them did not drain her energies at all. In a way they fed her, making her stronger. Making her capable of facing whatever lay ahead.

"She died giving birth," Sian said briskly. "My wife. She and the baby both died, and there was nothing I could do. The baby, a little girl, she came too soon and with many complications. All my training, all my worthless tricks . . . they could not even take away my wife's pain, much less give her or the child life. For more than a day I listened to her scream endlessly, helpless and frustrated and . . . terrified. And then the screams stopped, and that was worse."

Ariana wondered if knowing that there was a very real existence on the other side of this life would help Sian, but she suspected not. Not yet, in any case. Maybe one day.

"I once scoffed at your gift, but even when you were a

simple healer with nominal power and a bag filled with dried herbs, you possessed more magic than I will ever have."

"You're tired," she said, laying her head on his shoulder and closing her eyes. "And so am I. Can I sleep here, Sian? Will you hold me while I rest?"

She did not give him the opportunity to answer, but drifted to sleep while he held her naked body close.

HE HAD PROMISED THE DEPARTED EMPRESS A BODY TO call her own, if she would lead the woman who had the power to defeat him into his trap. Well, the Isen Demon had promised, and Ciro and the demon were now almost entirely one.

"I'm skinny," Diella complained as she felt her own breasts, squeezing and pinching herself.

"Eat," Ciro directed hoarsely. "You'll be fat soon enough."

"And my face is damaged." Her fingers traced the shallow cut he'd made with his teeth.

"It will heal in time."

"Could you not have chosen a more suitable body?" she complained.

Ciro did not possess an abundance of patience. "The body you now occupy is young and healthy, and it's yours. You have no need to share it with anyone. Isn't that what you wanted?"

Diella sat in the hard chair which dominated this dismal cabin they had taken. What remained of his army— little more than sixty men—waited outside, in the night. They did not deserve shelter, animals that they were.

The previous occupants of this small dwelling had

been disposed of on arrival and dumped behind the cabin they had called home. Ciro was still disappointed that there had been only two residents here, and they were both elderly. Neither did him any good at all, especially as they had both possessed white souls. Up here, in the middle of nowhere, two white souls which he could not yet take. He had drunk their blood greedily, but he craved yet another soul.

Something was wrong. He felt weakened. Almost . . . bereft. The reason for the weakness teased him, dancing just out of reach.

Diella left her chair and ran to him, crossing the short distance quickly and throwing herself at him. Instinctively, he caught her.

"I'm bored," she said lazily. She had riffled through the old woman's things in this simple home and had donned a plain, gray dress that was much too big for the body he had taken for her. The frock had been declared inadequate, but preferable to the sentinel's uniform she had been wearing when he'd found her. "And I have been sorely neglected in my years without a body. This body of yours seems fit enough." She ground herself against him. "How about a tumble?"

His body responded, but he set her away from him. "I cannot. My seed is for another."

She made a face of disenchantment and disappointment. "Don't be silly. Every man thinks his get is extraordinary, but one man's spurt is really no different than another's."

"In that case, you can find a willing companion outside." He gestured to the door.

She wrinkled her nose. "Your soldiers are not exactly the most handsome fellows in all of Columbyana, or the cleanest. Several of them have a tendency to drool. It's quite unseemly."

"I thought one man was like another," he said calmly, throwing her words back to her.

"But you're so pretty." She pouted, but Ciro stood firm. He was saving himself for Rayne. Once he was inside her, their son would be made. His fine, extraordinary son.

Our son.

Finally Diella sighed and turned away from him. "How about a touch of Panwyr? You do have some with you, don't you? Oh, I'll bet this body has never experienced the rush of that first Panwyr experience. It will be like starting the journey all over again. What fun! After my first dose, I imagine those dirty soldiers outside will look almost as pretty to my eyes as you do."

Ciro grudgingly shared his Panwyr with Diella, wishing he could just kill her and have done with it. The demon wouldn't let him. Apparently they still needed the former empress; she had not yet served her purpose.

Diella took a small amount of the Panwyr up her nose, sniffing it in an almost ladylike manner. Shortly thereafter, she began to dance. Hands that had recently explored her breasts and found them lacking explored once again as she danced. She caressed herself, fondling her own breasts and the crevice between her legs, readying herself for a sexual liaison with some unknown soldier—one of his Own—who would gladly give her what she wanted.

Ciro sat back and watched. Once, he even smiled. The body Diella possessed was pretty enough, and when she was properly dressed in expensive gowns that fit well, she'd be presentable. When the time came, if he didn't kill her first, she'd make a fine second empress and stepmother to his remarkable son.

He suspected they would remain in this cabin for several days. It was not as luxurious as the homes he was accustomed to—the Imperial Palace in Arthes or Fynnian's isolated home—but it would do. Here his soldiers could heal, and when Diella had finished having her fun, she could tell him more about the prophesy and the plans the woman Ariana had set into motion before he'd killed her.

His army was much smaller than it had been, but Ciro was not concerned. There were more of his Own out there, and they were coming. They were drawn to him, and for a few days, perhaps a week or two, he would wait here. When he closed his eyes, he could see them, making their way down dusty roads and through dense forests, each armed, each hungry—each connected to him, and to one another.

He missed knowing what those who wished to defeat him knew and planned, and in a way he wished he had made Diella wait for her body. She was not very good at waiting, and for some reason the Isen Demon indulged her.

He smiled as he heard Diella's frenzied laugh drift to him from outside his temporary home. Soon he would be so strong, the plans of his enemy would be insignificant.

16

ARIANA'S ARMY SLEPT AND HEALED. THEY CELEBRATED their victories and mourned their dead. Those who had passed into the Land of the Dead were buried. Their friends and comrades were buried with honor and emotion; the enemy dead were put into the ground out of necessity.

While Ariana rested . . . and Sian burned her clothes . . . two more enemy soldiers were found barely alive. As she had done with the first living enemy she'd recovered, she returned their souls, snatching them away from the Isen Demon with great effort. Each time, she experienced the same sense that she'd weakened the monster Ciro had become. Not significantly, but to some small degree. As he had done with the first of the soulless men, Merin dispatched the enemy once their souls were restored. This part of war was distasteful to Ariana, as a healer and as a woman, but she realized that it was necessary. The dark souls could be called back to the demon if the men were allowed to live, and she could not allow that to happen.

One day passed, and then two. The sentinels began to grow restless. They were waiting for her to direct them, Ariana knew. They were waiting for her to lead, as she had been chosen to do.

She knew without doubt that Sian loved her, and yet he denied his love so staunchly by his actions that she was confused and hurt, in a girlish way she could not afford to indulge. Since that morning when he'd bathed her and told her about his wife and child's deaths, he'd barely spoken to her. He didn't even look at her, and if he could manage to pass his time in the farthest part of the camp from where she found herself, he did so. He had all but cast her aside. Her broken heart meant nothing at a time like this, and yet . . . it was broken.

It seemed that everyone was treating her differently since she'd come back from the dead. She still felt a bond with the men who'd survived, but they remained distant and sometimes suspicious. Maybe they sensed that Diella, who was by far the stronger of the two of them, was gone, and she was now unfit to lead. Maybe they were frightened by her return from the dead. Some said she had only been stunned and had not been truly deceased, but those who had seen her die knew differently.

As she had been since the day following the battle, Ariana was clothed in the sentinel uniform that Sian had stolen before slipping from the palace and joining her assemblage, trying to blend in when he should've known that he was the type of man who would never be able to accomplish that task. There were a few farmhouses between here and the road which would lead her to Keelia, as well as a small village—if it remained untouched by Ciro and his army. She could probably find a dress of some sort there, and buy or borrow it. She certainly did not have time to sew herself another suitable outfit which included the trousers Sian insisted were better for her current task. Perhaps she could purchase a boy's trousers and shirt, as those of a fully grown man would fit no better than what she now wore.

She had become accustomed to the trousers and the loose shirt which allowed her freedom of movement, and the journey to come would be an arduous one. Sian's discarded uniform was worn and did not fit, but her vanity would have to be put aside in the name of practicality for a while longer.

It was time to move on. The men were miraculously healed, and Ciro had certainly not stalled in his quest. This war was not over. It had just begun.

Ariana called the soldiers together soon after a breakfast of hard bread and dried meat. Selfishly, she thought of the meals Keelia would serve in her palace when she reached The City. *If* she reached The City. Maybe once she was there, she'd have a night or two to sleep in a real bed, and take at least one long, hot bath. The small comforts she had once taken for granted now seemed like the greatest of luxuries.

Ariana hesitated as she looked at the suspicious and curious and awed faces around her. Without Diella, could she lead? Could she accomplish even this?

She stepped upon a fallen tree trunk, which had been taken down in a recent storm. The extra height she gained wasn't significant, but it did raise her up so that she could look across to the faces of her soldiers instead of looking up. "The first battle in this war to come . . . this war which has already come . . . is done," she began, "and while we did not kill Ciro, we accomplished much. We killed many

of his soulless soldiers." She swallowed. Her heart swelled.
Heavens above, she would not hide who or what she was
from these men who called themselves brothers. "We hurt
the demon himself by taking back a few of those souls.
We weakened him," she added in a softer voice.

From the back of the group, a leery voice offered,
"And you came back from the dead."

Ariana did not know who said the words, but the time
for denying what had happened was long gone. "Yes, I
did." She paced before them, studying the expressions of
the men. "I visited the Land of the Dead, and saw my ancestors waiting for me." She had told no one about the
words she'd shared with Emperor Sebestyen, and now
was not the time. What panic there would be if it was
known that Emperor Sebestyen had left behind not one
heir, but two. And was the information truthful? Or a departed spirit's mischievous trick? She wasn't sure exactly how to approach the knowledge he had given her.
Keelia would know what to do. Maybe she could even
discern where the heirs could be found, if they were indeed real.

She planted her feet solidly and securely on the tree
trunk. The uniform she wore was misshapen and too large,
with a rough length of rope serving as a belt and the hem
of both the shirt sleeves and the pants' legs rolled up. Her
hair had not seen a proper combing in so long she could
not remember when she'd enjoyed the luxury, and her always curling locks had become entirely unmanageable.
Instead of pretty slippers on her feet, she wore muddy
boots that might never be completely cleaned of dried
blood. Thank the heavens Sian had not burned that necessary part of her uniform.

What sort of picture did she present to these men? Did

they still think her a sister, or did they see her now as simply mad?

"I came back from the dead because this war isn't over and I have a part to play. You *all* have a part to play, each and every one of you. We are destined for this fight, and you have proven yourselves worthy of being called."

"As have you, sister," someone called. She thought it might be Merin, but she wasn't sure. A few soldiers added their agreement to the statement.

Ariana smiled wanly. "Thank you," she said softly. "I am not so sure that I am worthy, but I plan to do my best."

"Where do we go from here?" Merin asked.

This is where things could get tricky. What if she was wrong? What if the decisions she made led them all to their graves? Or worse. She had planned to take this army all the way to Keelia's City, where they would join with the Anwyn army. But Diella knew all the plans Ariana had made, so was it safe? Would Ciro and his army be waiting for them along the trail?

"The time has come for us to part company."

A few of the sentinels protested, but most remained silent and heedful.

"There are not enough of us to fight Ciro's army. We need more men. In addition, all the villages along the mountainside and on the path to Arthes must be warned. They *must not* be taken by surprise, as Lilia's village was. They need to arm themselves, form organized militias, and keep a constant watch for invaders. Lilia's village didn't have the opportunity to fight back. That can't happen anywhere else." She caught and held Merin's eyes. "Arik must be warned. He cannot under any circumstance allow Ciro access to the palace, or to himself." She had begun this meeting with trepidation, but she was filled

with the knowledge that this was right. They could stop
the man who had once been nothing more than an inef-
fectual prince and was now vessel to a demon. "Explain
to him that the thing wearing Ciro's face is *not* his son,
and hasn't been for a long time." According to Sian, the
emperor had already been told that Ciro was beyond saving, but Ariana wasn't sure that single warning was good
enough. What man could look into his son's face and see
the monster instead of the child?

"What of the journey to the Anwyn Queen?" Merin
asked.

"I will continue on alone," she said. The soft curse she
heard was most definitely Sian's. He stood to the side and
behind her, where she could hear but could not see him.
"An army is hard to hide," she explained, "but one
woman can slip past anyone if she's cautious."

Sian's sigh of disgust was unmistakable.

"I would love to be beside each and every one of you
when you fight again, but I am just one woman, and I can
only pray that I will be guided to those I need to heal
when the time comes. I love you all. You have become my
brothers, and I wish you the blessed guidance of your ancestors and an abundance of good fortune.

"We will meet here, at the site of our first victory, two
full moons from today." That would give them about six
weeks to accomplish their goals, if she was correct in her
figures.

The murmurings from the sentinels seemed less cautious than they had been before she'd begun to speak, and
more than one of them wished her good fortune as well.

She wasn't finished. "While this army is separated,
while you speak to others of the war we can no longer
hide, remember this . . . and share this bit of truth with all

those you meet. We cannot fear so fiercely what might come that we forget to enjoy the beauty of life. This war goes beyond one soldier meeting another, it goes well beyond sword to sword. This is a war of souls, brothers. It reaches every man and woman who treads upon this earth, no matter where they might be. With every scream of terror, Ciro wins another battle. Every time a good person hides, every time hope is lost, every time a soul shrinks and surrenders, Ciro wins. We must fight, yes, but we must also love, and laugh, and trust. Most of all, we must hope, and we must share that hope with all those we meet."

That statement was met with a round of war cries. It was a good enough place to end the speech. She'd said what she came here to say.

As the men turned to Merin for their assignments, Ariana caught the eye of one of the younger sentinels, and nodded her head crisply. Taran looked as if he was not much older than twenty years, but he fought well, and she liked him. His long hair was almost as fair as hers but was much more manageable, and he had pale blue eyes.

Taran saw her signal and all but ran to her, and Ariana smiled at him as she hopped from her perch. He blushed prettily. "I have a special assignment for you," she said.

He bowed in a courtly manner, sweepingly and with a manly elegance, as if she were a palace lady in a fine gown, not a grubby witch who had not seen a proper bath in much too long.

"Such formalities are not necessary," she said gently, offering him her hand. He took her hand and held on easily, as if he were afraid she would break. She led him away from the others. Sian made as if to follow, but Ariana shooed him back with her free hand. If he was going to all but ignore her, as he had in the past couple of days, she would not allow him to inject himself where he was not wanted. Indignant eyebrows arched, but Sian did cease following her and Taran. Her shooing did nothing to ease his glare.

"Your assignment is a very special one," Ariana said in a lowered voice. "It requires a most ardent discretion."

"Of course, sister," Taran said, a touch of excitement in his voice.

"Are you familiar with the Southern Province?" From his accent, she had deduced that he hailed from there, as she had.

"Yes." His eyes lit up. "I come from a small town near the coast."

"Are you familiar with Shandley?"

He shrugged his shoulders. "I know where it is, but I have never visited."

Good enough. "North of Shandley there sits a small mountain. It is not like these mountains before us, but is a very large, green hill. It is called Fyne Mountain."

Taran simply nodded.

"I want you to find my mother on that mountain. There is only one house, and it is my family home."

"You wish me to warn your family," Taran said, believing he understood his mission.

Ariana sighed. "No. Well, yes, since you will be there, you should tell them what's happened, but that is not the purpose of this task." She suspected danger to the Southern Province would not come for some time in any case, and if Ciro could be defeated, violence might not reach Shandley at all. Was he able to reach that far for his Own? She hoped not, but in truth she still knew next to nothing about the Isen Demon. She did know it was those who had the misfortune to lie between the Anwyn mountains and Arthes who would be the first in the path of danger.

Taran waited impatiently, and finally asked, "What is my task?"

Ariana steeled her spine. "Do you have a good memory, Taran?"

"Yes, sister."

"Good. This message is for my mother, and my mother alone. Repeat after me." Ariana took a deep breath. The question had to be worded just so, so that if Sebestyen's claim was true, Sophie Fyne would know what her eldest daughter asked, and why, but no one else would. "Ariana inquires as to the location of her father's sister and that sister's two children. It is of the greatest importance that she locates her . . ." The words caught in her throat, but she forced herself to continue. "Her cousins. There is a task ahead that only they can accomplish. A task they were born to."

Taran blinked. "That's it?"

"Yes. Repeat it, if you please."

He did so, very neatly.

"Again," Ariana ordered.

Without so much as a pause, Taran repeated the message. After he had done so four times, Ariana was satisfied.

"When you get your answer, do not write it down. Memorize it as you have memorized this inquiry, and when we meet here, you will give me and only me the answer."

"I don't understand," Taran said. "This is a family matter. Would I not be better utilized in informing the nearby villages of the dangers to come or in protecting the emperor?"

Ariana laid her hands on Taran's arms. "You do not see the import now, but trust me, brother, this is no family matter."

A light shone in his eyes. "It's a secret code, isn't it?" he whispered.

Ariana sighed and dropped her hands. "Near enough, brother. Near enough."

SIAN PACKED HIS FEW BELONGINGS IN HIS SADDLE BAG, as the sentinels did the same. They were energized, and no longer afraid of their *sister* who had come back from the dead. They smiled and joked, and they wished one another well if their assignments took them in different directions. One would think they were riding off to a tea party instead of rushing into what would be certain death for some of them.

Perhaps Ariana was right and Ciro could be defeated, but that victory would not come without a high price. That price would surely include the lives of some of these soldiers . . . or all of them.

Ariana readied her horse, as the sentinels did. Sian muttered vile words beneath his breath. If she thought she was going to travel alone, without *him*, she was sorely mistaken. He understood why she had chosen to do so, and the tasks she had given her men were necessary ones. But still, to travel alone was not only unnecessary, it was foolish.

He had been avoiding her for two days, since she'd slept naked in his arms. Since she'd told him that she loved him and hinted very broadly that if their liaison led to a child, it would not be a disaster. Two days since he'd stroked his hands down her naked back and kissed her. If there was a medal for restraint, he had certainly earned one.

As he stalked toward her, he could not help but wonder if her words this morning had been directed at him. Did she believe that he gave Ciro's darkness a hold when he abandoned hope? Did she think he fed the demon when he refused to take the chance that he might lose the woman he loved again?

When he was close enough for her to hear, he said, "I'm going with you."

She did not seem surprised. "If you'd like. I thought you might want to return to Arthes with Merin and his men, or take up residence in a nearby village to assist in making preparations for fighting Ciro's men, or . . . or go home." She continued to ready her horse, and did not so much as look at him. "Isn't that what you always said you'd do when I marched off to fight? Go home and wait it out?"

"You're a maddening woman," he said in a low voice.

"Me?" She spun and glared at him, completely unaware that her transformation made her even more beautiful than she'd been when she had the attentions of palace seamstresses and personal maids. He loved her hair down this way, wild and free. Even the too-large uniform was fetching on her body, and the flush on her cheeks and the fire of determination in her eyes made his heart clench. "You love me when you think I'm dead, but when love means dealing with a live, flesh-and-blood woman, you turn tail and run. *That's* maddening."

"I did not turn tail and run," he insisted calmly. "I'm right here."

The flush of her cheeks deepened. "You didn't run from Ciro or duty or the unpleasantness to come, but from me, Sian. From *me*."

He had explained his reasoning to her as best he could, and did not wish to discuss it again.

"I told you, I feel it is my duty to protect you."

Her face became impassive. "I release you from that obligation."

His jaw clenched. "I do not release *you*."

Even without his impossible feelings for this maddening woman, turning away from her now was impossible. There were still portions of the prophesy to be deciphered, and if he was able to discover something new, Ariana would need to know immediately. He doubted that there was anything he could teach her, magically speaking, since she had returned from the dead with heightened senses and healing abilities. Still, his strengths were different from hers. She might have need of his parlor tricks, as she called them, before she reached the Anwyn Queen.

He also wanted to speak about another matter, once they were well away from the sentinels. Most of the men seemed to have forgotten that Ciro had invited Sian to join his court. Why? Had it been a taunt or a serious offer? He did not want to consider the possibility that his soul was so badly damaged that he was fit to become one of Ciro's Own.

Those were the things that mattered. The war. The prophesy. The possibility that he might end up on the wrong side of this conflict. He could not conceive of joining forces with something so evil as the Isen Demon, but he imagined the sad and soulless man who'd died longing for a bloody kitchen knife had never thought of himself as a fiend either.

No, he would not stand by and allow innocents to be harmed, as those in Lilia's village had been, much less join in the violence. He would not allow anyone or anything to harm Ariana either. He was as much a soldier as any sentinel in this camp, but his strengths were different from theirs.

With all that on his mind, with the world on the brink

of taking a dark turn, what did love matter? What difference did his feelings or hers make? What Ariana wanted, what he wanted, didn't matter at all.

"I'll escort you to your cousin, the queen," he said, turning away from Ariana. "Once you're there and she has been informed of the prophesy and her part in it, her soldiers can escort you back to this place and your men, if there are any of them left by the rise of the second full moon."

"Don't say that," she whispered. "Don't stand there and tell me that everything I'm working for is going to come to nothing."

"I didn't say that."

"Didn't you?"

Sian took a deep, stilling breath. "No. If we face them before Ciro grows too strong, I believe his army can be defeated. Those we fought were merely human, after all. Soulless, violent men and women who can die, just as your soldiers and the people of Lilia's village can and did die. Anwyn soldiers will be a great asset, as will your cousin Lyr's Circle of Bacwyr. The war can be won, but it won't be bloodless. You musn't forget that, Ariana."

"Believe me, I can't forget."

"So I'm coming with you, whether you like it or not. I will protect you as best I can, until this part of your journey is done."

"What then?"

He hesitated. In truth, he didn't know *what then*. At the moment, he could not bear to look beyond today.

17

THERE HAD NOT BEEN A TRAIL INTO THESE MOUNTAINS which was fit for horses when her Aunt Juliet had first been taken there by the man who'd declared himself her husband. No, the trail had come later, when Queen Juliet's sisters had insisted on visiting, and their husbands had objected to making the entire hike on foot. It had taken years and the efforts of men and Anwyn alike to fashion this steep but passable road, and even that would only take them partway. They would finish their journey on foot, as did all who visited The City.

Ariana had been on this road many times, but never like this. Never with the fate of the world in her hands.

Diella knew where she was heading, and there was no other way to get to The City but this road. She had decided to bypass the village, but would that make any difference? Would Ciro and his men be waiting around the next curve? Would they jump down from hiding places high above?

Three days of travel, and so far all was well.

In one sense all was well. The trip had been uneventful and the weather had been pleasant—if cooler than it would be in Arthes at this time of year. Beyond that, all was not well. Not at all.

Ariana felt Sian behind her, even though she did not turn to look at him. What was she going to do? It wasn't the war that concerned her, nor was it Keelia and Lyr and their part in the prophesy. She worried about Ciro and his soldiers, but they were not constantly on her mind. She didn't even spend much time wondering if Sebestyen really had sons, and if they could be found.

Instead a much more personal matter occupied her mind. What was she going to do about Sian?

If the situation were different, perhaps she could seduce him. It wasn't as if he didn't want her in a physical sense. It wasn't even as if he didn't *love* her. If she were able to don an alluring gown and douse her skin in fragrant cream, he would not be able to resist her. Instead she was grubby and unkempt and dressed like a man. Her elbows and hands were rough, her feet ached, and her fair skin had suffered from the kiss of too much sun. It would be difficult to seduce even the most desperate of men in her present state.

Besides, the problem she needed to conquer was his fear, a fear of loss which had grown over the years since he'd buried his wife and child. If she could concoct a potion to keep them from creating a child, and if she could promise him that what they had was temporary and would soon end, perhaps he would not care that she looked like a battered and scrawny sentinel.

Little grew here, in this portion of the Mountains of the North, so she could not possibly gather the ingredients to make any sort of contraceptive potion. She certainly wouldn't lie to him and tell him that she considered what they had found in their hearts temporary.

So here they were, at an impossible impasse. What a fool she had been to think that love, when it came, would be enough to smooth all rough roads in her path.

They stopped for the night well before sunset. The horses were tired. They only had enough feed for one more day, but by tomorrow afternoon they would arrive at the way station where they would leave their horses while they continued on foot. The way station was also new, a necessity since there were now more visitors to The City.

Ariana remembered passing a night, with her mother and father and a few siblings, in this same spot many years ago. There was a small stream nearby, with cool, drinkable water. The rocky stream wasn't deep enough for bathing, and the water was too cold in any case, but she could wash the dirt from her face, at least. A shallow cave would provide shelter from the winds, should they rise in the night as they sometimes did here.

When she'd seen to her horse and washed her face—a true delight—Ariana laid out her bedroll so that she was situated in the mouth of the cave. The sunset was magnificent, and she watched it closely, and with wonder. So many things she'd taken for granted now had incalculable meaning, because she could not guarantee that she would be able to enjoy them tomorrow.

Sian settled down close by, but not too close, and spread before him the prophesy which was always close at hand, stretching the paper over the rocky ground. He studied the words as if he expected to see something new, as if he had not already memorized each word.

Ariana very quickly leapt up from her seat on the

ground, and crossed the short distance that separated her from the enchanter. He surely heard her footsteps, but as usual he ignored her. He could not very well ignore her when she pressed the dirty toe of one boot in the middle of the paper he studied.

Slowly, he lifted his head. Purple eyes, caught in the light of the setting sun, glared at her. "Yes?"

"Tell me that you love me," she insisted.

Sian's eyebrows lifted slightly, and he remained silent.

"I know you do, I can feel it, and you know I can feel it, so why do you insist on hiding your feelings?"

"Perhaps you are mistaken," he offered casually.

"I am not," she said in a lowered voice. Her toe remained in place. "I don't know if I will live for another day, or another year, or another hundred years. I do know that there is no time to waste, no matter what the case might be. No time, Sian. I love you and I don't mind saying so, even though I am basically tossing my heart out to be stomped on by a man who insists on pretending he doesn't care when I know to the pit of my soul that he does." Her voice grew more and more indignant as she delivered this speech.

Something new sparked in Sian's eyes. Something dangerous. "Speaking of souls, what do you think the state of mine might be, since Ciro so blithely invited me to join his court? How can you fight so valiantly for light, and still claim to love one whose soul is obviously dark?"

"Not dark," she whispered. "Damaged, perhaps, but not dark."

He did not seem soothed by the distinction, and returned his attention to the words her boot did not obscure.

Ariana loosed some of her anger and sighed as she

lowered herself to sit before Sian. She sat on top of the prophesy. Let him try to read it now.

A stone wall was at his back, and she sat very close. Unless he was willing to push her aside, he could not rise and walk away. She placed her hand over his heart, and he tensed. "Bitterness and regret make your soul gray. That doesn't mean you're not a good man, that doesn't mean you're fit in any way for Ciro's *court*. If he could, he would no doubt feed your bitterness, but it's not necessary. You do that quite well yourself."

"Ariana . . ."

"Let me finish, please." Her fingers rocked over his heart. "I never thought that I would love any man the way I love you, and even though that love has brought me aggravation and heartbreak and moments of anger so brilliant they blinded me, I'm not sorry that I love you. I have come to believe that love is the greatest power any of us will ever know. I think it will be the power that defeats Ciro in the end, if we don't allow him to take it away from us by filling all of us with fear, the way you have filled yourself with fear.

"I now have an incredible power for healing, Sian. You saw what I could do to the sentinels who had been wounded in battle. I've been wondering if it's possible that I can heal Arik, now that my powers have increased. I think maybe I can, and I pray he will live long enough for me to try. But when it comes to the soul, I can't help you. You have to heal yourself, and that healing can only come through love. You have to know that our day or week or hundred years together will be worth whatever pain love brings you. You have to believe with your heart and soul that our love is worth the risk that comes with it."

Ariana was tempted to lean in and kiss him, but she

didn't. She'd pushed hard enough, and the next step was up to him. Instead of kissing him, as she wanted to do, she stood and backed away from Sian and the prophesy his grandfather had written.

A MAGICAL FIRE LIT THEIR CAMP AND PRODUCED A small amount of warmth. The fire was more illusion than reality, but it served its purpose. It gave Sian something besides Ariana to stare at as he paced.

She pretended to sleep, but of course she did not. He was too tense even to pretend at this point. Besides, someone had to keep an eye on her. Ciro's men might be close by.

He didn't think so. He didn't feel the same tension that had come to him on the night they'd been ambushed, but in truth that meant nothing.

So he paced, and mumbled beneath his breath, and played out a thousand scenarios, past and future, in his head.

When he'd buried Jynna and their child, he hadn't thought it would be possible ever to love again. He'd closed his heart, he'd dedicated himself to the study of magic, he'd separated himself as much as possible from other people, and wallowed in the bitterness Ariana saw so well.

What Ariana felt from him was real. He did love her. He didn't want to, he didn't like it, and the timing was horrendous. But he *did* love her.

She feigned sleep just inside the shallow cave, her head turned away from him. The next move, if there was to be one, was his. In truth, his decision was simple. Did he continue to fall headlong into this uncertain world with Ariana or without her? Did he allow her to fall with or without him?

Sian turned his back on the fire and stalked to her, and when he was close, he dropped down to his haunches. The woman he loved deserved better than a rough bedroll and a chilly cave, so he gave it to her, in his own way. He waved his hand and a hint of wizard's light touched the cave. Her bedroll seemed to shift into a soft mattress covered in the finest sheets. The scent of fine oils filled the night. As long as he maintained his focus, this is what she would see and feel. Luxury. Comfort. A small portion of what she ought to have.

Ariana rolled over and smiled at him. "All the nights I slept on the hard ground, and you can do this?"

"For a while."

"It takes a lot of power, doesn't it?"

"Doesn't matter." He lay down beside her so they were on their sides, face to face and chest to chest.

Ariana glanced down at her own uniform-clad body. She touched a strand of wildly curling hair. "The least you could do is make me beautiful for you."

He tucked his finger beneath her chin and made her look him in the eye. "You are beautiful. Always, but never more so than right now." He kissed her, as he had longed to for days. He allowed complete surrender to wash over and through him. He could guarantee nothing. Not her safety, not his . . . not that of a child they might make, tonight or tomorrow or on some day far in the future. He could not promise that any of them would see tomorrow.

But they would see it together, no matter what might come.

He removed Ariana's sentinel's vest, and then unbuttoned her emerald green shirt. When it opened as far as it would go, which was midway down her torso, he lowered his head and kissed the soft skin that was revealed. Between her breasts, the pale globes, the rosy and pebbled nipples . . . he kissed them all.

Most of all, he kissed the place beneath her breasts, where Ciro's knife had pierced her skin. There was not so much as a mark to mar the perfection of her flesh, not a bruise or a scratch. It was a miracle. He held a miracle in his hands, and miracles should not be thrown away in the name of fear.

"I love you," he said as he moved his mouth to her throat. His lips brushed against the leather cord that bound them together in so many ways. "I tried not to. I tried very hard."

"I know," Ariana whispered as she clutched at his hair.

"I thought it would be best if I didn't. Couldn't. Wouldn't."

"Silly man," she responded dreamily.

He sat up, raised Ariana gently, and pulled the annoyingly inconvenient shirt over her head. Blond curls tumbled everywhere. Down her back, over her shoulder, even across one cheek. He was so distracted just by the sight of her that his wizard's light flickered, and for a moment she sat upon a scratchy bedroll meant for a battle-toughened sentinel. He regained his focus and once again there was a soft mattress beneath her.

She smiled, casting him a knowing glance and reaching out to unfasten a few of his buttons with slender fingers.

Sian suffered a momentary lapse. "A child at this time—"

"Is not a certainty," she interrupted. "Besides, my mother's magic was always stronger when she was carrying a child. Perhaps I inherited that trait from her."

"You are not yet safe."

"Who is safe, love? Who is really and truly safe?"

"No one."

She pulled his shirt over his head, as he had hers, and tossed it away without taking her eyes from his. "No one," she repeated. "Why, my mother carried Duran during the final months of the revolution. She marched with Arik and his rebels, and my father, of course. She never spoke of fighting, but she was there, with child, and somehow all was well."

He would keep an army between her and Ciro, if need be. Child or no child, he would protect Ariana.

SIAN UNDRESSED HER, AND SHE UNDRESSED HIM. THEY kissed and touched, like lovers who had been apart too long. His enchantment touched her, making her feel as if they were separated from reality, as if this place existed just for them and they were, for a while, completely sheltered from what had passed and what was yet to come.

All either of them wore were the bits of leather cord around their necks. Three strands, which had never been removed. Three strands, which bound them to one another at a soul-deep level.

Ariana knew the softness beneath her back wasn't real, but she enjoyed it for a time. She realized the scent of fine oils was not real, but it was nice all the same. As for the wizard's light and the enchanted fire—she loved them because they allowed her to see the man she loved as he lavished attention upon her.

"We will be married when we reach The City," he said as he kissed the soft and sensitive skin of her belly.

Ariana laughed lightly, and she shuddered deep. "If you wish it."

"I do." He lifted his head and glared at her. "Don't you?"

Conventions didn't seem very important at the moment. "Words spoken before others mean nothing to me. They're an insignificant formality. You're my husband. I claim you the way the Anywn choose their mates, and declare that it is so."

Sian continued to kiss her. He breathed deeply and raked the palm of one hand across her hip. "We are not Anwyn."

"No, but it seems a logical way to do things," she gasped when he suckled a nipple deep. Her trembling fingers wound through his hair, and her thighs parted. She wanted him now . . . she had wanted him since the moment he'd changed the direction of his steady pacing and come to her. "Besides, these leather chokers bind us more surely than any words spoken before a priest, do they not?"

His answer was a gentle moan.

Gradually, Sian's enchantment faded. The fire went out with a gentle pop. The sweet scent that had filled the cave diminished, leaving only a memory. The softness beneath her was replaced by the roughness of a blanket and the hardness of stone.

Everything of Sian was with her now. With them. He had no energy or concentration left for his magic.

He rolled over onto his back, dragging her with him. Ariana straddled his body, and he was right there, hard and throbbing. A shift and he would be inside her, but even though she was anxious, she was in no hurry. This was a night to be savored, not rushed. Like the sunset, she didn't know if the like would come again.

In the name of savoring, Ariana stroked Sian's length with her hand while she leaned down to kiss his neck and his chest. Her lips trailed across the throbbing vein in his throat and her tongue flickered there, tasting flesh and leather. The smell of his skin was more erotic than the magical scents which had filled the cave before she'd stolen his ability to create them. The taste of him was more luxurious than any mattress or fine sheet. The sensation of his hand on her body was more beautiful than anything she had ever thought to experience.

So many times she had looked into his eyes and felt as if she could fall into them. That was how she felt now . . . as if she was literally falling into Sian in ways she had not known possible. She closed her fingers around him and teased with a long stroke, softly and then harder, and then softly again, until he groaned and thrust up into her hand.

This was her enchanter out of control. At this moment he was hers, and hers alone.

Sian guided himself into her, and the sensation of him filling her trembling body took her breath away. The cave was dark, without the wizard's light, but she could feel so well. She could feel everything. She rose and fell, guiding him into her body and then rising up and away. Again. Again. His hands rested on her hips, and he guided her. Faster. Deeper. Everything disappeared but the way she felt for this man. Love, lust, friendship, need . . . joy. No matter what happened outside the walls of the cave, they all existed for her and for him.

She cried out as release washed through her, fracturing and fluttering through her body. Sian came with her, his body stiffening and shuddering beneath hers, the seed he was afraid to spill filling her waiting body.

Everything slowed, and she dropped down to lay her head on Sian's shoulder. Heavens, she could not breathe. Not yet.

Moments passed before she saw the purple tinge of wizard's light surround her. Later, still before a word had been spoken, the fire outside leapt to life again.

Almost lazily, Sian rolled her onto her side, and she realized that once again the softness of enchantment cushioned her. He brushed a strand of hair from her cheek. "I love you, Ariana. I have loved you for a long while."

"I love you, too, with all I have to give." She draped one naked leg across his and held him that way, as well as with her arms. "We are in the mountains of the Anwyn. Can I not simply call you husband now? Can I not claim you as they claim one another? I do not feel the need for the words of others. We are wed, in all ways that matter." She touched the leather at his throat.

"You may call me whatever you'd like. We're still getting properly married when the opportunity arises."

"If you insist," she teased.

"I do."

At that moment, Ariana saw something in the man she now called husband that she had almost given up on.

Hope.

SIAN HATED LEAVING THE HORSES AT THE WAY STATION with the young Anwyn male who looked a bit taller than he but was surely no more than thirteen years old. He'd heard that the Anwyn males were tall, but he was still taken aback. Not only was the boy large and possessed of Anwyn golden eyes, but he would turn into a wolf on the three nights when the moon was full.

He was sure the boy would take good care of the horses. The lad seemed quite capable. But to be on foot for days to come seemed barbaric.

Not that the horses could've handled the steep and rocky path he and Ariana walked upon.

He loved her. Maybe she was carrying his child, maybe she was not. She called him husband, but he still wanted a ceremony. Maybe in The City, maybe when they returned to Arthes. He wanted her bound to him in all ways. By heart, by body, by soul, *and* by law.

There were things he should tell her before that day came. He'd searched for the right words for days, but they would not come. *Oh, by the way, one day I might be emperor. Just thought you should know . . .*

No, he had to find the proper way to share the news.

The path before them had turned level for a stretch. "You mentioned that you might be able to heal Arik. Do you think it possible?"

"Maybe." She turned and smiled at him. "I believe his illness is somehow connected to the Isen Demon. If I can snatch back dark souls the demon has taken, then why can't I heal Arik?" She once again turned her eyes to the path. "After I deliver the Anwyn army to Merin, I'll return to Arthes and try."

"Will Arik live that long?"

"That is not in my hands," she said calmly.

The path grew steep again, and they stopped talking. The green trousers he had stolen before sneaking out of the palace were too big for her, held in place by a belt she'd fashioned from a length of rope, but when she climbed just so, the fabric molded to her backside and formed a pretty picture. He was tempted to rush to catch up with her, grab her, kiss her, and make love to her right here under the sun. It wasn't as if there was anyone around to watch, unless he counted the small critters that occasionally scurried from their path. He did not.

Sian rushed to get closer, but he did not grab Ariana. Not yet. "There's something I must tell you."

She glanced at him, suspicion in her eyes. "I don't like the sound of that, or the uncertainty that's pouring off of you."

"I had to fall in love with an empath," he said as he moved to walk beside her, as the current trail was wider than it had been to this point. "I don't suppose I will ever be able to lie to you."

She shrugged her shoulders. "You can try if you'd like. Now, don't make me wait. What is it that has you so tense?"

He took her arm and spun her about, bringing them both to a halt on the rocky trail. This was best said eye to eye, so he could better judge her immediate reaction. Besides, she was getting winded, and he knew she would not stop for even the shortest rest on her own account. "Before I left Arthes, Arik called me to his chamber. He said that he has another son, an illegitimate son who was kept ignorant of his true parentage for many years."

Ariana smiled. "That's wonderful!"

"Not really," Sian mumbled. He smoothed back a strand of wayward hair. "It's me, apparently."

He had not thought anything could take her by surprise, but this did. "I don't understand."

"Neither do I. All I know is that if you can heal Arik and he lives to father another son, this secret can remain a secret. I don't want to be emperor, but more than that, I don't want my mother's name to be sullied. I don't want the man who raised me as his own to be disrespected by gossip and supposition. Arik is not too old to marry and have more children."

Ariana sighed. "Even if I can't save him, even if Arik

doesn't have an heir, there might be a way to save you from this."

She seemed confident, but he could think of nothing but a miracle that would save him. Of course, miracles were possible. He knew that now.

"While I was dead . . ."

His heart leapt. "I wish you'd begin that sentence another way," he said. "Those are words I wish never to hear again."

She smiled lightly, understanding. "After my visit with Uncle Duran, I was . . . intercepted for a short time."

"Intercepted?"

"I was somehow pulled aside by whatever remains of Emperor Sebestyen," she added. "Not a ghost, not a soul at rest, but . . . a lost spirit, I suppose."

The idea was terrifying. To be in the hands of lost loved ones was one thing, but to come face to face with one such as Sebestyen . . . "What did he want?"

"He said he had two sons. Twins! They survived and have been in hiding all this time."

"Is that possible?"

Ariana shrugged. "I'm going to do my best to find out."

Before she could say more, they found themselves suddenly and completely surrounded . . . by the most hideous creatures Sian had ever seen.

18

IT HAPPENED SO FAST, FOR A MOMENT ARIANA DIDN'T breathe. What were those things? At quick glance she counted eight of them. They seemed to be half mountain cat, half man, standing upright but sporting vicious claws. They were primarily covered in hair that ranged from black to yellow and everything in between, but also sported sporadic patches of weathered skin that appeared to be human. Each wore a dark stone around its—his?—neck, but nothing else.

Were they animals or men? They appeared to be neither.

The creatures attacked. Ariana and Sian drew their weapons, each gripping a sword in one hand and a knife in the other. They adopted a back-to-back position, which was the only way to assure that neither would be struck from behind.

"Shield yourself," Sian ordered.

"I'm trying!" She did her best to cast the unreliable

shield not only around herself but around Sian as well. The magical armor gave her only a minimal advantage, but at the moment she'd gladly take it.

The animals moved in closer, wary of the weapons but certainly not afraid. Two dropped down and approached on all fours, and it seemed that one of them actually smiled. He showed yellowed, sharp teeth and a shine of spittle. Ariana's mouth went dry. The beasts would attack low and high. Even with their magic, how could they defend themselves well from all angles?

One on one, she could hold her own. This battle would not be one on one.

"It was worth it," she said in a lowered voice. "No matter what happens, having you was worth everything."

"Don't talk like this is over," Sian insisted, and then the animals pounced.

Ariana had taken her battle lessons to heart, and she wielded her blades as well as any sentinel who'd had no more training or practice than she. The first beast to move in was easily killed with a swipe of her short but sharp sword. The second to come at her slipped on a loose scrabble of rock . . . thanks to the shield perhaps? . . . giving Ariana the opportunity to dip down, lunge forward, and plunge her knife into the area where the heart should be, while holding another creature at bay with the sword. The creature she stabbed fell, and the one that came into contact with her sword blade backed away, one arm cut. She could not see how Sian fought, but his back remained against hers and she heard the screech of a wounded animal.

Again two came at her at the same time—the one she had wounded and another—and she tensed, lifting her sword to meet the one nearest the front. The blade nicked the stone that hung against a chest which was mostly covered with chestnut hair, and the spark that resulted was almost blinding. The wounded thing shrieked and jumped back, then landed on all fours.

"What was that?" Sian asked crisply.

"I don't know."

When a large brown creature tried to move in from the side, Sian waved his knife-wielding hand in that direction. A large rock flew up from the edge of the path and hit the creature in the snout. It dropped, dazed and bloody.

Ariana could not even think of trying to move a weapon with the magic Sian had taught her, while continuing to fight with her blades and maintain anything of the shield. There was no way she could concentrate enough to accomplish even sending a pebble into an attacker's eye. Her accuracy had never been consistent, in any case. No, she could rely only on the weapons in her hands and the protection of her empath's shield.

She knocked another creature back with her sword, and when he was down, she took a moment to assess the situation. Her heart lightened. At least four were dead. The wounded were backing away. She and Sian might actually win, even though when this battle had begun, the odds had been a disheartening eight to two. The catlike beasts were violent and had an advantage in numbers, but they didn't seem to have a plan and they did not work together. They just pounced and crouched, baring their teeth and slashing with their claws.

Just when Ariana was sure she and Sian would win this battle, six more of the creatures came over the hill, dashing her hopes. How many were there? How long would she and Sian come close to winning only to see more of the hideous creatures headed their way? For all she knew, there were hundreds of them, and they would keep coming and fighting until she and Sian were dead. All she could do was take them on as they came, one— perhaps two—at a time. She took a deep breath and resumed her fighting stance.

Without warning, rocks that had been lying on the ground all around them lifted into the air. Large, small, sharp, and round, they rose up off the path as if lifted by invisible hands.

Sian.

The beasts were taken aback by the display of magic, that was made clear by their tentative stances and puzzled catlike eyes. The floating rocks began to whirl about in a circle, effectively protecting her and Sian from attack. The rocks moved quickly, high and low, spinning in a defensive orbit. How long could Sian maintain this effort? Ariana pressed her back to his and did her best to assist him, to add her strength to his. After all, they were connected deeply, to the soul, to the heart . . . they were one in many ways.

One beast tried to break through the shield, and a stone whacked alongside its misshapen head. The thing squealed, making a horrible sound as it backed away. Ariana could feel the effort radiating from Sian's body and from his heart, but the stones which circled about did not slow or drop.

Another beast rushed forward, suffering only a minor collision with a smallish rock. Sian's sword was ready, and he cut the animal down with precision.

"I won't let them have you, Ariana."

"I know, love," she said. She believed him, she truly did, but she also knew that he could not defend them with these swirling rocks forever. If the beasts did not grow tired of waiting and run away, if they were not frightened away by Sian's magic, then she and Sian would eventually face them all with only their swords for defense.

Their swords, and their love, and their determination not to give up the fight.

Ariana expected the swirling rocks to slow or begin to fall as Sian tired, but they continued without pause. His back against hers seemed overly warm, and she caught an occasional tremble that passed through his entire body, but Sian did not give in to the exhaustion he had to be experiencing.

The rocks spun as if caught in a whirlpool, and eventually the catlike creatures began to back away.

Out of the corner of her eye, Ariana caught sight of an unexpected swarm of scantily dressed and very large men toting spears. Anwyn.

The feline creatures that remained alive scattered in the face of the new and less advantageous numbers. They screeched and bounded across rocks into the mountainside, scurrying away from the path. A few of the Anwyn made as if to follow, chasing the creatures away, but they quickly returned to the path to join the winded but unharmed couple, who gratefully lowered their blades.

Ariana turned her attention to the Anwyn in the lead, a very large man wearing a traditional short kilt. His dark hair was caught in a tight braid, and his striking gold eyes marked him as Anwyn more surely than the clothes or his remarkable size.

He offered a courtly bow, long leg extended and one arm sweeping. "Tryndad Romney of the Dairgol Clan, at your service. Queen Keelia sends her greetings to you and your husband."

"How does she . . ." Sian began, and then he paused and shook his head. "Oh yes. Psychic."

"Very," Ariana murmured. She extended a hand toward the body of one of the odd creatures. "What *is* that?" she asked the Anwyn, who was obviously this party's leader.

"I'm not sure." Tryndad's brow wrinkled. "We have seen a number of these atrocities over the past few months. The Queen says they were once Caradon, but some evil changed them. Now the creatures are lower than even the lowliest Caradon."

Ariana dropped down to study the rough stone that lay on one motionless chest. The talisman looked innocent enough, but since they each wore one, it probably had some significance. She reached out to touch the stone, but Sian's hand quickly caught her wrist.

"Don't touch that," he commanded.

He drew a square of cloth from his pocket, and used it to cover and protect his hand as he snatched away the talisman. He wrapped the rock securely and dropped it in his pocket. "We'll study the stone later, but you will not touch it or anything else related to these creatures. It might not be safe."

Ariana studied the area, searching for a wounded animal. Sian was insistent that she not touch anything connected with these monsters, and in truth she'd like nothing better than to follow that command. But could she snatch back a soul from one of these creatures? Had they ever possessed souls? Maybe they were Ciro's Own, like the soldiers the sentinels had defeated, but then again, perhaps they were simply a sign that the world was taking a dark turn. She saw a few dead creatures, but the wounded had escaped or been dragged away by their comrades, so there was no opportunity to find out.

"We will go now," Tryndad said. He turned and headed back the way he'd come, and Ariana and Sian followed. They were quickly surrounded by the men who had come to their rescue. No wonder the Anwyn had not given chase when the creatures fled. They had been sent here not to fight, but to protect.

After a few moments, Sian said, "You're very brave, Ariana."

"We must all be brave in the coming months and years. It takes great courage to love with conviction in difficult times."

Sian wound his arm through hers and pulled her close to his side as they tromped along the rocky trail. His smile warmed her heart. "Yes, it does, love."

CIRO HADN'T SLEPT IN MANY DAYS. MEN NEEDED sleep . . . the Isen Demon did not. He sat in the cabin he was already beginning to hate, and reached out for his Own, those who had not yet come to him. He saw what they saw. He spoke to them and soothed them and guided them.

When he saw what had happened in the mountains too near the Anwyn Queen, he barked a curse that had a curious Diella turning his way. "What's wrong, my prince?"

"The wizard Chamblyn is lost."

"Lost?"

"To us, he is lost," Ciro explained. "His soul no longer dances on the edge. He's turned, and that turn will not bring him in my direction."

Diella seemed unconcerned. "How very regrettable. I should've killed him when I had the chance."

"Yes."

"Don't be so gloomy." Diella closed the short space

between them and sat on his lap. "There are other wizards in Columbyana and beyond, and I'm sure many of
them have greater powers than Sian Chamblyn. You will
find the one you seek, in time."

Diella was trying to comfort him, which he found almost funny. He did not seek comfort from anyone. He did
not *need* comfort.

Inside him, what little was left of Ciro shuddered. This
bit of human that still remained, so precariously, needed
comfort. Rayne would offer that comfort to him when the
time was right. When she understood and embraced all
that they could be and do, she would gladly offer him all
that he needed.

"I know what will make you feel better," Diella said
brightly.

Ciro almost growled. If she offered him her body again,
he would kill her. He'd snap her neck and toss her outside
for his own soldiers to play with. He wouldn't even drink
her blood, such was his distaste for her at the moment.

But Diella did not offer her body. Instead she reached
into a deep pocket of the ill-fitting gown she wore and
drew out a vial of Panwyr.

Panwyr she must've stolen from him.

Ciro did not need or want sleep, the solace of a
woman's body, or the wizard Chamblyn. The Panwyr was
another matter entirely. His mouth actually watered. He
hadn't indulged in his weakness for many days, and looking at the offering, he realized that he had denied himself
for too long.

Diella put a healthy sprinkle of the drug on the palm
of her hand, and held it beneath his nose. Ciro closed his
eyes and sniffed the drug so that it traveled up his nose
and flooded his system.

The drug infused the body that had once been Ciro's, as well as the demon who had become addicted in the depths of Level Thirteen. Each soul it took there had been hopelessly addicted, so it was only reasonable to expect that the demon would share in that craving.

For a human, the advantages of the drug faded after a number of uses, though the addiction remained as it destroyed the body one day, one hour, at a time. For Ciro, for the demon he had become, each dosage took him to a finer, more exciting place. Mentally, all was sharp and colorful. Physically, it seemed that this body he possessed was finally truly alive. The power he sought flowed through his veins, making him stronger. Making him darker,

The faces and thoughts of his own soldiers and their failures faded, and he thought of Rayne. Thanks to the Panwyr, she seemed real for a moment, and he grabbed for her, finding Diella in the pretty village girl's body instead of the woman he planned to make his empress, the woman who would bear his child.

He opened his eyes and looked into Diella's face, and he saw Rayne.

"A man like you need not save his seed for any woman." Diella's voice—Lilia's voice—drifted to him from Rayne's face. "You'll make more before you are reunited with the woman you have chosen to bear the child."

"True enough." He caressed her breast through rough fabric.

She leaned into him and laughed hoarsely. "I knew we were meant for this, my prince. I knew all along."

He hated the sound of a voice that was not Rayne's coming from this woman who looked like Rayne, who felt, beneath his rough hands, as he had always known his chosen would feel. "Say another word, and I will break your neck."

Rayne opened her mouth to answer, and then closed it again. His answer was a simple nod of her beautiful head.

THE ANWYN SOLDIERS WHO HAD ESCORTED SIAN AND Ariana to The City and the Palace of the Anwyn Queen tried to take them to their assigned quarters before they were presented to the Queen herself. Sian could understand why. After so many weeks of travel, he and Ariana were not fit for being presented to a Queen or anyone else, but these difficult times called for a setting aside of common courtesies.

Ariana laid her hand on the big man's arm and insisted that she needed to see her cousin immediately. Tryndad apparently saw the determination in her eyes, and quickly acceded to her wishes.

They walked along a fine stone corridor, flanked by large men. Sian had always heard that the Anwyn men were of a size. Though he was tall by most standards, some of them stood a full head taller than he. He could only imagine what size they might be when they were transformed into wolves which would run beneath a full moon.

Sian knew a little about the Anwyn people, but not much apparently. He had certainly not been told that they preferred to pass the day more naked than not.

Ariana, who had once been so proper, seemed not to notice.

Raised voices reached their ears, and Tryndad tensed. His step increased, and soon they were all running down the corridor toward the alarming sounds. Sian and Ariana had to run hard to keep pace with the long-legged Anwyn soldiers, and soon they found themselves in one of the largest and most magnificent rooms Sian had ever seen. It was fashioned of fine stones, and sported columns which were true works of art. At the other end of the large room was a dais where two thrones sat, side by side. They were both empty. A petite blond girl was surrounded by yet more Anwyn soldiers, and she was obviously hysterical.

He was a little disappointed. She didn't look much like a Queen.

When the girl saw Ariana, she sobbed and broke away, running from the guards, who were now as agitated as she.

"Ariana, thank goodness you're here!"

Ariana tensed. "Giulia, dear, what's wrong?"

Giulia? Not the Queen, then.

The blonde threw herself into Ariana's arms and sobbed. Ariana wrapped her arms around the girl and did her best to soothe her. "What's wrong?" she asked again.

Tryndad and the other soldiers rushed toward an exit at the rear of the room, their visitors and the sobbing girl forgotten.

Giulia lifted her head and sniffled. "Someone took Keelia!"

"What do you mean, took her?"

"Took her! We were laying out our clothes for supper tonight, since we had a feast planned to celebrate your arrival. Keelia said we wouldn't feel like celebrating for a very long time, so we might as well enjoy this night. We were examining a selection of gowns which were laid across my bed, because I could not decide what to wear, and a man wearing a *mask* came up behind Keelia and grabbed her!" The girl's voice was quick and very young, excited and verging on breathless. "He told me if I screamed, he would kill her, and then come back for me and the rest of my family, so I was still and quiet. I thought the guards would stop them before they got far, or that Keelia would escape from his grasp. There are guards everywhere!" The small girl stomped one slipper-clad foot. "Why didn't they see anything?"

"A good question," Ariana said calmly as she cast her eyes at Sian.

He sighed tiredly. "I have another good question for you. How does one go about sneaking up on a psychic as extraordinary as the Queen of the Anwyn?"

ARIANA STOOD AT THE WINDOW OF THE PALACE ROOM she shared with Sian. Sunset was not yet here, but the sky had begun to turn brilliant with color, and it would be followed on this coming night by a full moon. She and Sian had been here for four days. *Four days*, and there was still no sign of Keelia and her kidnapper. Ariana could not believe that her cousin had been harmed. If the intruder had planned to kill the Queen, he could have done so in Giulia's room. He could've killed her in the hallway and left her body for someone to find. That would've been easier than escaping with a reluctant captive.

She felt sure Keelia was safe somehow. The Anwyn Queen had a part to play in the war with Ciro and his Own. As with the village Ciro had destroyed, Ariana felt things would be different if only they had arrived sooner. If only she had been able to ask her cousin about Sebestyen's twins, the crystal dagger, and how Ciro could be defeated.

If only.

Sian crept up behind her and wrapped his arms about

her in a gesture which spoke of love and comfort and protection.

"Tonight the Anwyn will change," Ariana said. Most had already moved beyond the walls of The City, walking into the hills, where they would truly be wild and free when night fell and the moon rose. A few still made their way toward The City gates, leaving their human wives, as well as the children who had not yet reached the age of transformation, behind, well armed in case the hideously transformed Caradon attempted to attack. So far the creatures had not come near The City, but the Anwyn couldn't be too careful. "It's quite a sight if you have never witnessed the change."

"It will last for three nights, correct?" Sian asked, knowing full well the answer.

"Yes."

"And when that is done, we will take the Anwyn army to our assigned meeting place."

Ariana nodded. "If Lyr hasn't arrived when the time comes for us to leave, I'll have to post a messenger on the trail. As there's only one road fit for horses leading here, that won't be difficult. Maybe we'll meet him on the way down the mountain." Or maybe she would not. Ariana closed her eyes. Would nothing go as it should?

She turned and looked up into the face of the man she now called husband. "What if we haven't found Keelia by then?"

"As pleasant as it has been to stay here, to eat well and bathe in hot water and sleep in a soft bed, we can't remain much longer. We can't wait. Merin and his men will be waiting for you when the *next* full moon rises." His eyes twinkled. "You could stay with your cousin Giulia while I—"

"Don't even suggest it," she interrupted.

He wasn't serious, though perhaps somewhere deep in his heart he hoped she would find a safe place and remain there. But he knew, as she did, that her part in this was not done. There were souls to be snatched from Ciro, and if she could heal Arik . . . what a triumph that would be.

Not for the first time, Ariana asked herself—why couldn't Aunt Juliet and Uncle Ryn be here? They would know what to do. Juliet might even know where her eldest daughter could be found.

But they were not here, and Sian was right. In three days, they would leave The City whether Keelia had been found or not.

"I'm not pregnant," she said, the words coming quick and low.

A light of something unreadable lit Sian's purple eyes. "Hmm," was all he said.

"Are you . . . relieved?" Had he released his reservations about creating a child? She wanted his baby so desperately, and yet she did not want to force a child upon him. While they were in The City, she could fashion another potion to prevent conception, if that's what Sian wanted. Should they wait until the world was once again a safe place?

He leaned down and kissed her forehead very quickly. "I am relieved, and also oddly disappointed." His jaw hardened. "Don't think this means we aren't getting married as soon as possible. Isn't there someone here who can perform a ceremony?"

"The Anwyn people say words before the Queen." A Queen who was mysteriously missing.

"Who performs the ceremony for the Queen herself?"

"A priestess of some sort, I have been told."

"Can't she—"

"I don't think it's allowed."

Sian sighed in evident disgust. "Then I suppose we will wait."

In her mind, Ariana imagined the wedding ceremony she wanted. Her parents and all her siblings would be there. She'd wear a beautiful dress, and Sian would be dressed entirely in black. He'd wear his hair down. There would be flowers and candles, singing and dancing.

It was a nice idea, but given the current situation, that dream wedding was as likely as Ciro surrendering before he ever marched on Arthes.

"Shall I prepare a potion to make sure I don't conceive until the time is right?"

Sian considered the proposal for a moment. "And when will that be?"

"I don't know."

"When Ciro is dead, and his soldiers are all gone," Sian said sharply, "when Emperor Sebestyen's sons have been found, and one of them is safely on the throne. When I can wrap you in a bubble of perfect and reliable shelter, where no one and nothing can ever touch you."

Disappointment welled up in Ariana's heart, hearing those words. Those conditions. Sian was still afraid.

And then he smiled at her and stroked her cheek with one finger. "Since that day will never come, I must say no to your potion, love. We'll take our chances. We will love with great conviction no matter what this war brings, and we will embrace hope as fiercely and completely as we embrace one another."

All she could say was, "I love you so much."

With her tucked close at his side, Sian turned to look out on The City, as Ariana had been doing when he'd found her. "We're still getting married soon."

"Yes, love."

"And while we're waiting here, your lessons will resume. We should not waste a moment. Your magical efforts in fighting the creatures that attacked us were dismal."

"If you insist."

"I do."

The sun disappeared, and darkness fell. A large and brilliant full moon lit the sky, hanging before them like a gem against velvet the color of Sian's eyes when he was angry. The war had just begun, Ariana knew that very well, and yet tonight their opponent suffered one small defeat. No, one *significant* defeat. While the demon's darkness reached for all that it could possess, hope survived. Love conquered fear.

In the darkness, a perfect and noble and wondrous light continued to shine.

Read an excerpt from

Prince of Fire

as the battle against the evil Ciro continues . . .

Coming from Berkley Sensation
April 2007!

SHAKING, TREMBLING TO HER BONES, KEELIA LIFTED her head and studied her own hands—pale trembling hands which were pressed against a chilly gray stone floor. Tangled strands of red hair fell past one cheek and pooled against the rough stone. A hint of panic welled up inside her, but she did not reveal that panic in any outward way, other than the tremble which she could not control.

Her mind raced, but her body remained very still. Without moving from the spot where she found herself, Keelia gathered her composure. No matter what had happened, she would show no fear. No weakness. The gentle shaking of her body ceased as she quieted her mind and took control, and searched for the memory of how she had come to be here.

She remembered standing over Giulia's bed studying an array of overly ornate gowns in the style her little sister preferred. Her mind had not been on the simple task at hand. Ariana was coming, and there would be a celebration of sorts, even though Keelia's psychic powers had warned her that there were not many celebratory times in the near future for the Anwyn or the humans in the lands below the Mountains of the North. An unspeakable evil was coming. No, that evil was already *here*.

She and Giulia had been studying the gowns, and Keelia's mind had been drifting, and then . . . and then, someone had grabbed her. Someone had actually dared to *grab* her, and then he'd done something to her throat and everything had gone black. Until now. She turned her head and studied the cave in which she had awakened. It was no ordinary cave but was a prison, a cell with bars built into a slender natural doorway. A narrow cot had been placed against one cave wall, but she had not awakened there. Whoever had brought her here had simply dumped her onto the floor. A chamber pot was discretely stored beneath the cot, and a crude wooden table sat near the rear wall. This was not a temporary facility, but one in which a prisoner might expect to remain for a long while.

An unwanted lump formed in Keelia's throat. How much time had passed since she'd been taken? Hours or days? Who had taken her? Who would dare? She was rarely confronted with mysteries of any kind, but at the moment she grasped no answers to her questions.

"Ah, the Queen awakes," a deep voice rumbled from the shadows beyond her prison.

Flaming torches lit the segment of the cave beyond the bars, but not well enough. Not nearly well enough. Keelia narrowed her eyes and attempted to focus, and finally caught sight of the man who spoke. He lingered just beyond the circle of illumination cast by the nearest torch so that all she saw was a shape, a distant and unclear silhouette. The shape was male, like the arrogant voice, but she could sense little else.

Her powers of telepathy were usually quite sharp. Though they were far from all-encompassing, those abilities were strong and reliable. At least, they had been until recently. What had once been crystal clear was now muddy. Indistinct. Dreams continued to come even when the visions did not, but she occasionally misinterpreted even them, until she found herself questioning everything that came to her. Something was interfering with her gifts. Her mother believed that if Keelia would search diligently for her mate and settle down, she would know a calm that had thus far eluded her and the visions would become clear once again. Keelia suspected there was something darker at work here, perhaps the very evil she sometimes dreamed of.

It was true that in the past few months she had not been able to interpret the meanings of her visions well, as she should, but even when her powers were not at their best, she could still reach into a person—any person— and know something of their thoughts. Were they scared? Angry? Well meaning? Frustrated? It was a finely honed instinct she had relied upon all her life, and she needed it now.

Keelia reached for this man who had dared to kidnap her, and received nothing in return. Not hatred, fear, or self-satisfaction at a job well done. Not arrogance or anger. It was as if he were a complete blank. She had sensed nothing of him as he'd snuck upon her either, which was alarming.

Accustomed to being able to understand the people around her, the emptiness Keelia was met with scared her more than finding herself in this cell. It was as if someone had taken away her very sight or her hearing or her sense of touch. Without her gifts, she was not herself, and she felt horribly lost.

"Who are you?" she asked sharply, refusing to show fear to her abductor. "What do you want? Are you a coward who always hides in the shadows?" Maybe if he moved closer, she'd be able to read something of his thoughts. Maybe if she could see his face, she could reach deeper and understand his intentions.

She did not fear death. If this man had wanted her dead, he could've killed her there in Giulia's room.

"One question at a time, my Red Queen," the man said, stepping forward so that the flickering flame of the torch illuminated his face.

Keelia's heart reacted fiercely to the sight of that face, skipping a beat and racing and thudding so hard she was afraid he would hear it. This was not possible. He was supposed to be nothing more than a dream, a figment of her imagination, a fantasy she called upon when her fertile time came and demanded that she find physical satisfaction. This man, this face she knew so well, he was of her own making, her own imagination. He was not real.

She closed her eyes tightly, wondering if she was caught in some kind of nightmare. No, the stone beneath her was real, the pounding of her heart, real, her inability to see into her captor . . . real. She opened her eyes, wondering if perhaps she had made a mistake. Maybe her abductor only favored the man of her dreams in some small way, and in her panic she had imagined that he was her dream lover come to life.

Her eyes flickered over him, from head to toe. No, it was not her imagination, not at all. The man who had kidnapped her had long dark blond hair oddly streaked with auburn. That distinctive ginger streak she had caressed in her dreams originated at his temple and shot back to eventually blend with the thick waves of the more ordinary blond. He was much taller than she, but a bit shorter than most Anwyn males, which had always suited her in her fantasies since, like her mother and sister, she was petite in size, and did not care for being completely dwarfed by the men in her life.

Her kidnapper wore plain brown trousers which fit loosely over long legs and were tucked into soft boots, and a worn leather belt which held a scabbard and dagger. He wore nothing else but a wide silver bracelet which graced his right wrist.

Keelia had been waiting for a long time for her mate to come to her. All Anwyn mated for life, and while the males had to move beyond The City to find their destined mates among human females, as Queen, she should have known for the past ten years or so who her mate would be. She was twenty-five years of age, and his identity remained a mystery to her. There were few mysteries in her life, and she had often wondered if this loneliness was the price she had to pay for her other abilities. Perhaps she would never have a true mate and know the love that came with such a union.

Her mother had always told her how she had been unable to read her mate's mind when they'd first met. The love that Juliet and Ryn shared had always seemed ideal to Keelia, and it was what she wanted most of all. More than being Queen, more than possessing remarkable powers like no other . . . she wanted what her parents had found. Was the fact that she was unable to read this man's mind a sign that he was her mate? Were the dreams and fantasies of him unrecognized visions of what was to be? She held her breath. Had she been dreaming about her mate all along? It was tradition for Anwyn males to abduct their mates, and while this scenario was extreme . . . perhaps he was the one. Perhaps her mate was a rogue who lived beyond The City walls, and he had finally come for her.

He wrapped his fingers around the bars that imprisoned her, and the bracelet he wore made a clinking sound as he settled his hands there. By the light of the torch, Keelia finally got a clear look at his face. The mouth was full and wide and wicked. In her dreams that mouth smiled often, but it did not smile now. The nose was perfect in shape, and the cheekbones were high and prominent. The eyes were slightly slanted and mysterious.

It was as she studied those eyes that Keelia put aside her wish that he might be the one she had waited for and she suffered her first real rush of fear. In her dreams, those eyes were as golden as her own. All Anwyn were graced with golden eyes, some deep amber and others brightly gold, with most colored somewhere in between.

Her captor's eyes were green. Not just any shade of green, but a deep and lively shade reminiscent of emeralds.

Her dream lover was a Caradon, and he was not a happy creature.

Keelia had always refused to accept that the ancient prophesy might be true, that the Red Queen would take a Caradon lover and thereby bring peace to her people. It had been told so many times, for so many years, it had obviously been twisted and misinterpreted. Her mate would be Anwyn, not a contemptible Caradon!

The Caradon kidnapper gripped the bars tightly with

large hands. Hands that had grabbed her, hands that had found a pressure point on her throat that had disabled her for hours.

In her dreams, her lover whispered only sweet things in her ear as he used those hands for happier purposes, but in reality he scowled and asked hoarsely, "What have you done to my people?"

JORYN GRIPPED THE BARS SO TIGHTLY, HIS KNUCKLES went white. The woman who lay on the floor, draped in soft gold fabric and tumbling flame red hair, looked innocent and harmless and even tempting. He knew she was not innocent or harmless, and he could not afford to be tempted.

"What do you mean?" she asked, her voice even, her strange gold eyes unflinching. "Explain yourself."

For the past ten years, he had heard tales of the powers of the Anwyn Queen, and when the Grandmother—the wizened old witch who had lived longer than any other Caradon—had come to him and informed him that the Red Queen was the one behind the horrid transformation of some of those among them, he had sworn to do all he could to stop her.

If he'd thought killing the Queen would end the dark magic, he would've done so already. Druson, another student of the Grandmother who had been present when she'd shared her knowledge, had suggested that Joryn kill the Anwyn Queen immediately. The Grandmother had strongly advised against such a dire measure. The Queen must be forced to undo the dark magic she had used to curse his people. If he killed her, those who had been turned into mutant creatures which had no name would be doomed to remain in such a state.

"You know very well what I mean, my Queen. Undo what you have done, and maybe I won't kill you."

She huffed prettily, showing no fear as she rose up into a more rigid sitting position. Even with the floor as her throne, she appeared regal. Unshakable. "I am not *your* Queen, Caradon scoundrel, and I have done nothing which needs to be undone. I command that you release me immediately."

Joryn said nothing for a long moment. It was almost funny that the Red Queen believed she could command anything of him. He owed her no allegiance, no explanation, and she was in no position to hold any authority over him—or anyone else. But she did look pretty, sitting there issuing orders as if she actually expected his obedience.

The Anwyn Queen was beautiful, but he could not afford distractions.

He wanted more than her cooperation; he wanted answers. How was such bad magic possible, and why would she go to such lengths when most of the Caradon left the Anwyn in peace? Only a few outcasts felt compelled to annoy and on occasion attack the Anwyn beasts. Most were content to leave the wolf-people who shared these Mountains of the North alone.

In the beginning, only a few of his people had been infected. They had been cursed by this woman and wore talismans—stones hanging from thin leather cords—to mark them as bewitched. Not that anyone who saw them wouldn't know that they were no longer as they should be, but the talismans made it clear that whatever had happened was no mistake—no freak of nature. No, they had been purposely ruined.

Terrible as it was, that curse had been only the beginning. Those Caradon who had been turned into evil, monstrous things were now spreading their disease. Joryn had recently learned that a number of innocent Caradon who were bitten by the monsters became like those who had lost their spirits to this witch, and on the rise of the next full moon after the attack they, too, were affected. Those who had been bitten began to change, as they always did beneath the full moon, but the transformation did not complete.

The infected ones were horribly caught between mountain cat and man. No longer human, but nether animal, they were twisted in mind and body. Some of them lost their minds entirely and ran into the mountains alone or threw themselves from cliffsides to their deaths. Others joined the rampage of the monsters who cared for nothing but violence and murder.

"As you do not care for being called Queen, perhaps 'witch' will suit you better." He clanked his bracelet against one metal bar that imprisoned her. "Do you wonder why you can't read my mind, witch?" He could tell by the flicker in her eyes that she did wonder, very much. "Your evil magic doesn't work on me because I am protected by the power of the ancient Caradon." The bracelet he wore had been fashioned by the Grandmother, and he had been warned not to take it off for any reason. Even when he shifted into a mountain cat, the bracelet would remain in place, and he would be protected from the Queen's probing magic.

"I am a witch," she confessed, "but I am not evil." Moving with a gentle grace, she unwound her body and stood.

Anwyn men were quite large, but apparently the females were small. The Queen was not much more than five feet tall, he would guess, and the other female who had been with her when he'd taken her was no bigger.

Even her bones were small, as evidenced by the tiny structure of her wrist and the delicacy of her hands. She did not look at all powerful, but then he had been warned that she was well practiced in deceit and dark magic.

"If you are not evil, then why did you curse my people?" Joryn asked, his patience growing thin. "Only a creature with a dark soul would infect the innocent as you have."

A light of awareness came into her eyes, and she took a step toward him. "Oh, I understand."

She looked innocent enough, but he would not be fooled. "Of course you understand."

The Queen moved forward and stopped close to the bars of her cell, but not close enough to reach out and touch him. "The creatures you speak of have been changed, but that is not of my doing, I swear. Something terrible is happening, not only here in these mountains, but in the lands below. An evil is spreading to all corners of the land. I have dreamed of it. I have seen the growth of this evil in my visions, and the abnormality of your people is a part of that growing darkness."

Joryn didn't want to believe her, but he searched for deception in her face and saw none.

"Why should I believe you?"

The Queen was immediately incensed. "Because I do not lie!"

"Ah, a virtuous Anwyn. Of course you do not lie."

"Do not patronize me, Caradon."

"My name is Joryn, witch."

Her eyebrows lifted slightly. "I do not care what you call yourself. Your name is of no consequence. Release me this instant."

"No," he said calmly.

The Queen stamped her small foot and glared at him as if her stare alone would undo him. "I demand that you release me!"

He was unaffected by her anger. "You issue commands like a woman who is accustomed to having them obeyed."

Her lips thinned, slightly but significantly.

"Does no one ever defy you, witch?"

"No one."

She looked at him oddly, almost as if she recognized him. He was certain their paths had never crossed, but he would admit—to himself, not her—that there was something familiar about this beautiful redheaded woman.

Maybe she had crept into his head with her magic, in spite of the protection of the bracelet. Maybe her powers were stronger than he, or the Grandmother, realized. At this moment he wished she were older, uglier, and lumbering. It would be easier to do what had to be done, if that were the case. The Anwyn Queen was the kind of woman any male of any species might wish to call his own and protect.

He could not afford such fancies.

"Are you waiting for your mate to rescue you?" he asked. "Is that why you feel you're in a position to issue commands? I can assure you, no one will find us here."

Her eyes narrowed slightly. "An entire army is searching for me."

She did not mention her mate, and he found that strange. It was the weakness of the Anwyn, that they relied so completely on their mates. They were all but crippled by the connection, as if they were not whole without their other half. The Caradon had no such weakness. Joryn could not imagine being so dependent on another being that he could not function without her.

The Anwyn and the Caradon had been enemies forever. They shared one trait: they shifted with the rise of the full moon, three nights out of the month. The Anwyn transformed into wolves, the Caradon to mountain cats. Beyond that, they had nothing in common.

The Anwyn lived and ran together, congregating in their City and shunning all those who dared to be different. They mated for life, choosing one partner and pledging themselves to that one person for a lifetime. They worshipped their Queen and relied on their army to protect them. The Anwyn people very rarely birthed girl-children, but produced large males who were forced to kidnap mates from among the humans below. There were rare females, like the Queen and her mother and her sister, but they were so unusual they were all but worshipped.

The Caradon ran free, beholden to no one and unfettered by cities or clans or marriage. There was no Queen, no King, no army, no unnecessary rules to bind them. They mated with whom they chose when they chose, and very few spent their entire lives with only one mate, though a few chose to do so. They also birthed many girls. Joryn's mother was Caradon by birth, a direct descendant of the Grandmother. His father had been a wandering human from Columbyana who'd caught her fancy for a few nights, before she'd disappeared, taking his unborn son into the mountains with her.

Joryn enjoyed the freedom which was his birthright as a Caradon male. When his duty to his people and the Grandmother was done, he would return to the life he had enjoyed before the curse. He would study and increase his inborn magic, run wild beneath the full moon, and love with abandon.

Not that he was indiscriminate. Far from it. Joryn was a lover of beauty, particularly where women were concerned. Not many were as beautiful as his captive—not that he cared to touch her in any pleasurable way. She was, after all, Anwyn.

The Queen's expression softened, and she clasped her small hands at her waist, well beneath her small but very nicely shaped breasts. "There has been a terrible misunderstanding. Release me and I will return to The City on my own and tell no one of your mistake. You will not be harmed for your foolishness." She spoke to him as if he were a small child, or an imbecile.

"I'm not going to let you go," Joryn responded. "Ever."

Her mask of innocence dropped, golden eyes flashed with anger, and she rushed toward the bars, and him. Joryn stepped back as one small hand shot through the bars. There was not yet a full moon, but that arm . . . the arm only . . . shifted in a heartbeat to that of a russet wolf, complete with wicked claws that missed him by mere inches. Only that one arm shifted, and it was under her complete control.

He had heard that the Anwyn Queen had such powers, but he had not believed it was possible.

"You . . . you . . . *Caradon*!" she said as she swiped at him. "How dare you! You will release me, or I will have your head. Release me *now*, or I swear . . . I swear . . ."

"You swear what?" Joryn asked from a safe distance away from the bars.

Her eyes shone, but she did not shed a tear. "You will be sorry."

"Somehow I don't think so, *witch*."

Indignation rose within and around her, as if she infused her humble surroundings with her dignity. The arm she had tried to attack him with transformed into a delicate, female arm as quickly as it had become a clawed weapon. "You will address me as Majesty or Queen, you . . . you lowly Caradon kidnapper. I am your superior and you will address me as such."

"Yes, Your Wondrous Magnificence," he responded with an exaggerated bow, smiling at her before he turned and walked away. She continued to shout after him, using surprisingly vile language to describe him and his people. It was very unqueenlike behavior, in his opinion.

Joryn did not yet have what he needed from the Anwyn Queen, but he would in due time. Perhaps she was a powerful and fearsome sorceress, a Queen accustomed to having her every desire fulfilled at the snap of her fingers, but she was also a female like all others. She was small and weak and afraid, and with the protective bracelet he wore to keep her from peeking into his mind, and the bars on her cell to keep her from touching him, she was powerless.

And best of all, she was his.